WHEN WORLDS COLLIDE

2D VS 3D

BY MERYL MCCURRY

Copyright © 2021 Meryl McCurry Publishing

All rights reserved. No part of this publication may be reproduced, distributed, or transmitted in any form or by any means, including photocopying, recording, or other electronic or mechanical methods, without the prior written permission of the publisher, except in the case of brief quotations embodied in critical reviews and certain other noncommercial uses permitted by copyright law. For permission requests, write to the publisher, addressed "Attention: Book Rights and Permission," at the address below.
Published in the United States of America

ISBN 978-1-7358010-8-7 (SC)

Meryl McCurry Publishing
222 West 6th Street
Suite 400, San Pedro, CA, 90731
www.stellarliterary.com

Ordering Information and Rights Permission:
Quantity sales. Special discounts might be available on quantity purchases by corporations, associations, and others. For details, contact the publisher at the address above.

For Book Rights Adaptation and other Rights Permission. Call us at toll-free 1-888-945-8513 or send us an email at admin@stellarliterary.com

CONTENTS

The Concern 5

True Love 14

Soul Mates 23

The Brawl 33

Ryan's Miracle 41

The Bribe 49

Old Friends 58

The New Offer 74

The Set Up 82

The Search 94

The Chase 102

Kyle's Regret 114

The Dolphin Club 120

The Stadium 128

We're Getting Close 135

The Battle Begins 140

Ryan's Arrival 149

Jewel's Sacrifice 158

William's Surprise 166

The Revelation 173

The Escape 178

The Rescue 185

The Final Fight 194
Good-Bye Old Friend.. 205
A New Beginning.. 208
A Whole New Beginning 215

CHAPTER ONE

THE CONCERN

On a nice casual sunny day, the birds are chirping and the children are playing peacefully at the park. It is a vast, friendly park where citizens frequently come to relax and enjoy themselves. Some dined on hot dogs from the food stand, while others walked their dogs along the cobblestone plated trail of the park, and young children played in the sandbox, jungle gym, and swung from the swing sets as their parents cautiously speculated from nearby benches. Then after a while, two unusual characters known as Ryan and Kyle walked into the scene. Kyle was a 2D (traditional hand-drawn animated) pterodactyl which fashioned a peach color with turquoise and purple stripes. Ryan however, was a 3D (CGI computer-animated) fox with a deep reddish-orange tint accompanying two sets of chocolate-colored paws. Most foxes have a white complexion under their stomach and the tip of their tale but Ryan's color was light yellow. Kyle was the same height and size as Ryan. They were best friends, but Kyle was less enthusiastic while Ryan was the happier character. Ryan ran ahead of him while Kyle dawdled in the back.

"It sure is a beautiful day, isn't it Kyle?"

"Whatever. But I didn't want to come to the park. I wanted to go to an amusement park instead."

Ryan had to keep himself from laughing out loud. "What are you a kid?" he asked joyfully.

Suddenly Kyle stopped dead in his tracks when he noticed a penny on the ground. He smiled with satisfaction. "Maybe this is my lucky day after all. I hear if you pick up a penny heads-up it will give you good luck."

Ryan looked at Kyle with much concern. "I don't know Kyle; I thought it was bad luck to pick up a penny."

"Oh what do you know."

Just as Kyle bent down to pick up the penny, an enormous demolition missile plummeted down from the clear blue sky and landed directly on top of him. It caused an immense earthquake which shook the whole park. Suddenly the film came to a screeching halt as a director yelled at one of the actors revealing that the park scenery and everything else was only part of a Hollywood movie set. There were humans and realistic props on the set, but there were also animated characters to fulfill the fantasy part of the show and movies. Charles was the producer of the television series whereas Ryan and Kyle were the stars. Apparently something went wrong and the frustrated film-maker's blood boiled as he snatched up his bullhorn to verbally bash Kyle. He was a brilliant film-maker but also a difficult individual to collaborate with, especially for 2D characters who rarely seemed to satisfy him.

"Kyle! I told you for the hundredth time, you're supposed to pick up the penny before the missile hits you. Is that so hard for you to do? It takes only five seconds before the missile lands on you. And here I thought you 2D characters were supposed to be faster. What am I going to do with you?"

Ryan felt bad for Kyle so he decided to stop Charles from butchering him any longer. "Gee whiz boss, give Kyle a break!"

"I'll give him a break alright; I'll break his legs and then his wings. How about that!"

"That won't be necessary boss; he's already broken up enough as it is. That missile you dropped on Kyle left him completely unconscious. Please at least give him until tomorrow to get it right."

"This picture should've been done yesterday, now I have to air another pathetic rerun. That doesn't make our production look too good."

Chapter 1: The Concern

"We've always worked through this before, just give it more time," Ryan begged mercifully.

Charles paused for a moment as he contemplated Ryan's request and very much aware of the pot-bellied, middle-aged man's temper, it was nearly impossible for the cast and crew to tell if he was going to accept Ryan's plea.

"Fine. We'll complete it tomorrow right on schedule, but you better give a pep talk to your so-called 2D friend cause I could easily replace him with a 3D character any day. Tell him he's required to perform with utter perfection with no screw ups."

With that, the entire staff wrapped up their filming and proceeded to put all of the equipment away, as extras that depicted citizens in the park began to relocate from the set, but no one even bothered to assist Kyle by removing the missile that remained nestled on top of him. Ryan was the only one kind enough to aid Kyle in his dilemma. The lively, dedicated creature hoisted up the distraught bird hastily as he stretched like a piece of gum and by the time his dear friend freed him, his body was tangled like a rubber band.

"You okay pal?" he asked him.

Kyle only answered with mumbling and gibberish.

"Hang on pal; I've got your back." He immediately called for a medical stretcher to get him to the nurse's room and when they got there, Ryan looked down on his friend while inquiring with concern. "You hanging in there Kyle?"

"Oh—my aching head. Th-They always give me the worst lines, they treat me horribly, and h-how come you never get hurt on any of the sets, but I do?!"

"Well—that's how the script was written for the production. A noble and bright fox who never gets hurt and his pal the pterodactyl who always seems to get into nothing but trouble."

"Don't sound so stuck up like Charles, besides, you know the real reason and so do I. It's because you're 3D and I'm 2D!"

Ryan always knew this conversation would become an ugly argument, so his ears dropped down while he held his shoulder tightly. "Please Kyle don't start with that again," the frustrated 3D animal pleaded as he abruptly attempted to end the conversation.

"But it's true, back then I used to get the best parts and the best lines, I was even a director of my own show. But since you 3D characters became so popular, we 2D's are the underdogs now. We're treated as second place and get no respect from anybody anymore!"

Kyle accidentally cracked his back when he let his anger get the best of him, as a result, he screamed in agony as Ryan helped him into the nurse's office.

"Calm down Kyle, you need to rest. Starting tomorrow, you're going to have to do the whole script all over again, and just remember, do the part right and this will be the last time you'll have a missile dropped on your head."

"Thanks Ryan, I feel so much better now." Kyle shrieked sarcastically.

"Now that you're here you'll be taken care of but as for me I have to go because I need to talk to Joseph, then head on home."

"What do you want to talk to Joseph about?"

"Just some personal business matter. Gotta go, I'll catch you later Kyle."

Ryan left the nurse's office heading down the hallway of the studio when Kyle turned to the nurse who was heading towards him with a thermometer. Kyle cracked a devilish smile when he saw how beautiful she was. "Nurse when you're finished taking my temperature, I'll be ready for my sponge bath."

The nurse glared at Kyle angrily for a brief moment but shortly after a devilish grin spread across her face. "Sure thing, sir."

A few minutes later, the nurse wheeled Kyle into the room where he was to be bathed as he waited patiently in the wheelchair.

"Maybe getting hurt on these sets isn't so bad after all! I could get used to this."

"Are you ready for your sponge bath sir?"

"You bet baby. Bring it on!"

"Alrighty then."

Chapter 1: The Concern

Suddenly a large 3D gorilla crashed the door open and bellowed a frightening gorilla roar that was devastating and made Kyle jump out of his skin. Kyle became paralyzed in his wheelchair, obviously feeling helpless and terrified.

"This will be the gentleman that'll give you your sponge bath."

"Oh no, no, no, no! I change my mind!"

Without listening to him the nurse just left the room and only remarked, "Have a nice bath."

As soon as she left, Kyle slowly focused his attention on the gorilla who smiled wickedly at him. The gorilla began punching a sponge in his hand as if he was getting ready for a fight. "You'll hate baths by the time I'm through with you."

"I hate my life…" Kyle cried in despair.

Meanwhile, an annoyed Ryan trotted down to Joseph's office. Joseph Roberts was the CEO of the animation company which was called Cartoon Studios, where all the films were produced. The dark-haired, brown-eyed, physically fit professional who always wore an impecUberle suit was a reasonable businessman that allowed 2D and 3D characters alike to star in television series or movies together. Although 2D animation wasn't as popular as it used to be, he was still generous enough to give them a second chance in the spotlight. Ryan slowly approached Joseph's front door and took a deep breath, then he respectfully knocked on the door waiting for Joseph's response.

"Yes, who is it?" Joseph called from the opposite side of the door.

Ryan poked his head through the door and answered, "Excuse me sir, but do you have a minute to talk?"

"Oh, Ryan, come on in. I didn't know I had an appointment with you today."

"You don't boss, but I just need to talk to you about something. It shouldn't take too long."

"Very well Ryan, I always have a minute for you, after all you're one of my best actors."

"Thanks boss," Ryan said as he took a seat that was placed right next to Joseph's desk.

"What can I do for you Ryan?"

"Well you know boss, I am really thankful to work for you but some of the people that I work with don't get treated fairly."

"What do you mean?"

"I mean the 2D characters; they don't land great parts in movies anymore. They're underrated, considered as underdogs, and no one treats them with respect anymore. Today our producer, Charles, was extremely hard on Kyle and it was completely unnecessary. I believe the 2D characters should get the same respect as the 3D characters."

"I know where you're coming from, and I'm sorry about that, my friend. There's very little I can do nowadays you see, the future is always progressing ever so quickly and 3D animated characters are of the modern age while apparently, the 2D characters are of the former age. I did the best I could by at least allowing several 2D characters to star here at my studio when no other studio for miles around would hire them, but their ratings aren't doing me any good. The critics don't care much for 2D anymore and unfortunately, they're causing me budget cutbacks. The only reason why my company is still prospering is because of you 3D characters."

"It's unfair the way 2D characters get treated; they were here long before 3D characters were even created. It's similar to how everyone got rid of puppetry animatronics and upgraded to everything being CGI. At least with puppetry you knew people crafted those special effects by hand and had to come up with techniques that couldn't be done back then. You also have to consider the fact that at least you knew something was in front of the camera instead of the computer doing everything. People seem to forget the memorable classics of the golden age of animation and begin to uplift the advanced, future technology of the new age."

"So in your opinion, you think the 2D's are better?" Joseph inquired.

"I'm not saying that at all, I'm just saying why can't we all get along? We're both good at what we do, I just wish the critics and audiences could see that."

"Literally if it were up to me Ryan, 2D and 3D characters would always be famous for what they do. There wouldn't be any competition between the two."

Chapter 1: The Concern

"Well, no one could be as generous as you anyway. If it weren't for you then there would be a lot of 2D characters out of work, I just wish there was something I could do to change everything."

"You hold that thought Ryan, maybe you'll be able to do something after all."

"Really, what?"

"Due to your talents as animated beings, cartoon characters of your caliber have always been equipped to wriggle your way out of hectic situations. Just wait for the right moment and an opportunity will approach sooner or later."

"I hope you're right boss. Well—I guess that's it then, I'm sorry if I took up any of your time."

"Nonsense Ryan, you're always welcome, but I am an extremely busy man so next time you come in, make sure to make an appointment first."

"You got it, boss. I'll see you around."

Ryan jumped from the chair and headed out towards the door when he almost bumped into a tall man who just entered Joseph's office. It was William, mostly known to everyone as a heartless and notorious gambler that built an empire based on his wagers as a bookie, which was odd considering his line of work and showing up at an animation studio. Coming in right beside him was a fully grown 3D female polar bear named Miriam. She was intimidating enough to give Ryan a startle who immediately walked right past her. William knew Joseph personally and would occasionally visit him from time to time, especially when he was at work. However, Joseph disapproved of William for the simple fact that everything he heard resembled the cash register jingle and everything he saw resembled dollar signs. He was a dirty scoundrel with readiness for gambling and only cared about making more money for himself, even if it was illegal and unscrupulous. William politely walked into the office wearing a flawless suit while his sidekick polar bear stood by as a personal bodyguard.

"Excuse me," said Ryan as he left the office. William then closed the door behind him and focused his attention on Joseph.

"Mister Roberts, it's great to see you again."

"What's so great about it?"

"Let's get down to business, Joseph. You know why I'm here."

"Yes, I know. Again, my employees aren't the sort of people who will do well in your racketeering ring, William. They're cartoons, not wagers."

"But you said so yourself, the 2D characters are depleting your finances and that's not good business for you. Eventually, you'll be in debt with your company. You should let me take them off your hands so you don't have to be caught in the middle anymore."

"The 2D characters do their best in my studio despite the critic's receptions and I'm not going to hold that against them."

"I don't understand why you continue to put yourself through this mess."

"Call it what you like but somebody's got to care."

"What year are you living in? Nobody cares for each other anymore. We're living in a new century where everyone is out for themselves."

"Only someone as greedy as you solely cares about themselves. By the way, why do you want the 2D characters? They're not so good in the spotlight anymore so what could you possibly want them for?"

"My friend you could always bribe anyone with anything as long as you manipulate them. Sure 2D animation isn't popular anymore but I have an advantage to working around that."

"As corrupt as your gambling is, I could only imagine the hazardous situations the 2D characters would be getting themselves into. So again the answer is no."

"Stubborn fool, people who know me would never turn down my offers. I'm giving you the deal of a lifetime; you better take it while you still can."

"I believe your time is up William. Good-bye."

Disappointed that he could not convince Joseph with his proposal, he angrily headed for the door with a sly look plastered on his face and turned back towards his stubborn foe. "You know Joseph, as charitable as you are, I'm sure your 2D characters aren't happy working here with all the criticism they get. You may speak for them now but I'm sure everyone is

Chapter 1: The Concern

entitled to their own opinion. When things get harder we shall soon see what happens. In due time my friend, in due time."

William left Joseph's office with Miriam closing the door behind them.

"Let's hope it doesn't come to that. Of all the people I know, I surely wouldn't want to see them in his hands," Joseph said to himself as he got back to his paperwork.

Outside his office, Miriam raised her eyebrow towards William saying, "So you were never going to tell him?"

"It's not my intention to do so. No matter. I'll still easily assemble as many 2D characters as possible. And you do the same, do you understand?"

"Uh boss, I know you've been planning this for quite some time now but I'm conflicted on going through with this plan. These are my people and it would kill me to turn against them like this considering what you have in mind."

"Miriam, this is the second time you question my authority. Don't ever let me catch you doing it again or else you know what will happen," William threateningly warned the polar bear.

"Yes sir," Miriam said submissively.

CHAPTER TWO

TRUE LOVE

Although the workday was over for the cartoons, the majority of them spent their time in a big cafeteria that was in the center of the studio. They constantly served fantastic food for the humans and the cartoon characters alike. Everyone would always sit down with each other involved in different conversations but the 2D and the 3D characters would never sit with each other. They would always sit with their own kind separated from the other class. Most of the animated characters were animals and creatures while a few of them were people. This is how it was every day at Cartoon Studios, but Ryan and Kyle seemed to be the only ones who sat with each other at their own table. Ryan wanted to head home after talking to Joseph but he got kind of hungry so he headed for the cafeteria behind the rest of the staff. When he got there he spotted Kyle sitting at their table and decided to go and talk to him, quickly sliding into the seat right next to his friend.

"Hey Kyle, are you okay?"

"Am I okay? Am I okay? AM I OKAY? Are you kidding me?! You must think I'm a practical joke! An idiotic bird brain!" Kyle shrieked in anguish.

"Calm down buddy, I just came here to see if you were okay. What happened?"

"Where do I begin? Well for one, a missile dropped down on my head, second, they're going to do it again to me tomorrow, thirdly, next week

Chapter 2: True love

they're going to smash fifty anvils on me, and fourth… aww forget it. It's too embarrassing to even talk about."

"I'm sure it couldn't have been as bad as all that."

Kyle looked at Ryan furiously and showed him his severe wound marks from the sponge bath.

"Whoa, what happened to you?"

"As I said, I don't even want to talk about it."

"Well as I always say, tomorrow is a new day. It might turn out better for you."

"Please don't make me hurt you. You can prance along and play mister happy-go-lucky every day, but it's always a nightmare for me tomorrow. Apparently, things have gone down the toilet for us 2D characters."

"I know, I know, I know, Kyle we have this conversation every day. Can we please just talk about something else for once?"

"There is nothing else to talk about when those 3D characters are stealing the fame and glory from us. They think they're so tough and better than us. But the reality is… they're all just a bunch of jerks."

"Including me?"

Kyle focused his attention on Ryan and felt guilty for what he just said. "I—I—I'm sorry Ryan. I didn't mean you. You're the only good 3D companion I have, it's just that I get sick and tired of being treated this way and it's especially due to them!"

"What you need is a nice refreshment. I'll get you some coffee."

"Coffee? Apparently, caffeine is your thing; I'm not very fond of it."

"Trust me pal, when you get into caffeine like me, you'll never feel dry ever again. In your case right now, it's just what the doctor ordered."

As Ryan left the table to head for the food section, he wasn't looking where he was going causing him to bump into somebody who dropped their food tray. Ryan felt completely embarrassed; his first reaction was to pick up the food that had fell on the floor. "I'm terribly, terribly, terribly sorry; I've never done this before. Let me clean up this mess for you, it's all my fault."

"It's quite alright, mister."

Besides hearing what the individual said, Ryan's attention was on the voice which was the most attractive, joyful, mesmerizing voice that he had ever heard. Before he continued picking up the food, he first noticed the female's feet which were two sets of a dark-reddish color then slowly inch by inch he gradually brought his head up until he got a clear look at the character. His nose then met hers causing him to blink rapidly as if to make sure he wasn't dreaming, but to his astonishment, it was a female fox. Oddly enough, the most amazing aspect of it all… she was a 2D character. Her fur was a refined light orange color and white stomach which hypnotized him like a sideshow magician's trick. Ryan's heart began to vibrate uncontrollably, for he had never fallen in love before. Nevertheless, he had tried in the past to meet the right girl but he never found her… until now. It was strange and unusual at the same time; no 3D character in history had ever fallen in love with a 2D character or the other way around. Staring at her was like finding one's soul mate, the one person you've been searching for your whole life. No doubt about it, Ryan had fallen in love with a 2D character. His mouth began trembling, his ears started to droop, and he started sweating profusely as the food he held quickly dropped back onto the floor. He honestly didn't know what to say, all he could do was gaze at her. It was like everything else around the room became blurry, except for her, she was a dream and fantasy come true. The female fox felt uneasy the way Ryan was looking at her so she decided to speak.

"Are you alright? Umm… I'm Jewel by the way, it's a pleasure to meet you," she said respectfully.

But Ryan still couldn't answer; he was still caught up in a bewildered trance. As the staring continued, Jewel grew more uncomfortable so she decided to leave.

"Alrighty then—ummm… I'll just get myself another food tray. See ya around—weirdo."

As Jewel turned around Ryan could feel her silken tail run across his face smelling the fragrance of sweet royal roses blooming in the spring and felt an extremely heartwarming sensation that pierced right through his soul. Ryan knew at that exact moment that Jewel was meant to be with him, he didn't care if she was 2D. He saw something in her unlike any 2D

Chapter 2: True love

character before. He could care less if his kind wouldn't approve but he wasn't even deliberating about that now. Ryan eventually snapped out of his love trance, keeping his entire focus on Jewel and in so doing tried to follow her until a 2D Doberman Pincher named Rex jumped directly in his path preventing him from getting to the 2D's section of the cafeteria.

"Hey buddy, aren't you on the wrong side of the cafeteria," he viciously growled.

"I'm sorry, I just wanted to…"

"Get back on your own side, or things will get real ugly."

Rex barked furiously at Ryan and nudged him back on the 3D's section of the cafeteria giving him another snarl before leaving. Though Ryan stayed in his section, he still kept his eye on Jewel as she gracefully retrieved another tray of food and began to take her seat with the other 2D characters. Still fixated on the beautiful fox, Ryan failed to notice that Kyle was speaking to him. The impatient pterodactyl shoved him repeatedly trying to get his attention.

"Hellllllloooooo! Hello, hello, hello! Ryan is anybody home in that brain of yours? Have you finally had a breakdown buddy!?"

Unable to tolerate Kyle's constant nagging, Ryan focused his attention on him.

"W-what? What do you mean have I finally had a breakdown? I was never on the brink of having one."

"Well, judging by your spaced-out nature, peculiar mannerisms, and your apparent deep thought, my personal opinion would be to see someone that can help you."

"I think I already have," Ryan sighed.

"What are you talking about?"

"I want you to take a look at something for me okay?"

"Okay," Kyle agreed feeling slightly concerned.

Ryan grabbed Kyle by the wing and directed his attention towards the 2D's section of the cafeteria.

"You see that female fox on the left side of the table over there?"

"Yeah? So what."

"Who is she? I've never seen her around here before."

"Of course you wouldn't, don't you know the identities of 2D and 3D are kept confidential from each other." Kyle tried not to laugh, as Ryan rolled his eyes.

"Just tell me who she is."

"Okay, okay, from what I know her name is Jewel and she started working here last week. She mostly keeps to herself but she's alright—I guess. Why do you want to know about her? She's 2D for crying out loud."

"She's gorgeous Kyle. My heart is literally aching for her; I've never seen such a beautiful work of art before. She's better than any 3D fox I've ever known. I honestly think that… um… that I'm in love."

Kyle looked at Ryan as if something contagious just struck him. It was already shocking enough that Ryan made friends with him but he couldn't comprehend what Ryan was even imagining. A 3D character falling in love with a 2D character was outrageous and unheard of.

"Oh my gosh! It has finally happened. This is worse than a breakdown, your health is out of control, you need a doctor quick. I'll take you to the nurse's office—umm… on second thought forget about the nurse's office. I'll take you to a real hospital instead."

"Kyle, will you knock it off! I'm not sick; in fact, I've never felt better in all my life."

"Poor thing, you've been around 2D animation for so long, it seems they've contaminated your brain to the point of utter stupidity. But it's a good thing because if a cartoon character was ever sane then we would be as sensible as humans. A terrible thought to think about, being exactly like them… yuck!"

As Kyle's words spilled out, several humans passed by and were greatly offended by the pterodactyl's comment. He immediately noticed them and giggled shamefully. "Uh, no offense to you guys of course! Just be glad my intelligence is lower than yours."

"Kyle, can you put aside your deranged mentality and understand what I am saying," Ryan claimed aggressively. "I think I'm in love—with Jewel."

The words descended into Kyle's head. At first, he thought Ryan was mentally ill and he couldn't believe it as his eyes widened and his mouth dropped open. "Oh my Gosh! You're serious aren't you?"

Chapter 2: True love

"Dead serious."

The anxious pterodactyl flapped his wings hysterically then grabbed Ryan by the tail with his claws.

"Hey Kyle what are you doing!"

Kyle placed Ryan underneath their table and quickly joined him.

"News flash Ryan, when in history has a 3D and 2D character fallen in love? It can never happen, I don't know if you noticed lately but we're at war here. We can never get along as one race."

"None of that matters to me Kyle, my heart is telling me to follow Jewel and that's exactly what I am going to do. I'm not going to deny who I have feelings for."

"You're sicker than I realized. You don't need a doctor; you should be committed to an insane asylum."

"What's wrong with falling in love with somebody?"

"Someone who is not a 2D character, Einstein!"

"Leave Einstein out of this. This is Jewel we're talking about."

"Ugh shut up, look the point is you're walking on eggshells here. You're going to start something deadly."

"Why should our looks determine who we should or shouldn't be with? I'm sick and tired of all of this ugly prejudice. We are all cartoon characters and as long as we're animation we are one race."

"Powerful speech my brother, however, it's still not going to make a difference. Your kind won't approve of your feelings. They'll stop you at all cost if they have to."

"I'd like to see them try," said Ryan as he got up and strolled over to the 2D's section of the cafeteria.

"Ryan stop! You stop right now!" Kyle yelled anxiously. "Sit, stay, stay! Ugh, a dog would be more obedient."

But Ryan didn't stop. He completely ignored his nervous friend and kept on moving forward.

"Crap, that idiot is going to get himself killed. This is what I get for making friends with a 3D character," Kyle cried miserably.

Of course, Ryan didn't get far because Rex was ready for him and he jumped in his path again.

"Either you have a really hard time listening or you're just really stupid," Rex snarled.

"Listen, I have no beef with you, I just want to talk to someone."

"No you listen! Do you see this line? You are not supposed to cross it. This is our section. Understand!"

"There's no need for this argument. I don't want to fight you; all I want to do is to talk to somebody."

Amazingly, Ryan put his foot onto the 2D's section. The aggressive dog couldn't believe how suicidal he was, causing him to stare in astonishment, then growl furiously. "You just signed your death warrant," he whispered disturbingly.

Unexpectedly, Rex bit Ryan on the leg and threw him back over to his side of the cafeteria causing Ryan to yelp in pain, but he wasn't seriously hurt. The sudden commotion attracted everybody's attention triggering all of the 3D characters to become irritated when they witnessed Rex's action. Every 3D character got up from their seats as well as the 2D characters, obviously ready for a real fight. New to the company, Jewel remained seated at her table unaware of what was going on. She became worried for a brief moment as Ryan directed his concentration towards her despite his injured leg. Kyle immediately flew into the picture to be by Ryan's side.

"I told you to stop Ryan! Why are you so hard-headed and don't listen? Maybe now I should take you to an insane asylum."

"Kyle?" Rex said surprised.

Kyle blew a little sigh of relief when he recognized Rex. They weren't close friends but they were frequently good buddies from time to time.

"Hey, Rex my brother, what's up? I'm sorry about Ryan, he just isn't himself today but I'll take full responsibility for what he just did."

"Mmmmm—very well. You're off the hook this time; fox, only because Kyle said it's okay. But next time, we might not go so easy on you."

"Or what!" said a random 3D lizard.

"Yeah, or what," said a 3D owl.

"You don't want to mess with the old school. We know every trick in the book," Rex snickered.

Chapter 2: True love

"YEAH!" all of the 2D characters roared.

Suddenly every 2D and 3D character was staring each other down while remaining silent and completely still. They were anxiously waiting for someone to make the first move until Joseph abruptly entered the cafeteria. As soon as they saw him, every single one of the 2D and 3D characters got back to their seats and tried to continue as if nothing happened. They put on fake smiles and even tried gobbling up their food while Joseph stared at them, suspicious of what they were about to do if he hadn't come into the cafeteria.

"I sure hope no one was about to start anything," he declared to them. "It wouldn't look good in the media, now would it? Besides, you'll have to answer to me."

"Sure thing boss," everyone answered.

Then the cartoons began to talk all at once, Joseph couldn't understand any of their babbling. "Let's hope whatever you guys were about to do won't happen again," he announced.

Satisfied, he grabbed an apple from the food section and left. Once he was gone the cartoon characters breathed a sigh of relief. They wanted to fight each other more than anything, but they weren't going to risk losing their jobs, especially inside Joseph's studio. Rex just glared back at the 3D's section and whispered, "We'll finish this some other time." Everyone agreed by just nodding their heads. Kyle aggressively grabbed Ryan and placed him back at their table.

"Nice going Romeo, your stupid romance almost caused a big fight in here," Kyle bellowed angrily. "Are you trying to get us all fired or something?"

"You guys are at risk for getting yourselves fired with your hatred for each other but nothing is going to stop me from talking to Jewel."

"The girl must have possessed you with some kind of love spell that made you lose your brainpower. You're more stupider than I realized."

"You don't put more with stupider Kyle, besides call it what you like, but I'm determined to make her mine."

"RYAN! Please come back to me! I don't want to lose my best friend! Stop right now while you still have a chance!" Kyle cried out shaking him.

"Kyle, will you relax? I'm not going to stop until I talk to Jewel and that's final."

"What Jewel needs to do is to give you a good smack across the face for a reality check."

Ryan then jumped from his table and left the cafeteria. Kyle's head just dropped on the table with a sour and depressed look on his face.

"Poor Ryan, I could've sworn that some unnatural being was inside of his brain controlling him. Oh well, if he doesn't survive this, perhaps the producers will be willing to give me a 2D partner to replace him."

CHAPTER THREE

SOUL MATES

Once evening approached, Cartoon Studios was finally closing up for the day. Ryan waited patiently outside the studio for Jewel. After the confrontation he faced earlier, he'd rather wait until she was alone to finally talk to her. All the humans and cartoon characters were leaving and heading for home but Ryan still didn't see Jewel. The only character he noticed leave the building was a large 3D dragon. He was a tall red-orange dragon with two large bat-like wings behind his back, razor-sharp claws for his hands and feet, and was another one of Ryan's best friends whose name happen to be Fangs. In his roles, he always played a vicious and scary dragon but off the set, he was a gentle character and he immediately noticed Ryan on his way out.

"Hey Ryan. What's up?"

"Hey Fangs. How are you?"

"I heard you almost caused a fight in the cafeteria today. You keep that up and everyone will be out of work by the end of the week."

"Gee Fangs, thanks for your input," Ryan scoffed.

"Don't mention it. You know, no one fires 3D characters anymore—unless they deserve it, of course. So anyway what are you doing out here?"

"I'm waiting for—someone, nothing important you need to know about."

"If you say so, just stay out of trouble next time. Oh by the way, how did your filming go today?"

"Same ole, same ole. It's just my partner Kyle who was on the back burner."

"The back burner—oh I see. I think I know how Kyle feels."

"Really? I don't know how that's possible; he's 2D and you're 3D. No doubt your lines are better than the 2D characters'."

"True but they always have me play the bad guy. I'm either tearing up a city, fighting Knights and Vikings, or destroying anything good. For once I would like to play the good guy because that's who I am."

"Oh, well you do look pretty intimidating—no offense. I guess that's why they get you to play the bad guy all the time."

"Still I would like to play the good guy for once! That's why I think I know how the 2D characters feel by not getting the best lines in movies. They just want a second chance to be heard from again and so do I."

"I'm sure you'll get your chance one day, just like I hope the 2D characters will get noticed again."

"Yeah—but what I think I really want is a mate."

"You?! You want a woman?"

"Why not? I'm pretty lonely and just want someone to share my life with. A gorgeous female reptile that will complete my life. Someone who I could relate to, someone who eats meat, especially small critters, they're my favorite snack. The squirrels, raccoons, chipmunks…."

Ryan was getting very uncomfortable with the conversation and started shaking like crazy. He decided to cut Fangs off and quickly change the subject. "Well—good luck with that pal. I hope you find the right girl for you someday and I'm sure you will, just keep a low profile."

"You too—I guess." Fangs scratched his head for a brief moment then began to thrust his wings open. "Gotta go pal, I'll catch ya later."

In a quick flash, Fangs took off towards the sky without looking back. All Ryan could do was wave good-bye as he was blown away from the gust of wind brought by the dragon's wings. After that, Ryan thought his patience had finally paid off when he spotted Jewel. He watched her as she walked out of the studio, however, she wasn't alone. Rex was with her. Why did it have to be that same dog that bit him on the leg earlier? He was by her side every step of the way. At first, Ryan felt a little worried,

Chapter 3: Soul Mates

nevertheless, he wasn't going to let it stop him; he'd been waiting all day to talk to her. Ryan got himself prepared by taking a big deep breath, then he licked his paw and wiped his hair down to make himself look more presentable. Suddenly a hair flung itself up, Ryan just sighed annoyed. Ryan saw Rex and Jewel were walking in his direction so he hurried to intersect them.

"Excuse me Jewel and Rex, I don't mean to bother you."

"You again! You must be eager for a death wish!" Rex growled. "I'm going to call the hounds on you to begin an early foxhunt on your hide."

"Please I just want to talk to Jewel for a minute; I don't want to cause any trouble."

"Pal, you've got trouble! I told you to stay away but you just don't listen. Prepare for agonizing pain and torture. I hope you made funeral arrangements."

Before Rex could do anything, Jewel stopped him by grabbing his shoulder with her small paw. Rex quickly turned to Jewel bewildered as to why she interrupted him.

"Rex that's enough! You're overreacting too much. I'm sure he means well. You don't have to protect me anymore," she answered.

"What! Come on, Jewel. I don't trust these 3D morons, they hate us 2D animation because they think they own everything now."

"I'm sure all of them are not like that. I promise you I'll be alright, you may leave now Rex."

"Good for nothing 3D animation, controlling the world with their CGI crap," Rex angrily mumbled under his breath as he left the studio without Jewel.

After Ryan and Jewel made sure Rex was gone they both focused their attention on each other.

"Sorry about that, Rex is my new bodyguard—I mean my watchdog. But it's not just me, he watches over the other 2D characters as well, especially newcomers. He's very overprotective of us. It's hard to get him to appreciate 3D characters."

"That's quite alright. I've worked for this company for a long time and I already know the 3D and 2D characters hate each other. It's a good thing you've got someone to watch over you."

"You're not a stalker are you?"

"Oh heavens no! I'm nothing like that—it's just uhhhhh…I just wanted to apologize for knocking your food over today and causing that argument which could've ended up in an ugly fight."

"Well that's a start but you didn't cause anything. I do admit though, you kind of embarrassed me by the way you were constantly staring at me."

"Yes—ummm… about that. That's why I wanted to talk to you," Ryan said humiliated as he grabbed his tail. "Would you like to—uh… talk?"

"You mean talk, as in you want to get to know me better?"

"Yeah—something like that."

"Well I'm in no hurry to go home yet so… why not."

"Really! That's great! Uh—I mean—I meant, thank you."

Ryan felt excited, nonetheless, tried to contain his excitement. He finally had the time to talk to the female fox he already loved. He was also pleased that she didn't mind talking to him because he was 3D, so he would make it the best time he possibly could. No matter how things turned out he was determined to win Jewel's heart. Ryan and Jewel spent the entire night together walking around the streets of the city. They soon entered the park which was calm and pleasant. It was during the winter season where there was snow and an ice rink around the lake area. All of the citizens were gone from the park now and it made Ryan and Jewel feel truly special to have it all to themselves.

"Are you cold?" Ryan asked Jewel considerately.

"No I'm fine, thank you Ryan."

"So how did you come across Cartoon Studios before you started working there?"

"A friend of mine recommended Cartoon Studios to me when she told me they still hired 2D animation to star in movies and shows. Of course, I don't have a big role but at least it's better than nothing."

"I get what you mean that none of the 2D get big roles but I respect Joseph. He's a reasonable guy that likes 2D and 3D characters, even

Chapter 3: Soul Mates

though 2D animation gets poor reviews from critics, which is bad for his company."

"You know Ryan; you're unlike any 3D character I've ever met. Let alone had a chance to talk with, since no 3D has ever even tried talking to me before."

"Personally Jewel, I like 2D and 3D animation both. I have great respect for the 2D generation; they made things what they are now. They were here from the early 1900s until now. Some people just forget the true agelessness of masterpieces. They're generally called traditional animation but everyone around here calls them 2D for short like we're normally called CGI but called 3D for short. Also not to mention, if it weren't for 2D animation then none of us 3D characters would even be here. Through the process of development, we always come out as 2D in the beginning, and then when we're in the final stages we're 3D animation."

"Storyboarding right?" Jewel presumed.

"Exactly," Ryan smiled with affection.

"I admire your compassion and understanding. You're probably the only decent guy I know who doesn't want to start fights with 2D animation. You must have a special 3D female character who's lucky to have you."

"Yes—well to tell you the truth Jewel, I don't have a partner. Let alone a 3D fox. I haven't found the right girl yet."

"Oh I'm sorry, I didn't know. But don't you worry, I'm sure you'll find the right 3D girl someday."

"Maybe it's not a 3D girl I should be looking for."

Jewel suddenly became silent and started to stare at Ryan thinking he was crazy but she could look deep into his eyes and see that he was serious. Her whole life she'd been wishing for someone like this, someone with a compassionate personality, someone who appreciates 2D and 3D animation but she never thought it would be a 3D character. Never in history had this ever happened and Jewel felt scared for her life. Not that she was in any danger but she felt a sense of guilt for betraying her kind if she got involved with Ryan. She could only imagine if anyone found out about them how dreadful the consequences could be, so she decided to change the subject by running onto the ice.

"Hey Ryan want to skate?" she asked happily. As she ran onto the ice she accidentally slipped and fell on her stomach, provoking Ryan to immediately come to her aid as he steadily slid on the ice and gently helped her up.

"Jewel, are you okay?"

"Guess I'm not as good at this as I thought I would be."

"Well, I could help you if you want. I starred in an episode once where Kyle and I were stuck in Antarctica freezing in the snow. Unfortunately, poor Kyle got frostbitten, attacked by vicious polar bears, and frozen countless times falling into the icy cold water but I skated on the ice with no problem."

"Okay," Jewel giggled trying to hold back her outburst from Kyle's unfortunate dilemma.

Ryan easily held Jewel under her shoulders helping her stand on her feet. Although Jewel's feet kept on slipping Ryan held her steady to keep her from falling.

"It's okay, just take it one step at a time," he whispered to her.

Jewel calmly took a deep breath and tried to remain stable as she stood still on the ice. She had her eyes closed the entire time but she eventually opened them up realizing she hadn't fallen again. She was steady on her feet as long as she remained calm; this made her feel relieved and satisfied. Ryan continued to hold her feeling an irresistible temptation that was making him fall in love with her more by the moment. He felt his heart beating faster again by just being this close to her but he fought hard to keep his cool and remain calm.

"Alright—I'm going to let you go. When I gently push you aside, just gently slide with your paws instead of running. It's pretty simple once you get the hang of it."

"Are you sure I can do it?"

"There's no doubt about it. You 2D characters are born for these natural things, it's in your ink. Besides, I'll be right here to catch you again if you fall—that is if you don't mind."

Chapter 3: Soul Mates

"As long as you don't try anything funny."

"My paws are sealed," he promised her.

"Alright, I'll give it a try."

Jewel got herself ready just as Ryan gently pushed her aside. Jewel closed her eyes, fearing she would fall again but actually found herself truly skating on the ice. Ryan was right after all, it was pretty simple once you get the hang of it. Jewel stopped running for a bit and just easily slid in circles around the ice. The way she danced made it seem as though she was a natural at it. Ryan was completely captured by her personality. This was a moment he would treasure for the rest of his life.

"You got it Jewel," he congratulated her. "I knew you could do it."

Jewel took a few more turns and spun around in circles like a ballerina. She was enjoying this happy moment realizing she was possibly falling in love with Ryan too but decided to keep it hidden. After one more spin Jewel stopped when something caught her attention. She witnessed a snowflake float right in front of her. Ryan looked up and noticed that it was snowing, but neither Ryan nor Jewel were cold. The snow just made it more romantic for their joyful time together. Ryan looked back at Jewel then smiled as he slid near her. He brought out his paw to her hoping she would take his. Respectfully, Jewel smiled back at Ryan and took his paw just as he had hoped, then both of them slid on the ice together. They both danced on it as though they were dancing to soft romantic music being played in the background. While they persisted skating, Ryan and Jewel were both enthralled by each other's beauty. Jewel became mesmerized by the sight of Ryan's soft 3D fur and his charming handsome good looks, while Ryan became fascinated with her 2D feminine beauty, her delicate blue eyes, and attractive orange fur blowing in the winter snow. Both of them stopped skating believing that their strong love for each other would cause them to break all the rules in animation history, like Romeo and Juliet. Ryan and Jewel were defeated and overwhelmed by a powerful loving feeling, as they continued to stare at one another. Then remarkably, both of them leaned up against each other and gave into their infatuation. They both kissed each other directly on the lips under the falling snowflakes. Their kiss sparked a deep connection that brought them closer together, unlike any romantic couple. Ryan passionately embraced Jewel as he wrapped his tail around her not wanting the moment to ever end. The kiss seemed as though it were lasting for a lifetime but hurling back to reality and realizing what she was doing, Jewel quickly removed herself from Ryan by pushing him away.

"No! We shouldn't!" she shrieked.

"Why not?" Ryan asked very heartbrokenly.

"I'm sorry Ryan. We never should've done this, it's wrong."

"Why? Because we're a little different. Jewel—just for a moment pretend the 2D and 3D conflict doesn't exist. Would this even be an issue if I was 2D instead?"

"Of course not Ryan, it's just that…"

"I'm not trying to force anything on you Jewel, but I can't help the way I feel about you."

"Do you realize if any of this ever got out, you and I could be in serious trouble? 2D and 3D will never get along with each other and it could only escalate into something much worse. They will never let us be together."

"They are the least of my problems; my only problem is if I'm not with you."

"But Ryan, you don't even know me. I'm pretty sure this is just a simple crush. You'll pretty soon find the right 3D fox when she comes along. Trust me; you don't want somebody like me."

"Jewel—I've honestly never felt this way before. I want to get to know you because I don't want to be with anybody else but you. This is not a simple crush, it's something much more powerful which I can't control. I must follow it or else I wouldn't be able to live with myself. My heart is forcing me to tell you that… that I love you."

Ryan gently pushed Jewel off of the ice and followed her. She sat on the cold wet grass while Ryan stood in front of her.

"Listen Jewel. I thought it was just me but after what happened, it's obvious you feel something for me too. It's like we were meant for each other. I don't care what the 2D or the 3D animation think, but I believe our love for one another is more important. I've met many 3D girl foxes

Chapter 3: Soul Mates

and my heart never ached for them as it did for you. I almost got myself killed today because I couldn't stay away from you. It's like you're my one and only true soul mate."

Jewel looked deep into Ryan's eyes. No one had ever been this direct and truthful to her. She admittedly felt the same way about him but she couldn't help thinking about their rival families who would keep them from seeing each other.

"You'll be willing to stay with me no matter what?" Jewel asked.

"Till the end of times."

"What if I were to say no?"

"Then I'll respect your judgment—and just leave if that's what you wish," Ryan said sadly as he turned to walk away. Deeply caring for the woman he loved, he would be willing to do anything for her, even if it meant leaving her alone. Jewel just watched Ryan leave for a minute but couldn't bear letting him go this way.

"Hold on," she cried stopping him. "Okay—let's just say for the sake of argument if it was possible, how could we get away with it?"

"Simple. We could keep it a secret," said Ryan.

"The old secret trick?"

"That way no one will ever find out about us. Things could go on as always but our secret will be kept for our own safety."

"This is crazy—I don't know."

"Please give it a try, my love. Life is way too short to worry about what others will think of you. Sometimes you gotta live your wildest dream before it's too late, especially when following your heart."

"You really know how to pursue a woman—umm you'll forgive me for feeling a little hesitant but I'm really bewildered by all of this."

"Please, I know it doesn't mean anything to you now but I promise you that you'll never be alone. I promise to take care of you till the end of time; I want a chance to be a part of your life and for you to be a part of mine."

After staying silent for a brief moment, Ryan presumed Jewel was unwilling to accept him. He sadly ducked his head down in defeat.

"Okay," said Jewel.

"Okay! Really! You mean you really want to go through with it!?" Ryan cried happily wagging his tail.

"I can't hide the fact I'm probably in love with you too Ryan. I've never found the right 2D male fox for me either, although most of them tried taking me out none of them captured my heart as you did. At the same time, it will be a new experience because 2D and 3D have never been with each other before."

"I'll be willing to take any chances just to spend the rest of my entire life with you Jewel."

Ryan and Jewel happily embraced each other. Their bond was now forever strong and could never be separated. They were going to stick together and stay with each other as long as it took, even if it meant breaking the rules from their rival families. If Ryan was never happy in his life before then he certainly had a reason to be happy now.

CHAPTER FOUR

THE BRAWL

Three months later life hasn't changed for the bitter conflict between the 2D and 3D dilemma. They were constantly at each other's throats, ready to kill one another if necessary. They respected Joseph enough to never let it get out of hand at the studio. Joseph had his hands full dealing with the finances for his company so he really didn't have the time to stop the little clashes between the cartoon characters. Although the struggling bigotry was still an issue, life had become much healthier for Ryan. He and Jewel were still together, happily enjoying their lives with each other, and then shortly after got married in secret. Although it seemed like a frightening experience for Jewel at first, she was glad she went through with it because Ryan was everything she had hoped for. Throughout the whole three months they had been together, Ryan had proven to be a good husband, always watching over her, protecting and supporting her, never getting into arguments and constantly finding ways to be romantic. Ryan always lived in a residence by himself before he met Jewel but since she had become his wife, they now lived together. He couldn't ask for a happier existence but he just wished the conflict would stop between 2D and 3D animation.

One late afternoon, Kyle headed out of the studio to the nearest public restaurant in the center of town. The restaurant was called "EATS." It was a nice fancy café where citizens would often come to eat some of the chef's finest foods, including 2D and 3D characters. Kyle walked inside with a grumpy look on his face taking a seat at one of the nearest tables where his

2D dinosaur friends known as Ralph and Stan were waiting for him. Ralph was a Long Neck dinosaur while Stan was a Triceratops. They were Kyle's best friends outside of Cartoon Studios because they had different jobs in town but they were always there for him if he needed their company.

"Hey Kyle, how was your day at work?" Ralph asked.

"Don't even ask," Kyle remarked. "Is it just me or are things getting worse for the 2D generation?"

"I don't know Kyle," Stan said happily. "I'm happy with my life. My boss just promoted me to assistant manager at the construction site. Sure we probably don't get the fame and glory like we used to, but things could be worse."

"You're kidding me aren't you," Kyle shrieked angrily. "Today on the script a 3D dog told my director Charles that the audience might get more laughs if the pterodactyl would get more injuries done to him."

"The pterodactyl?" Ralph asked confusingly.

Kyle sighed and groaned irritably. "Me you idiot! I'm talking about me!"

"Oh of course," Ralph laughed a little nervous. "Continue."

"Today there was a script of me and Ryan running across some telephone wires," Kyle continued. "I was only supposed to get electrocuted once but thanks to that dog's request I was electrocuted twenty-five times, chased by dogs, bitten by dogs, thrown in the dumpster, smashed by a plane, hit by a car…"

Kyle continued through a whole list of terrible things. Ralph and Stan had to keep themselves from laughing. It was horrible for Kyle; however, it was quite amusing to them. Kyle finally stopped when he noticed his friends were snickering.

"Oh, so you think this is funny huh!?" Kyle asked furiously.

"No—no—no," Ralph and Stan both answered.

"I'd like to see you two laugh when the same thing happens to you!" Kyle yelled. "And it's all because of that 3D jerk! The 3D generation are all a bunch of scumbags!"

Every 3D character in the café stopped eating, immediately becoming very annoyed by Kyle's conversation. They began to stare at the dinosaurs

Chapter 4: The Brawl

like they were ready to jump them, some even bawled up their fist, while others were slamming their hands on the table. Ralph and Stan became petrified, unlike Kyle who liked getting into fights they preferred to avoid them. On the opposite side of their table, there was a small 2D sparrow bird named Carlos who was pecking on bird seeds but instantly stopped when he heard Kyle's talk of 3D characters. Carlos was a troublemaking, loudmouth bird who enjoyed being a nuisance. He became very excited and flew on over to the dinosaur's side of the table where he landed directly on top of Kyle's head.

"Hey don't stop on my account, continue please," he spoke quickly.

"Get away bird; this isn't any of your business!" Kyle yelled annoyed.

"Hey we're family, you're 2D and I'm 2D right. Am I right or am I not right?" Carlos asked.

"Oh yeah, he's right," Stan said.

"Definitely right," Ralph also said.

"Besides I'm a bird, and you're a bird too," Carlos stated proudly.

"I'm a pterodactyl," Kyle groaned.

"The same thing, you're part of the bird family, so go on. Continue with your conversation, pretend I'm not even here," Carlos said rapidly.

"It's pretty hard to pretend you're not here with you on top of my head loud mouthing away," Kyle grunted feeling very aggravated.

"It's cool brother, it's cool. You were saying something about the 3D characters," Carlos said trying to get back on the 3D subject.

"Yeah—I was. They think because they're the new popularity now they get all the attention. The human's decision revolves around 3D animation, they get all the attention, the reputation, the fame, and glory but the reality is—they like to degrade us 2D to the lower level. As if we already don't feel humiliated enough by the constant tease and torment we get from them every day."

Now all of the 2D characters in the café were listening to Kyle. They started to get emotional and could relate to what he was saying. Some were getting angry, while others were sniffling and blowing their noses with a tissue.

"Yeah—I feel for you my brother, they think they're better than we are," Carlos cried. "We are disgraced, cast aside like yesterday's garbage but we will not be ignored!"

The 3D characters were becoming awfully irritated, incapable of containing themselves while listening to Kyle's remarks about them and Carlos' big mouth. At that moment a 2D cow named Diana who was a waitress at EATS came by to serve the customers their food and drinks. Soon enough she came by the dinosaur's table.

"Alright, let me guess, the usual for you three you boys. Three servings of pepperoni and cheese pizza, right?" Diana asked as she had her notepad and pencil out writing everything down.

"Right again Diana," Stan said happily. "You know us too well."

"You forgot about me," Carlos stated.

"Sorry Carlos I didn't see you there," Diana said noticing him on Kyle's head. "I thought I already gave you your order. Two servings of bird seeds right?"

"Right you are sister, but I want something else," Carlos stated.

"And what will it be?" she asked.

"How about some nice warm milk?" he asked joyfully.

Diana became infuriated by Carlos's remark moaning in frustration.

"No really, I want some warm milk, and chocolate milk, and strawberry milk, and also a nice cold chocolate milkshake. With utters as big as those, I bet you can whip up all different types of flavors. By the way—aren't you doing something after work baby?"

In the blink of an eye, Diana squirted some milk at Carlos. It shot him off of Kyle's head like a violent water hose leaving him unconscious in the process. Kyle, Ralph, and Stan stood stunned for a moment looking at Diana and Carlos. Shortly afterward the aggravated cow mooed a terrible sigh and just left.

"Why do I even bother working here?" she mumbled to herself.

Unlike the cartoon characters having their ugly disputes against each other, the humans always got a kick out of their comedy. It was always fun and amusing to them, especially for the children.

Chapter 4: The Brawl

"They are always so funny, it's better than watching them on TV back at home," a little girl remarked.

"I think the 2D characters are funnier, they have more class," said a teenage girl.

"No way, it's the 3D characters with the new style," a teenage boy commented.

With a bunch of feathers flying all over the place, Carlos finally came to. "What happened?" he asked. "Did I get her number?"

"Take it from me pal," Stan mentioned. "Don't have a cow."

"See, that's just the type of humor you don't see any more these days," Kyle stated assertively. "The 3D characters have destroyed that flavor from us with their constant burp and fart jokes. All they care about is crude humor now instead of true creativity."

"No offense Kyle but 2D has sometimes had a reputation for crude humor as well," Ralph remarked.

"It doesn't matter!" Kyle argued. "They will continue to do so until there is none of us left."

"That would be great," said a 3D German Shepherd dog named Rascal. He was sitting on the exact opposite left side of their table. Of course Kyle became furious and directed his attention to the new adversary.

"Hey buddy, if you got something to say to me then why don't you say it to my face," Kyle snarled.

"Bird brain, take a good look around you," Rascal laughed. "No one cares for the old garbage anymore. People always move on to bigger and better things."

"Oh yeah, what makes you guys think you're so special?" Kyle asked angrily.

"Oh man, where do I began," Rascal said sarcastically. "Well first of all, the critics like us better of course. Not to mention we're more advanced than you guys will ever be. People love the new age of CGI now. We're more realistic, cartoonish, easier, and much more entertaining."

All of the 3D characters in the café began clapping after Rascal's speech. Feeling proud of himself he stood on top of the table and took a few bows. Carlos immediately flew back on Kyle's head and told him, "Are you going to let him get away with talking to you like that? Show him who's boss, Kyle! Show him we're the real masters around here!"

Kyle stood up on his table and looked directly at Rascal.

"So you think you're better than us," Kyle shouted at the top of his lungs. "Well for your information butt sniffer, we 2D characters were here long before you guys were even born. We made movies what they are today, despite the critics disliking us; we got their attention in the past. The only reason they don't like us any more is because of you guys corrupting our reputation. I'm sure I speak for all of us 2D characters, we just want a chance to be known and discovered for our talented attributes to entertain audiences around the world like we used to."

Then after Kyle's speech, all of the 2D characters began clapping for him but he didn't take any bows like Rascal did, however, all of the clapping and cheering in the café left the prideful dog angry.

"Take a good look around you buddy," Rascal barked. "No one likes you guys anymore, that's why we star in all the movies and television series now these days. The future is moving on up and we are the future! You guys are old stuff, the elderly ancient generation; you're over and finished with!"

The way Rascal aggressively barked at Kyle made every single 2D character in the café assemble themselves on the dinosaur's side of the table. This instantly made all the 3D characters gather up on Rascal's side of the table. Rival groups were on opposite sides of each other ready to start a real fight leaving the whole restaurant in complete silence; even the humans remained quiet.

"This always ends up badly," Ralph cried as he hid underneath the table.

"Next time we should just get fast food," Stan whimpered under the table with Ralph.

"I've got twenty bucks that the 3D characters will trash 'em," a teenage boy told another.

"You're on," whispered the other teenager.

Within seconds a big battle erupted between the cartoon characters. Some were flying all over the place, while others threw food at their targets.

Chapter 4: The Brawl

Rascal was chasing Kyle around the café and bit him on the tail once he came into contact with him. Kyle screamed in pain but eventually used his wings and flew out of the jaws of Rascal. He flew above the café like a stealth aircraft and looked below him searching for Rascal in the commotion. Once he caught sight of him he instantly zoomed at the dog knocking him up against a table. At that moment Kyle had Rascal in the grip of his claws strangling him senselessly while the dog was gasping for air.

"I had my share of enough bruises and broken bones on the filming set today," Kyle yelled. "But as much as I hate you guys, I'll be willing to end up in the hospital just to rip you guys apart!"

"Really, well you might want to start by wearing a bandage strip over your face," Rascal said.

Leaving Kyle confused for a moment, Rascal immediately removed himself from Kyle's claws and punched him directly in the face. Kyle fell back and held his face from the soreness. When he removed his hands, Kyle revealed the discolorations of two black eyes.

"That's a good look for ya, you should do it more often," Rascal laughed as he strolled away.

"I'm going to kill that dog!" Kyle yelled furiously as he flew after him.

Some of the humans were getting frustrated when all they wanted to do was come here and eat, so they decided to leave while others stayed enjoying the fight. It was mostly the teenagers and kids who were enjoying the amusement. The 2D and 3D characters were always careful to make sure no humans would ever get hurt in their madness; it was in their nature to hurt each other but never a human. Humans were always important and precious to them because their destiny is to entertain and humor them till the day they died. Carlos was suddenly thrown across the room like a baseball and fell on one of the customer's table, accidentally knocking their food over. One of the teenagers flicked Carlos across the head to wake him up. After getting himself back together Carlos shook himself off and smiled at the teenagers.

"Wuss up guys," he replied. "Be sure and tell your friends about me, I've got connections with a lot of people. Oh yeah, and don't miss my show, Saturday mornings at 3:30 a.m."

"Saturday mornings at 3:30 a.m.," the teenager said to himself. "No wonder 2D animation isn't as popular as it used to be. It kind of makes me feel sorry for them."

"I think the only popular 2D animation is Flash now," said the other teenager. "Flash is still 2D animation but it's used off the computer. Traditional animation like these guys are hand-drawn old fashioned."

"How do you know that?"

"I went to the Art Institute," he replied.

Carlos quickly flew back into the brawl. "Anarchy!" he called enthusiastically but within seconds was easily thrown into the front counter where the waitresses served the customers their food. He fell right into a pie which Diana was about to serve but stopped when she noticed him fall inside of it.

"Hey baby—how about that ch-chocolate milk?" he asked wearily, and then fell unconscious all over again. Diana quickly focused her attention on everyone in the café witnessing the whole brawl. She groaned in frustration again walking over to the telephone.

"Why didn't I listen to my dad and become a farmer instead," she said upsettingly as she dialed a number. "Yeah get me the police, we have another fight."

CHAPTER FIVE

RYAN'S MIRACLE

Simultaneously while the fight was taking place at EATS, Ryan was on his way home. He usually took Ubers for transport because the driver who frequently drove him was a friend of his named Grace. She was a red 2D alligator with short black hair wrapped in a blue band matching her tomboyish personality. She didn't care much for 3D characters but didn't mind driving Ryan to his destinations. She respected Ryan as a descent friend because of his kind-hearted nature but Grace like many 2D characters, was upset with her lifestyle, she actually hated driving Ubers. She was once a famous actor who starred in plenty of television series but her career was ruined when the filmmakers decided to replace her with a 3D alligator. There was also a human lady named Alexandria Anderson in the vehicle with them. She was a top-notch lawyer, with a reputation for winning many cases. She was also Ryan's lawyer and an endless workaholic who always seemed married to her cell phone. Alexandria had him sign some papers she urgently needed within a few days. Ryan flipped through the stack of paperwork, hoping it would end soon, his paw feeling like it was stinging with arthritis.

"My goodness Anderson, how much more of this paperwork do I have to sign?" Ryan asked anxiously.

But Alexandria wasn't even listening to him; as always, she was too busy talking on her cell phone. "Now Carl, you need to reschedule Joshua's appointment to Friday afternoon cause I won't be there in time," she demanded. "Their case isn't that serious so tell him there's nothing to worry about. As for Jeremy Willis, reassure him that I've dealt with this kind of situation before. It's going to be a difficult case but be I'm sure we'll accomplish it."

Ryan looked at Grace in the review mirror as they both shared the same expressions of aggravation.

"I still can't imagine how you got her as your lawyer," Grace remarked.

"Long story. Yes, she's hard and quite difficult but I'm lucky to have her," Ryan replied. "Yo' Anderson, I know you're a very busy woman but don't you have any relaxation in your life."

"When I'm old and wrinkled, then I'll rest!" Alexandria stated.

"Are cases all that matter to you?" Ryan asked. "I swear if you had no one left to sue you'd probably go after your own family members next?"

"Been there, done that," Alexandria said without even blinking an eye. "Alright, did you finish all of the paperwork yet?"

"Yet?" Ryan cried. "Woman you've given me a hundred papers to sign and you ask me am I finished yet. By the time this is over I'm going to have to soak my paws in ice-cold water for a week."

"Are you done complaining?" Alexandria inquired. "And don't forget your wife needs to sign some papers too."

"I'll take them home with me to have her sign them then I can return them to you later," Ryan said.

"Hey speaking of which, how come none of us has ever seen your wife Ryan?" Grace asked.

"Because she's shy—very shy, she doesn't like to go outside at all," Ryan said worriedly.

Grace could read Ryan's expressions as easily as a book and knew he was keeping something confidential; he didn't want anybody else to know about it. "I can tell you're hiding something," she scoffed. "Trust me, one of these days I'll find out the real truth."

"Fine, but she still needs to sign these papers," said Alexandria, as she handed Ryan the documents.

Grace stopped the car once they arrived at Ryan's house. She parked the vehicle on the sidewalk in front of his driveway, as he stumbled out of

Chapter 5: The Miracle

the Uber; his paws looked like skeleton bones and still felt sore as he clutched the paperwork in his arms.

"Now Ryan, I want that paperwork done by tomorrow and pronto!" Alexandria demanded.

"Yes your highness," Ryan replied. "That is if my paws will still be able to function properly."

Alexandria was about to reply until her cell phone started ringing. She instantly got back on it and started chatting again as Ryan rolled his eyes and looked up at Grace who poked her head out of the car.

"Ryan, what are you really hiding," she asked anxiously. "You can trust me, I can keep a secret."

"How do you even know I have a secret?"

"I can tell from the way you're acting. You never hide secrets and for you to have one it must be very serious."

"Grace please, you'll only disappoint yourself when you find out that I don't have a secret."

"I thought you trusted me Ryan."

"I trust you as a good Uber driver—nothing more."

"Ryan! I'm ashamed of you. I have been your transportation for a long time but I thought we were friends and that we at least developed a sense of trust with one another. I thought you were different from the other 3D characters—but I guess I was wrong."

Ryan felt guilty for what Grace just said. He would take the secret to his grave before he would tell anyone; nevertheless, he did consider his good friends who probably could've kept the secret with him. In a way, he sensed himself being selfish and not trusting his friend's judgment which was a side of his personality he didn't like. Before he could say something to Grace, she angrily rolled up the window and started the Uber driving off in a quick flash. All Ryan could do was watch the Uber disappear in the distance, sighing, and feeling terrible for the way he made Grace feel.

"Stupid," Ryan complained. Thinking to punish himself, he slapped his head and squeezed his mouth shut from the torment, as his eyes began to water. He immediately realized that it was his tender paws he had slammed against his head and it suddenly felt like he broke them.

"AHHHHHHHH!!!" he screamed to the universe.

When Ryan made it to his front entrance he closed the door behind him collapsing on the carpet floor and let the paperwork just fall next to him.

"Yeah—I deserved—that," he whimpered to himself.

Jewel quickly came around the corner of the hallway when she saw Ryan by the door.

"Sweetheart, are you okay?" she asked. "I thought I heard you screaming from outside."

"Trust me baby, that wasn't even the least of what I deserved after what I did," Ryan said as he stood up on his feet.

"What did you do?"

"My friend Grace wanted to know about us but I wouldn't tell her anything. She felt I couldn't trust her. I really might have lost one of my good friends because I couldn't trust her decision. Not to mention I could've caused Grace not to trust 3D characters anymore because of me."

"I think you're beating yourself up way too much but I do agree if you have a close friend that you could trust, then maybe you should consider telling them."

"I really don't want to risk our safety, especially yours."

"Well—I did tell someone about us Ryan."

"WHAT! Who, when?!?"

"Three months ago, after you proposed to me, it was Rex I told."

"REX?"

"He wanted to know why I was keeping secrets from him and he was really concerned about me. Eventually, I told Rex that I would never tell him anything unless he kept the secret to himself. He promised me, so I eventually told him. Of course when I told him about us, he was furious. More than anything all he wanted to do was go after you. But he didn't, you know why?"

Ryan shook his head no.

"Because he knew I was pleased with you, all he wanted was my happiness. And for three long months, he has never broken his promise. He kept our secret safe and sound without telling anyone. Yes, he may still

Chapter 5: The Miracle

hate you and other 3D characters but despite his nasty nature he still has his heart in the right place."

"Jewel—why didn't you ever tell me?"

"For one, Rex didn't want you to know that he knew. He told me he preferred it if you didn't know about him. Second, I was afraid you would be angry with me—because I know how much you wanted me to keep this secret just between us."

Ryan smiled and passionately hugged her. "Jewel—I could never be angry with you," he said. "You're my life and my only reason for living."

Ryan then gently removed himself from Jewel smiling with happiness.

"I'm really grateful for Rex keeping our secret all this time. I honestly didn't think I could trust someone like him because of his hatred towards me and my kind. But now—he's proven me wrong. It just makes me feel even worse because I could've told Grace or Kyle all this time. After all, they're good friends of mine."

"You still have a chance honey, it's not too late you know."

Ryan still felt a little depressed but was gradually warmed by Jewel's confidence. If Jewel could trust someone like Rex then he could certainly trust one of his friends as well. Ryan then looked down at his wife's stomach which was plump and fat. He knelt down near her stomach gently resting his head on her belly.

"So how has our little guy or girl been doing today?" he smiled rubbing her stomach.

"A little feisty but he or she is fine," she said proudly.

"I can't wait until we have our first kid. From the moment I found out you were pregnant, it was one of the happiest moments of my life."

"Mine too."

Since the day the two had found out they were going to become parents, Ryan would have never thought in a million years that he would ever become a father. He didn't even think it was possible for him and Jewel because of their distinct differences. Now, they were about to have a baby that would be the first cartoon character in history, crossbred from 2D and 3D animation, not by the hands of animators but by the creation of two creatures coming together to create new life. However, the two didn't want to overthink it. It could easily be a 2D baby or just a plain 3D baby. Still, they weren't sure about anything, other than that they were completely thrilled about this miracle.

"The only thing I'm still worried about Ryan is when we have this child, we won't be able to keep our secret hidden anymore," Jewel said worriedly. "Everything will be out in the open. The horrible revelation is if someone found out about our child they might try and destroy it, especially our rivalry families. They always despised each other so they wouldn't tolerate anything that would be a combination or a hybrid of their enemies."

Jewel slowly took a seat at the nearest sofa and wrapped her arms around her stomach. Ever since she found out that she was pregnant, she felt actual fear and terror for their child. She couldn't bear any harm or prejudice to ever come to him or her. Ryan could see the discomfort in her heart and he knelt down right beside her as he wrapped his arm around her shoulder.

"Jewel, I felt the exact same way for the first time you told me you were pregnant but this should be a happy moment for us. Our child wouldn't be born for a reason if he or she couldn't exist. I'll love him or her no matter what they'll come out looking like and I promise you that no harm will ever come to you or our child. Besides we already planned and discussed if necessary we'll leave town if we have to. We'll move to a nice and little decent town where the population is really low and where we could live peacefully."

"Even if it means sacrificing your job at Cartoon Studios and all of your good friends?"

"You and our child are more important to me and that's all that matters. I'll throw all of this away for you any day."

"That's so sweet of you Ryan but remember I don't want you to decide that unless a drastic situation called for it. If the risk will be too much for our child, I'll go away with him but I still want you to keep your job and friends at Cartoon Studios. You built your career there and I couldn't bear it if you threw it all away. I wouldn't want to move too far away from this

Chapter 5: The Miracle

town, that way you can still always come over and be the supportive father I know you'll be."

"Don't worry baby," Ryan assured her as he kissed her on the nose. "We'll find a way to make this work and we prepared for it."

Jewel honestly didn't know how things were going to turn out but she appreciated her husband's support every step of the way. She gradually embraced him around the neck giving him a whole bunch of kisses.

"I love you Ryan."

"I love you more Jewel,"

"It shouldn't be much longer now. Three months is the deadline for our kind when it's about time to have a kid," she mentioned. "I just hope it won't interfere with any plans we might have scheduled."

"For whatever the baby is involved, I'm willing to drop any plans if necessary."

Getting up from the sofa, Ryan strolled across the room and grabbed two suitcases where he began rechecking their belongings which were packed for emergencies whenever Jewel was ready to give birth. "Everything is still packed and ready just as the day we planned it. Anything else that needs packing?"

"Not that I could think of," Jewel said calmly. "Maybe a new crib would be nice."

"Already arriving in the mail baby, along with the other baby appliances."

"You always think ahead don't you?" she smiled.

Suddenly the telephone rang which gave Ryan quite a jump. He quickly picked up the phone and answered it.

"Hi this is Ryan. Oh Joseph it's you. Yes. Yes I understand. Really—now? But—but I—okay I understand. Is it that important? Okay. Yeah—yeah, I'll be there."

Ryan hung the phone up with a sad look on his face.

"Honey, what's the matter?" Jewel asked.

"I need to head back to Cartoon Studios. Joseph said it's urgent."

"Well, then you should go."

"But what about you?!"

"You act like you never left me alone before, I'll be fine Ryan."

"That was before we are now cutting it close to having our kid. I don't want to leave you and take that risk when the baby could be due at any moment. Please Jewel let me stay here with you."

"You already told Joseph you'll be there. You must go to Cartoon Studios and help your boss out. I promise that I'll be okay and trust me, the baby won't come while you're gone."

Ryan didn't like the idea at all but eventually gave in. "Alright—but if you feel anything, anything at all don't hesitate to call me."

"You know I will."

Before Ryan headed out the door, he gave Jewel a big hug and embraced her as though it was their last moment together. He was afraid of leaving her and the baby's side.

"I promise you I'll be back before you know it," he said as he held her tightly.

"You go on and take care of your business, I love you Ryan."

"I love you too Jewel, with all my heart."

CHAPTER SIX

THE BRIBE

Apparently, the fighting at EATS eventually landed Kyle, Ralph, Stan, and Carlos inside of a prison cell. Kyle was looking miserable sitting on the side of his bunk bed feeling annoyed by the irritating Carlos.

"Hey don't sweat it pal," Carlos assured his comrades. "I've been in worse situations than this. I was the only sibling in my family who fell out of the tree at birth and I hit every branch on the way down and I turned out just fine. But that battle back there was awesome; I loved the way you handled that 3D mutt, he didn't even have a clue what hit him. And all the others, boy, didn't we have them on a roll. I love it when we go into combat; it teaches the 3D scum not to mess with the real big boys. We should do this more often. Two days a week no—three, four days a week."

Kyle's dinosaur buddies, Ralph and Stan couldn't stand Carlos's loud mouth anymore. They both ran towards the prison bars pleading for mercy.

"Let us out of here!" Ralph cried.

"We had nothing to do with the fight! We didn't even hit anyone!" Stan cried.

"Calm down you two, we'll eventually get out of here," Kyle said rationally.

Outside the prison bars, Rascal walked by and quickly flicked Kyle on the nose. The irritated pterodactyl held his beak not realizing what just hit him.

"Hey!" he cried.

"Hey is for horses and cows," Rascal laughed. "But I wouldn't count on you guys leaving so you might as well get comfortable."

"What are you talking about?" Ralph pleaded.

"As I said before, everyone likes 3D animation better so none of us have to face any charges," Rascal replied rudely. "But the charges against you 2D characters are severe this time and you won't be getting out of this one so easily. I'll be sure to send you guys a telegram. Ha, ha, ha, ha!"

Rascal continued laughing as he headed out of the prison walking down the hallway.

"I hate that dog," Kyle groaned as he held the prison bars tightly.

After hearing what Rascal just said, Ralph and Stan began to cry in misery.

"We're done for!" Stan wept.

"Who'd ever thought eating in a restaurant would end up with us spending time in prison," Ralph cried. "I hope this doesn't go on my record."

"Oh it's not so bad you guys, I spend half of my life in prison," Carlos said happily. "But don't worry, they're usually nice to newcomers, they give you gifts like a brand new sledgehammer. And the inmates are somewhat generous... they'll only break one part of your back instead of turning you inside out."

"I want my mommy!" Ralph screamed. His scream was so loud it could be heard throughout the entire prison.

Inside the front office of the police station, Lieutenant Elliot Strode approached his front desk. As a lieutenant he'd been doing this job for quite some time; however, he didn't seem to mind. Besides managing a whole police force he had two assistants which were Roberto and Maya. They were the only 2D characters in the entire department. Roberto was a blue medium-sized 2D octopus who was basically a respectful citizen and only wanted to do the right thing, not to mention he's very helpful due to his eight arms. Maya on the other hand was a small 2D chipmunk who's the exact opposite of Roberto. She worked with Roberto in the same department and loved her job but always hated breaking up fights between

Chapter 6: The Bribe

the 2D and 3D characters. In her opinion, she preferred they be taught a lesson crucially. The only thing that symbolized the two cops were the officer hats they always wore on their heads. Lieutenant Strode looked at the recent paperwork from the commotion caused earlier in the café. His assistants Roberto and Maya were the main ones who brought the trouble makers in but it was Roberto who mainly did all the work.

"How are you today, boss?" Maya said happily.

"What are you so cheerful about?" Lieutenant Strode asked in a less enthusiastic voice.

"We took care of some business downtown today," Maya commented. "I think you'll be delighted with our results."

"So what do we have here?" Lieutenant Strode said looking at the paperwork.

"Same old thing, boss. 2D and 3D characters fighting each other again," Maya replied.

Immediately, Lieutenant Strode became upset and slammed the paperwork on the table looking directly at Maya. She jumped for a second because he almost hit her.

"Was it something I said?" she asked a little terrified.

"Maya, how many times do I have to make this perfectly clear to you?" he scolded. "For the hundredth time, my prison is not meant for cartoon characters, only humans!"

"I told you he wouldn't approve of this Maya," Roberto remarked.

"Shut it Roberto, nobody asked you anything! Listen boss, they don't have prisons out there for 2D or 3D characters," Maya cried. "But they should because we get into fights just as much as you humans do."

"You guys are cartoon characters," Lieutenant Strode explained. "The fights you guys get into are meant for audiences to laugh and enjoy. It's in their nature to act the way they do."

"No boss, you don't seem to understand," Maya clarified. "The conflict between 2D and 3D animation is getting out of control. The only way we can teach these idiots a lesson is by making them understand the law and it starts by locking them up in the joint if they deserve it."

"Listen here you little rat!" Lieutenant Strode yelled. "Don't you dare challenge my authority, I'm the boss around here and I call the shots! You are to let every single 2D and 3D character out that you've locked up and don't let me catch you locking up any more cartoon characters in here again! Only humans! Do you understand me?"

"But—but I…" Maya protested.

Lieutenant Strode gave Maya a firm look as a warning sign. Feeling scared and defeated she eventually agreed.

"Yes sir," she sighed.

"Now if you'll excuse me," he stated, "as you all know I have to leave the department for today. Although I'll be back tomorrow I'm depending on you and Roberto to take care of things until I return."

"Yes boss," Maya and Roberto said at the same time.

"And don't you do anything stupid Maya. If she does Roberto, don't hesitate to tell me," he warned them both. Lieutenant Strode then walked away and threw the paperwork into a trash can on his way out, leaving Maya frustrated as she hopped on top of Roberto's head and thought diligently for a moment.

"What are you thinking about Maya?" Roberto asked. "Whatever it is, I'm sure it isn't good."

"The only way to get the message across to those idiots is to make them pay attention," Maya said.

"Huh?" Roberto cried.

"The boss will never know as long as he doesn't find out," Maya smiled devilishly. "For those cartoon characters that are still in lock-up—leave them in there."

"But the boss said…"

"I know what the boss said but I'm going to do things my way from now on to stop this conflict between our families."

Roberto used one of his octopus tentacles to get Maya off of his head and set her down on the floor so he could look at her face to face.

"Maya, you're starting to sound like a corrupt cop. This isn't how you do things by the books around here to get your message across."

Chapter 6: The Bribe

"Well I'm going to go through with it Roberto, everyone has always walked over me my entire life just because I'm a small helpless little chipmunk but when they see this badge—that's when they should get scared."

"Don't do it Maya, I'm begging you. You make us 2D characters look bad when we already have a bad reputation with 3D animation taking over."

"I'm doing it anyway Roberto, with or without your help."

"Well I can't let you Maya—I'll—I'll tell. I don't want to because I've worked beside you for twenty years and you're my partner but I can't let you use authority to your own benefit. It makes us and this whole department look bad."

"Very well, if you tell on me—then I'll have no choice but to tell the boss you were the one who inked in his office two weeks ago."

Roberto became frightened by what Maya said and accidentally inked himself all over the floor. Roberto squirmed in embarrassment.

"You know about that!"

"Oh Please Roberto, you're the only one who inks enough ink around here."

"It was an accident—I—I was sleepwalking. I didn't mean to walk into the Lieutenant's office and use it as the bathroom. I was only dreaming."

"Not to mention you also wiped up after yourself using his important documents."

Roberto grabbed Maya in hysteria and pleaded with her anxiously. "Please don't tell him Maya! Please, I beg you!"

"If you only go along with what I tell you."

Slowly and gently Roberto set Maya back on the floor and felt miserable. He felt himself caught up in a situation where he knew there was no possible way out but to agree with it.

"Whatever you say Maya."

"Good, now let's go deliver the good news to the inmates!"

Before Maya could continue into the next room, she found herself stepping and slipping all over Roberto's ink.

"Roberto! Please clean up after yourself will ya!"

With Lieutenant Strode gone for the day, Maya had taken over the whole police department. The rest of the officers hated taking orders from a cartoon chipmunk but they knew Strode left her in charge, so they had no choice. Roberto also hated the fact of being blackmailed by this headstrong chipmunk but didn't want to risk losing his job over his stupid mistake. About an hour later, a big 2D tiger named Jackson entered the police station. He was completely calm, nonetheless, extremely serious at the same time. He wore a black jacket that covered most of his body and looked around the police station giving everybody a scare, even the humans. Then he slowly approached the front desk meeting Maya and Roberto face to face.

"May we help you sir?" Maya asked him.

Jackson gave Maya a frightening stare but answered her question with a very deep and low voice.

"I heard you locked up some trouble-makers that started a fight in a restaurant today," he said.

"You're right," Maya said. "But they're not getting out. They're serving their time… isn't that right, Roberto!"

Roberto wrapped his tentacles around his body shamefully and didn't even want to answer but Maya aggressively nudged him.

"Right," he answered in a low voice.

"How much is their bail?" Jackson asked.

Maya never thought about bail before but she saw this as another opportunity to get more satisfaction for her greedy nature.

"Oh I don't know. Ummmm—how about fifty hundred?" she asked.

"Maya! That's ridiculous!" Roberto yelled. "The boss wouldn't even put the bail that high unless an inmate really deserves it. You're treating our own kind very unfairly!"

"I'm calling the shots around here now, Roberto," Maya scolded.

But to Roberto and Maya's amazement, Jackson immediately threw the exact amount of money that Maya specifically asked for in front of them. The aggressive tiger slowly paced around then walked down the hallway to Kyle and the other's cell.

"Well I'll be," Maya said happily. "This must be my lucky day."

Chapter 6: The Bribe

"The boss doesn't know about that money" Roberto replied. "What are you going to do with it?"

"Oh I don't know," Maya thought. "Buy a lot of nuts."

"Don't you mean donuts," Roberto corrected.

Within a few minutes, Jackson approached Kyle and his friends still waiting inside their chamber. Kyle, Ralph, and Stan suddenly became scared at the unknown figure who was giving them the same stare as he did everyone else.

"Oh no, I hope he's not our new cellmate," Kyle said worriedly.

"Oh please, Dear God no! Just kill me now!" Stan yelled.

"You can take anything you want, just don't hurt me!" Ralph pleaded. "Hold on, I don't have anything."

"I made bail for all of ya," Jackson said.

"You did? Not that I'm ungrateful but why? We don't even know you?" Kyle asked.

"The name is Jackson," he replied deeply. "My head boss, known as Christopher sent me here to get you guys out."

"Why?" Kyle asked once more.

"Is it true that you guys started a fight with the 3D characters?" Jackson inquired.

"Oh yeah it's true," Carlos responded happily. "Guilty as charged I'm afraid but very proud of it. We had them running for their lives. They didn't even know what hit them."

"Oh you're one to talk," Stan complained. "You're the one who was thrown across the café like a baseball countless times."

"Christopher is organizing 2D characters that will be willing to assist him in getting rid of the 3D characters once and for all." Jackson announced. "He wants you to join him in an alliance. In the process, you won't end up in prison ever again and you'll get paid twice as much than you were normally working. This is the opportunity of a lifetime and I suggest you take it. So are you in or are you out?"

Kyle suddenly felt like his prayers had just been answered. He was extremely grateful to be a part of something big that would forever get rid of the 3D animation. He considered it was finally payback and he would probably get the recognition he deserved. Kyle no longer wanted to be treated like the underdog, even if it meant quitting his job at Cartoon Studios.

"We're in!" he said gladly.

"Heck yeah!" Carlos added.

"Good," Jackson smiled mischievously. "When you're ready, meet me in my car out front."

When Jackson left the room, Ralph and Stan didn't like the idea and just felt themselves getting deeper and deeper into an uglier situation.

"Oh, so you just speak for all of us, right," Ralph shrieked.

"But I like my job," Stan objected, "I just told you I got promoted to assistant manager. I don't want to throw all that hard work away."

"This is an opportunity I've been waiting for all my life," Kyle declared. "Finally for once, I will get treated with some respect. You know the old saying—no more mister nice guy."

"It's not natural for something like this to happen," Stan commented. "We could be getting into something much more dangerous. For all, we know it could be a trap."

"Please Stan, the guy just made bail on us for crying out loud," Kyle remarked. "And he promised to pay us double the amount than what we get paid at our normal jobs. What's not to like?"

"It could merely be a part of his darker plans," Stan said worriedly. "I don't like this at all, besides this Christopher guy sounds dangerous. If his bodyguard is a tiger then what do you think he is?"

"I really don't want to know," Ralph exclaimed. "I've got more than I bargained for on this day so far."

"Alright work!" Carlos chirped. "I've never held down a single job before but if it has to do with us getting back at those lousy 3D characters, I'm so there!"

"Just think of it boys," Kyle said gladly. "Pretty soon we'll get our reputation back and the 3D characters will be defeated."

"If the 3D characters are defeated then the only thing I can see is an entire mob of people chasing after us with flame torches," Ralph wailed miserably. "We'll never see the end of it."

Chapter 6: The Bribe

"Ditto," Stan added.

"Kind of like Frankenstein, right?" said Carlos.

"Right," Ralph sighed upsettingly. "We're the monsters."

CHAPTER SEVEN

OLD FRIENDS

Ryan eventually made his way back to Cartoon Studios because Joseph had some urgent news to tell him. He was determined to get back home to his wife. All he could think about was Jewel and his unborn child. When he finally arrived, he noticed there weren't many 2D characters roaming around the studio. The 2D and 3D characters always roamed around the back lot of Cartoon Studios which was an occasional pastime so it would be unnatural not to find any of them wandering around the place. Without hesitating Ryan made his way to Joseph's office and quickly opened the door, without knocking, as he normally would, he just walked inside finding him sitting at his desk as usual.

"I'm here Joseph, what is the urgent news you wanted to tell me?"

"Good, you're here. Ryan—three months ago, remember you told me you just wish there was something you could do to change everything and I told you to hold that thought. Would you still be willing to do something to stop the conflict between 2D and 3D animation?"

"Yes, you know I would sir."

"Well early this morning, most of the 2D characters in the studio quit their job."

"What?"

"Including Kyle not too long ago before you got here."

"W-what's going on?"

"I honestly don't know Ryan, that's why I called you."

Chapter 7: Old Friends

"Me?"

"You said you wanted to do something to stop the conflict between your brothers and sisters. Someone might be deceiving the 2D characters into a trap while they don't even know it and pretty soon the 3D characters will all be gone from Cartoon Studios as well. I can't do anything about the situation but you can. It's in your cartoon's nature to go on adventures and dangerous missions. If you find out the mystery behind this, you might be able to bring the 2D and 3D conflict to an end. It might be their only choice to work together if the situation gets out of control."

"You think the situation could be that serious?"

"Ryan, half the employees don't quit their jobs in a whole day without a reason. Not to mention, I do believe William is behind all of this."

"William? Is William that big-time gambler dude with a 3D polar bear assistant?"

"I'm afraid so. He occasionally comes here trying to convince me that the 2D characters would be better off with him instead. He always warned me that he would get them sooner or later."

"I—I don't know where to start sir?"

"You're smart Ryan, you'll figure it out. That is—if you're still up for it?"

Three months ago Ryan would've wanted to solve this case more than anything; however, he was more concerned about Jewel instead. His baby could be due at any minute and he didn't want to miss the arrival of his baby, but he did promise Joseph that he would try to stop the conflicts between 2D and 3D even before he met Jewel. Under these circumstances, Ryan felt it was his duty to solve it; on the other hand, he would never dismiss his wife over the situation. He would constantly check in on her and quit the mission if the baby was ever to arrive.

"Yes, I'm up for it sir. I'll get to the bottom of it."

"You don't have to do it on my account Ryan, it's more important for your 3D family instead."

"You're right boss; it's about doing the right thing to stop this conflict."

"You sacrifice so much to help 2D and 3D characters alike. I don't have many employees like you, which is what I like about you Ryan and I respect you for that."

"Thank you sir."

"Just—make sure you don't get yourself killed."

"Killed! Wait a minute now, I—uh… I'll—I'll try."

Joseph gave Ryan a satisfactory smile and waved good-bye to him as Ryan waved back to Joseph on his way out the door. Heading back outside, he leaned up against one of the buildings and pulled out his cell phone.

"I gotta call Jewel," he exclaimed frantically. "I hope she's alright."

After hearing nothing but silence for a few seconds she finally answered.

"Hello?" she responded.

"Hey baby it's me, are you okay?"

"Oh Ryan, of course I'm alright, why wouldn't I be?"

"You know why. Feel any different, anything, anything at all?"

"I'm fine Ryan; just tell me what the urgent news was about?'

"Well, most of the 2D characters quit their job here. No one knows why but that's the reason Joseph called me. He wants me to get to the bottom of it."

"Great that sounds like a lot of fun."

"Jewel—I really don't want to go. I'd rather be at home with you and the baby."

"Remember the confidence you gave me Ryan?"

"Yeah."

"Just keep that same faith with you. I assure you that everything will be okay. I promise you if anything happens I won't hesitate to call you."

"But Jewel…"

"Ryan. Do it for me and do it for Joseph."

Ryan hated being away from Jewel when all he wanted to do was be with her, but if the situation Joseph called him for was bigger than any of them, then he knew he had to do something about it.

"Are you sure?"

Chapter 7: Old Friends

"Yes Ryan. You go on and find out the big mystery and take care of yourself."

"You know I will. If you say so then. I love you Jewel."

"I love you too Ryan. Good-bye, and take care."

Ryan heard Jewel hang up the phone first, then he gradually closed his cell phone. When Ryan stepped back he almost got stepped on by one of his tall friends. He looked up right behind him and noticed it was Fangs.

"Hey Fangs watch where you're stepping," Ryan cried.

Fangs brought his head down and spotted Ryan underneath him.

"I'm sorry Ryan, I didn't see you there," he said apologetically. "I guess I should be careful where I walk."

"That's okay, hey listen—did you know that most of the 2D characters are leaving the studio? Joseph wants me to find out what's going on and hopefully get everyone to come back to work."

"That's a bummer. I know it should make the 3D characters happy but not me, I liked having the 2D characters around."

"Since you say that, would you like to solve this case with me? It would be better than just having one individual, besides it might be more dangerous than we expect."

"Oh—tempting Ryan, uh—I really don't know."

"Awww, come on Fangs. When have I ever asked you for anything?"

Suddenly, Fangs wasn't even listening to Ryan anymore; his mind was focused on a 2D character which just entered the studio.

"Yo Fangs! Wake up! Aren't you even listening to me?"

"Whoa—who is that?" Fangs said feeling smitten.

"Huh?" Ryan said.

When he turned his head around, he noticed Fangs was looking at a female alligator but it wasn't just any alligator, it was Grace. At last, this could be his chance to make it up to her and apologize.

"Grace!" Ryan called.

"Grace?" said Fangs. "Oh, what a beautiful name."

Ryan wasted no time running up to her but she didn't even know he was there until he was right in front of her.

"Ryan? What are you doing here?"

"I work here remember."

"Oh—right."

"What are you doing here Grace?"

"It's none of your business but if you really must know, I was just dropping off an employee here. Now if you will excuse me, I must be on my way."

"Wait Grace!" Ryan pleaded.

Grace stopped before she could get back inside her Uber and wondered what Ryan wanted.

"Listen Grace," Ryan spoke apologetically. "I'm sorry how I made you feel. You were right about me and I don't blame you for being angry. It was wrong of me not to trust you. I don't just see you as my Uber driver. You've been a trustworthy friend I could really depend on for a long time. I still want us to be friends and I want nothing to change that. Please forgive me."

Grace looked deep into Ryan's eyes and could tell how truly sorry he was.

"Just to show you there are no hard feelings, I'll tell you everything you wanted to know," Ryan said.

Then he brought his paw out to Grace wanting to shake her claw as a truce.

"Friends," he said hopefully.

Grace couldn't stay mad at Ryan for too long. As much as she hated 3D, she still really appreciated Ryan so she brought her claw out towards his. "Friends," she said respectfully as they shook on it.

"Seeing how you were keeping your secret, you don't have to tell me if you don't want to," she said.

"No, I want to," Ryan said eagerly. "It'll make me feel better just to get it off my chest."

Ryan first looked around him to make sure no one was listening, and then satisfied he turned back to Grace and told her quietly, "Well here it is—I'm—I'm married to a 2D fox."

Grace was silent for a minute, but to Ryan's surprise she burst out laughing hysterically.

"What's so funny?" he asked nervously. "I thought you would be horrified that I could do something like this."

Grace tried getting herself together, recovering over her laughter. "I thought—I thought it was something much more serious than that," she laughed calmly. "I thought you might have been working for the CIA or might have been a spy working for the government."

"It is serious," Ryan protested. "Since when in history have you ever seen a 2D and 3D character together?"

"I guess you're right but I still thought you could've been hiding something much more serious than that," Grace stated.

"You promise not to tell anybody?" Ryan demanded.

"Of course Ryan," Grace stated. "Your secret is safe with me."

"And me!" Fangs remarked.

He scared Ryan and Grace for a brief moment because they didn't know he was right behind them.

"Fangs!" Ryan angrily shrieked. "Were you eavesdropping?"

"Sorry, I couldn't help it but I had to know what was going on?" he said remorsefully. "But I wanted to know what you were saying to that beautiful reptilian creature."

"Are you referring to me?" Grace inquired.

"Yes I am," Fangs spoke without hesitation. "I must say, you're the most beautiful reptile I've ever seen. Allow me to introduce myself, I'm Fangs."

"Fangs? That explains the sharp teeth," she scoffed rolling her eyes.

Fangs looked at the sharp teeth sticking out of his mouth and embarrassingly tried to hide them.

"Yes well um—my animator gave me that name when he created me," Fangs confirmed.

"All the same, I guess it's nice to meet you too," said Grace. "But I'm surprised you're even talking to me because I'm a 2D character or haven't you noticed yet?"

"Trust me, I've noticed and I don't care."

"You don't? Why not?"

"I'm pretty much like Ryan. I don't care about the rivalries between 2D and 3D animation. It's a whole bunch of rubbish. Do you agree?"

"Uhhh—I—I uh… I'm afraid I don't care much for 3D animation," Grace said shamefully. "My whole career was lost because of a 3D character."

"But you made friends with Ryan."

"Only cause I trust him above any 3D characters I've known."

"Not all 3D characters are bad. Are you going to blame all of us because of what one 3D character did to you? So can you trust another?"

Grace slowly glanced up at Fangs. His words gradually descended into her frame of mind. She couldn't help the fact that he was right, punishing every 3D character just because of one. Besides this conflict must come to an end sooner or later. Ryan could see that Fangs and Grace were getting more acquainted with each other and feeling mighty proud because maybe he wouldn't be the only 3D character that has fallen in love with a 2D character for the first time. This could be a sign that they all could get along as one. He decided to leave them alone for a moment but he didn't walk far because he suddenly caught sight of a familiar character. Ryan first rubbed his eyes to see if he was dreaming. When he opened them again he realized he wasn't. This familiar character he noticed was an old childhood friend of his, which was a large 3D rhinoceros named Russell. It had been a long time since Ryan had seen him, like about five years.

"R-R-Russell—is that—is that you?" Ryan called.

Russell heard Ryan's voice and thought he was dreaming himself. He looked around the studio and spotted him a few inches away. It was truly a miracle seeing each other again after all this time. Russell honestly didn't know what to do; all he did was stand in his position. Cautiously Ryan walked up to Russell, as much as he wanted to hug him; he knew Russell had a tough nature so he didn't even touch him. He was never the affectionate or sympathetic type; he had an explosive temper and was very irritable. Ryan looked up at Russell with delightfulness but Russell didn't say anything, he just stared down at him with a gruff. Ryan decided to speak first since he knew his old angry friend probably wouldn't.

"Long time, long see—huh Russell."

Chapter 7: Old Friends

"Yeah—how long has it been, three, four years?"

"Five."

"So—it's really been that long?"

"Yeah. So, how have you been? What are you doing here?"

"I wanted to see Joseph about something. He and I go back a long while just like us."

"Yeah, remember the day when we first bumped into each other."

"I try not to."

"It's not that bad. I'm the one who should wish not to remember."

Everything gradually switched to a flashback to seven years ago that started at an animation school in Hollywood. This animation school was only meant for 2D and 3D characters but some humans who created the characters were known as the principals. The main teachers of the school were 3D characters and the substitute teachers were 2D characters. This school was very different in comparison to a normal school because the students in this school are taught to act comical and humorous. They learn very little intelligence because it's all part of the process for cartoon characters to be dim-witted. These kids are trained to be hilarious and side-splitting at an early age so when they get older they would be able to star in movies or television series to entertain audiences around the world. Human students from normal schools were always jealous and envious because being in an animation school was so much fun. Most of the time it was fun but it was regularly dangerous due to most of the stunts the teachers would have the students do. For example, getting blown up by dynamite, getting smashed by anvils, being shot through rockets, chased by dangerous animals, etc. was the norm. Cartoons can handle these hazardous abilities but it always gave them major wounds and a splitting headache in the end. The teachers were once actors that starred in movies and teach their students everything they know. Ryan was just a young pup then. He was cute, innocent, and always minded his own business but if other children wanted to play with him, he would join in as well. He always had such a free spirit which made him a talented actor in Hollywood. He was usually the teacher's pet which made him a great target for the 2D rivals; nevertheless, he never let it affect him. One early afternoon, Ryan sat at his desk along with many other 2D and 3D students. Their teacher was a 3D dingo named Drake. He was very comical like many of the other teachers but he was Ryan's favorite. Every time he had a class with him he felt excited and happy.

"Alright class!" Drake said. "Pay attention and take a look on the board. Our lesson for today is to learn how to make shapes appear around your head."

On the board, Drake drew all types of symbols like stars, bells, birds, anvils, food, and many other things. These symbols represented the objects that are supposed to emerge from a character's head once they get hit with a hard object. The students thought it was fun but didn't know how it was going to happen.

"I like the birds!" a 2D otter called.

"I want a pizza symbol!" a 3D chicken cried.

"No I want the pizza!" a 2D mouse shrieked.

"I'm going to get all of those symbols at once," said a 3D chimpanzee.

"Calm down class," Drake ordered. "You all can have any symbol you want but you need to concentrate on how to get it first."

"You mean we can make our own symbols appear like magic?" Ryan asked.

"That's right Ryan. Every single one of you has a special skill to do this but, trust me, it won't be easy."

"I'm sure it can't be that hard," the 3D chimpanzee claimed. "Tell us how to do it."

"Very well," Drake said amusingly.

The entire class watched Drake as he reached down from his desk and pulled out a humungous mallet. Everyone shrieked in horror. They knew whenever they saw weapons like those they were in major trouble. Drake swung the mallet in his hand smiling back at his students. He always got a laugh out of their reaction.

"First things first," he stated. "Once a hard object comes into contact with your head, a symbol must pop up. Depending on whatever hits you or if it's something that you've been thinking about for a long time should

Chapter 7: Old Friends

mainly appear. Also make sure that you have more than three or four symbols."

"At the same time!" a 3D squirrel cried.

Drake nodded his head with a clear smile as he held the mallet around his shoulder like a baseball bat.

"I don't think I can make one symbol appear, let alone three," the 3D chimpanzee complained.

The whole class groaned in frustration. Everything they tried for the first time was hard for them.

"Relax class," Drake declared. "It'll get easier once you get the hang of it. Now watch carefully because I will give you the first demonstration as always."

Drake raised the mallet high above his head and then got ready for the real pain. He immediately rammed it into his head about three or four times. He instantly collapsed to the floor dizzy and injured. Everyone carefully and patiently watched Drake as he tried to get back up. He clumsily brought himself up but held on to his desk for support. In the process, his face was jacked up with a swollen purple eye and his tongue sticking out but incredibly, he had eight Christmas bells spinning around his head. They were even jingling with holiday Christmas sounds. The entire class cheered joyfully.

"Jingle bells Mr. Drake!" Ryan cried. "That was cool, how did you do that?"

Drake had to shake his head to get back to normal. He was still pretty dizzy and wobbly; nonetheless, he was still able to guide his students through the lesson.

"Full concentration Ryan. If you concentrate really hard, you can do anything. Alright class, now grab your own mallet from underneath your desk and do the same thing."

Everyone groaned annoyed, but all of the students pulled out their very own mallets. They would always hesitate before they did anything, so the teachers would always give thcm a minute.

"Okay class—whenever you're ready," Drake ordered.

Knowing they couldn't wait any longer, every single one of the students raised their mallets and slammed it into their heads. Some of them only did it once while others had to do it two or three times. Half of the students fell unconscious while others sat at their desks in a battered daze. Drake walked around their desk to see if any of them had symbols popping up. Most of them did but only one or two at a time.

"Very good Zackary, a star—but try to come up with four or five stars next time. Stan, a bubble? Unusual but—good. Alfred—how could you think of &%$#@! as your symbol? Mmmm—Laura, a heart? Do you have the hots for someone around here—not bad?"

Drake roamed around the whole classroom till he finally came to Ryan.

"Very good Ryan. Four mallets. The perfect symbol to imagine; the very object you got hit with."

Drake stood in front of the whole classroom reaching for something inside of his desk. Eventually, he brought out an ice pack for his head. "Very good students. For your homework, I want you to practice this new technique. Just make sure you don't give yourselves brain damage and make sure you always put an ice pack on your head afterwards."

During recess, it was constantly a fun time for the animation students. Their jungle gym equipment in the school playground was literally like an amusement park combined with a water park. The equipment represented the cartoon's skills of getting around and being clever at getting out of situations. Since the students were only kids, it was nothing but fun to them, but once they got older it improved their abilities of skillfulness. Ryan gracefully ran through the jungle gym like a real fox and then headed over to the sandbox. For a while, he was happily building sandcastles until someone knocked them over. Ryan looked up and before him stood a big 2D grizzly bear with his two thugs; a beaver and a wolf. These 2D bullies wanted to get back at Ryan for being the teacher's pet. It annoyed them for so long and they were ready to torment him. This was all new to Ryan because no one had ever bullied him before. He was terrified and didn't know what to do.

"H-hi—m-my name's—R-Ryun," he squirmed.

Chapter 7: Old Friends

"Ryun? Ha, ha, ha!" the bear laughed along with his sidekicks. "He's so dumb he can't even get his own name right."

As the bear commanded, the beaver clutched some of the sand on his flat tail and then the wolf blew it into Ryan's face. Ryan fell backwards rubbing his eyes anxiously, of course leaving him crying in the process. All the bear and his comrades did was laugh the whole time.

"Listen teacher's pet, this is our playground! Go and find your own—Ryun. Ha, ha, ha!" The bear laughed gleefully.

While Ryan continued crying something else happened. Russell unexpectedly walked up from behind him. The bear and his comrades got scared; even when Russell was little he was still pretty big. He gave the bear a frightening blow from his nostrils. The smoke blew into the bear's face knocking him to the ground. His partners, the beaver and wolf slowly helped him up. Russell angrily walked over to the bear and had his face up against his, looking at him dead in the eyes.

"Listen you," Russell said angrily. "If I catch you bothering anymore 3D again then I'll rip you to pieces so badly your mommy wouldn't be able to recognize you!"

The bear was so scared he didn't know what to do; he never had anyone stand up to him before. It made him feel powerless and humiliated at the same time. The bear commanded his sidekicks to assist him but before he knew it they were gone in a quick flash, abandoning him. All the bear could do was look at Russell helplessly. After Ryan stopped crying, getting all the sand out of his eyes, he witnessed Russell charging at the bear with his big horn. The bear tried running for his life but Russell was always right behind him. Eventually, Russell heaved a big push into the bear's butt which made him fly high into the air. Once the bear landed back on the ground he was caught up in a terrible wedgie hanging from Russell's horn. His fur was like a pair of pants while his bear pink butt was shown clear as day. Completely traumatized the bear wailed out like a baby as Russell carried him away. "Mommy!" he cried.

Moments later Russell came back to check on Ryan as he politely helped him up. "Are you okay?" he asked him.

"I just got a little sand in my eye," said Ryan. "Thank you for helping me."

"It's okay," Russell replied. "We 3D have to stick together."

"3D?" Ryan said confusingly.

"Your mom or animator probably hasn't told you about this yet," Russell stated. "You see, we are 3D characters. You and me. The bear and his bullies picking on you were 2D."

"What's the difference?" Ryan asked.

"From what my mom told me," Russell confirmed. "We 3D are C, umm, CG—something. Wait! Let me think for a minute. Uhhhh—oh I know, I know, we're CGI!"

"W-what's CGI?" Ryan asked again.

"It's what we are," Russell said. "3D characters are CGI. We're realistic looking and cool. The 2D characters are flat hand-drawn cartoons. My mom said they're called frame by frame, like flipping a lot of pages or something like that. Anyway, my mom said that we 3D characters are better because we're the new age of animation, while the 2D characters are the old age. The 2D characters are jealous because when we were born no one cares about them anymore."

"That's sad," Ryan said.

"It is not, stupid," Russell said angrily. "The 2D are the bad guys. Didn't you just see what they did to you? If it wasn't for me, then you would've been eating sand for the rest of the day."

"My name's not stupid—it's Ryun," he declared.

"Ryun?" Russell repeated. "What a stupid name. Well, I'm Russell."

"Thanks Russell," Ryan said. "So—do you want to build sandcastles?"

"No!" Russell groaned.

"Alright, I'll teach you. It'll be fun, you'll see," Ryan said happily as he pushed a reluctant Russell into the sandbox.

"Whatever," the rhino replied annoyed.

Since that day Russell and Ryan became friends, an unlikely friendship but still friends. The flashback finally ended with Ryan happy to relive the good moments with his old buddy but Russell didn't like to think too much about it.

Chapter 7: Old Friends

"I have to admit if it wasn't for those bullies then we probably wouldn't have become friends," Ryan mentioned.

"I saved your butt because of those bullies!" Russell growled. "You still couldn't understand that, even till this day."

"Russell, we're only at war here because we choose to be," Ryan claimed. "It doesn't have to be this way. Indeed, 2D animation doesn't get the popularity like they used to, but it's not their fault, they feel hurt. Maybe if we stop criticizing and degrading them we could understand their pain, besides would it hurt if we supported them instead?"

"After all these years, you still haven't learned anything," Russell snarled. "2D animation are enemies! We 3D characters are the new generation of animation in the modern century and we should be the ones in charge. Don't you understand Ryan, if you and I form our own gang of 3D characters we can conquer the 2D animation and have the humans fully devoted to us. We are the future now! The 2D characters are the ones who poisoned your mind."

"Wrong Russell," Ryan said. "They're misunderstood; no one understands them because they choose not to. Besides, your mom was the one who poisoned your mind. She had you believe the 2D generation was a sickness. If you ask me the only sickness is this war that is between us."

Suddenly Russell became enraged. Smoke blew out of his nostrils and he aggressively stomped his foot on the ground leaving Ryan puzzled for a minute.

"Russell—what are you doing?" he asked concerned.

Without warning Russell instantly charged at him. Ryan suddenly found himself running for his life from his old childhood friend. But Ryan didn't get very far when he accidentally tripped and slammed up against one of the nearest studio lot buildings. Ryan frantically looked for a way out but it turned out to be a dead end. When he looked at Russell he could see red in his eyes. There was no use reasoning with him or stopping him. Russell was just about to attack him, until unexpectedly Fangs and Grace jumped right in front of Ryan, protecting him. Fangs gave Russell a frightening roar as a warning to stay away. He snarled with his sharp teeth as he thrust his wings out with smoke coming out of his mouth. Seeing he was defeated and no match for Fangs, Russell stopped his assault on Ryan and finally calmed down. Ryan ultimately got up and stared at Russell in shock not believing what he just did.

"Nobody talks about my mother that way," Russell roared. "She was the only one who had enough sense to teach me the truth about 2D animation. After everything I've done for you and this is the way you thank me. You're nothing but a traitor. A traitor and a disgrace to your own kind."

"Russell—it's time for you to leave," Ryan said sadly.

"With pleasure," Russell replied. "I'd rather be caught dead in the streets than spend my last moments with you."

"You've got too much hatred in your heart," Fangs remarked, "and you need to change that right now."

"The only hatred I have is towards 2D animation," Russell bellowed. "And if individuals like yourself love 2D characters so much then you're the enemy too."

Russell leisurely turned around and walked away without looking back as he left Cartoon Studios. Watching Russell walk away seemed to take forever for Ryan. He was still in complete shock after what his old friend just did. This is one of the main reasons why Ryan ended his friendship with Russell because of his unbearable discrimination. However, his other friends, Fangs and Grace, tried to comfort him through his trauma.

"You okay Ryan?" Grace asked worriedly.

"Yeah," Fangs said. "I thought he might have tried to kill ya."

"I—I—don't know what to say about him," Ryan said with disappointment. "He's too far gone, I can't reach him anymore. I feel hurt because of what he just did, he's a hard rhino on the outside but, I know there's still good in him on the inside. He just won't admit it."

"So what are you going to do Ryan?" Grace asked.

"I can't worry about Russell right now," Ryan replied. "I need to find out why all of the 2D characters are quitting and once I'm done with that I must return to Jewel."

"Is it that important?" Grace inquired.

"She's pregnant and the baby could be due at any moment," Ryan said.

Chapter 7: Old Friends

"You're having a baby!" Grace shouted happily. "Congratulations Ryan, you're going to be a daddy!"

"Uhh—thanks Grace," Ryan said quietly.

"If the baby will be due at any time, then you need someone with you to help solve this case and I'm in," Grace insisted.

"Really Grace?" Ryan remarked thankfully. "You'd be willing to help me?"

"Hey that's what friends are for, right?" she asked.

"Count me in too," Fangs added.

"You too Fangs?" Ryan said surprisingly. "Hold on, I thought you said you didn't know."

"Now I know," Fangs demanded. "You two need a big and strong muscular bodyguard with you and that's me of course. Besides I'm up for playing the good guy for once."

"Is that really the reason or are you just trying to impress Grace?" Ryan suggested.

Fangs quickly started to sweat and noticed Grace was staring at him confused. Feeling embarrassed he decided to change the subject.

"Well there's no time to waste!" Fangs spoke rapidly. "We must hurry up and solve this mystery, the sooner the better."

CHAPTER EIGHT

THE NEW OFFER

Late that night, Kyle along with his friends were being accompanied by Jackson who was taking them to meet Christopher. They were all relaxing and sitting in the back seat of a nice big fancy limousine while Jackson was driving upfront. Kyle and Carlos were comforting themselves with beverages while Ralph and Stan were still scared about the whole situation, remaining terrified.

"You guys should learn to relax more," Carlos said contentedly. "I tell you it can't get any better than this. Not only do we have a new job but we get all the comforts and joy with the life of luxury. Isn't that right Kyle?"

"You bet bird brain," Kyle replied. "Quitting my job at Cartoon Studios was the best thing that happened to me in a long time. I never thought I would feel so free."

"How could you say that Kyle?" Stan asked. "Maybe you didn't get the best part in the movies but you at least had a job and good friends like Ryan."

"True," Kyle admitted, "but this job is so much better. We get all of this and we get to live amongst our own kind."

"Kind? You mean us 2D animation?" Ralph mentioned.

"Who else?" Kyle snapped.

"But what about your friend Ryan?" Ralph asked. "If you're going to become a part of this deal fighting against 3D characters that means you'll have to battle against your best friend too."

Chapter 8: The New Offer

Kyle thought for a moment and didn't like the idea. As much as he hated 3D characters, Ryan was one of his best friends and he couldn't imagine it if he got into a fight with him, even if he didn't, he wanted to assure his safety.

"Well I, uh—I'll make sure Ryan won't be a part of this," Kyle said.

"How's that possible?" Stan asked. "As big as this plan sounds it looks like every 3D character might be involved."

"He must never find out what's going to happen between us 2D and 3D characters. I'll think of something to get him out of the way," Kyle declared.

"Oh I don't like this plan," Ralph cried as he squirmed. "Something bad is going to happen, I just know it. All I want to do is go home!"

"Me too!" Stan confirmed. "We never agreed to be a part of this battle in the first place!"

"Come on you guys," Carlos said holding his drink in the air. "Show some backbone. Think of this as a new beginning. 2D will reign again and we will triumph."

"It will be the end for all of us," Stan cried helplessly. "3D and 2D will both be deceased. Before you know it, they'll have 4D as a new beginning."

"What's 4D?" Ralph asked.

"I don't know, I just thought if there was 2D and 3D then 4D must come after it, right?" Stan asked.

After a few minutes, Jackson stopped the limousine and parked it near the sidewalk of a back alley. As he stepped out of the limo, he opened up the car door for Kyle and the others. When they exited the vehicle they looked at their surroundings. It seemed like a terrible part of town; there wasn't a single soul in sight and garbage was being blown everywhere by the wind. The buildings around the area looked condemned with broken windows and wrecked structures.

"Find a happy place! Find a happy place! Find a happy place!" Ralph repeatedly cried to himself.

"Are you sure we're in the right place?" Kyle questioned with much concern.

"I'm sure," said Jackson without looking at him.

"Hold on a minute now!" Carlos interrupted. "If this Christopher guy is so rich and has a fancy limo and everything else, why in the world would he live in a place like this?"

"I never said he lived here," Jackson replied. "This location is his secret headquarters where he discusses business with you 2D characters. It's kept hidden from all of the 3D characters."

"Um… excuse me, for a minute mister Tiger, but just how big is this Christopher guy?" Stan asked frightened.

"You don't want to know," Jackson moaned disturbingly. "All I can tell you is, if you dare to cross his path, then you'll never be seen or heard from ever again."

After hearing Jackson's words, the next thing Stan knew he had wet himself while Ralph fainted right behind him. Kyle realized his two friends were always the sensitive type and only hoped he would get through this humiliation.

"Ralph, Stan, come on you two, pull yourselves together will ya? You're embarrassing me," Kyle groaned. "You're dinosaurs for crying out loud, you're supposed to be tough and mean."

"We're herbivores, you need meat-eaters for that, like a T-rex or Velicoraptor," Stan declared.

"Maybe I will replace you two guys with a T-rex and a Velicoraptor if you won't get your act together!" Kyle shrieked irritably.

"Let's get back to business you guys," Carlos shouted. "We're about to meet one of the best 2D characters ever. He might be a Mafia gangster for all we know. Wouldn't that be great!"

"Shhhhhhh! Not so loud you big mouth!" Kyle whispered. "You want to tell the whole world?"

"Yeah, as a matter of fact I do!" Carlos responded. "The whole world should hear of what we're a part of."

Jackson slowly walked up to one of the old buildings and opened the front door with his paw. He turned his head back at Kyle and the others expecting them to make their move.

"Right this way," he spoke softly.

"Uh—coming," said Kyle feeling a little on edge.

Chapter 8: The New Offer

Stan eventually woke Ralph up by slapping him across the face.

"Come on buddy," Stan cried. "We need to get through this mess together; I can't do it without you."

"Uhhh—am I in a happy place," Ralph muttered trying to get back to his senses.

"No, you're still in nightmare land for now," Stan proclaimed sadly.

Little by little, Kyle and his friends started to walk near the entrance of the building. Once they were inside Jackson closed the door behind them with a large thud. The loud noise immediately made Ralph and Stan hold on to each other like frightened children. Jackson walked ahead of the others and continued to lead them deeper inside the building. There was dust and filth everywhere which made Carlos constantly sneeze.

"ACHOO!! You sure could use a maid around these parts," he mentioned.

Ultimately they came to a front office, but before entering Jackson knocked on the door.

"Come in," said a voice inside the office.

Jackson was the first one to enter the room while Kyle and the others followed right behind him. He forcefully closed the door behind them. The office itself looked quite professional compared to the rest of the building. Kyle and his friends saw Christopher sitting at his chair positioned in front of his office desk. To their amazement, Christopher was nothing but a little squirrel. A flying squirrel at that, but he rarely flew unless he needed to. Although he was small and cute he was still an intense hoodlum. He was smoking a cigarette and wore a black gangster suit. Surprisingly sitting right next to him was a young beautiful human woman named Brittany Garland. She had beautiful long flowing blonde hair, plump red lips, and legs as long as a giraffe's neck, she was impecUberly dressed, a real knock out. It was unusual because most humans didn't associate themselves with 2D or the 3D characters, but Brittany enjoyed her life with the 2D generation. Because of her beauty, she'd generally have men pursue her; nevertheless, Brittany preferred to stay with Christopher even if it was weird and bizarre.

"Wow! Just wow!" Carlos yelled excitedly. "I've seen many attractive women in my life but you take the cake!"

Brittany just tilted her head and smirked at Carlos. "You're cute. Not very smart, but cute," she replied.

"Hey, when this fighting is all over, do you want to have dinner later on!?" Carlos asked eagerly.

"Watch it pal, that's my girlfriend you're talking to," Christopher snapped.

The situation made Kyle feel mortified and he decided to speak before something happened that he would regret.

"We're extremely sorry for him boss, he just has a big mouth," he apologized, "but I assure you it won't happen again." Then he immediately grabbed Carlos in the grip of his claws and covered his mouth to keep him from talking. "First of all, I just want to say th-thank you for um—bailing us out of prison."

"Well, we 2D have to stick together, right?" Christopher replied.

"I agree!" Kyle answered.

Kyle turned his head around and noticed that Ralph and Stan were still holding on to each other trembling in fear. He then gave them a firm look, hinting for them to agree with Christopher's conversation.

"Oh yeah! Definitely!" Ralph cried out.

"Absolutely! I totally agree!" Stan responded.

"Good, so since we're all on the same page here, you guys do know what you're getting yourselves into?" Christopher asked.

"Yeah uh—to fight against the 3D characters," Kyle reacted nervously.

"What Christopher means is that this is no ordinary fight between cartoon characters. This will be an epic battle, a severe and serious one that will probably cost you the lives of some of your friends," Brittany stated with much sophistication.

"Brittany's right my friends," Christopher said. "We 2D characters are fed up with CGI running the world with their new fancy technology. You've seen it out there how things have rapidly changed over the years. Pretty soon there won't be any of us left. People might have liked us in the past but now that 3D has come out, we're treated like yesterday's rubbish. But we will not be ignored or allow the insults of critics to destroy us. We're here to send a message to the scum out there, including the humans

Chapter 8: The New Offer

and if this is what it's going to take to get their attention—then so be it! This will be a battle that no one will ever forget. It'll be in the history books when we're finished, something unforgettable that will take the world by surprise. So again, I ask you, do you know what you're getting yourselves into?"

Kyle stood puzzled and scared for a moment not realizing how serious the situation was. His friends Ralph and Stan were extremely terrified and just held on to each other even tighter. Kyle understood that he agreed to go along with it in the first place and decided to go all the way. Besides, he couldn't go back on anything now, not after Christopher helped him and his pals out of prison. He felt he at least owed him that.

"Yes, my friends and I will be willing to assist you in this serious battle," Kyle said.

"Smart man," Christopher said looking at Kyle with a sly demeanor. "I like the way you think. Your friend on the other hand might get himself killed right away with that loud mouth of his—then again it might work to an advantage."

"In my honest opinion I don't want to see any of you 2D characters get killed," Brittany declared. "You're a traditional legend that'll last throughout history and nothing will ever change that. Just be cunning and clever with your cartoon personalities. Obviously, the 3D characters will be aware of your skills."

"Yep, and another thing," Christopher remarked. "Only the 2D characters know about this. The 3D must never find out. I called numerous 2D characters to be a part of this and they all agree to go along with it. The one who will help us conquer the battle against the 3D characters is William."

"William? That big-time merchant who gambles a lot?" Kyle asked.

"Correct," Christopher said. "A few weeks ago he came to me with an offer I couldn't refuse. He told me he owns an enormous stadium where the fight will take place. Because of William's advertisements, humans will come to watch the battle. Of course the humans will have their own opinions of who they want to win, nevertheless, it won't change anything.

We're going to arrange for the 3D characters to come there, then we'll catch them off guard and finally defeat them once and for all."

Stan fainted with Ralph this time, for the both of them were unable to take the sudden news any longer.

"Hey are your two friends alright? They don't seem like they're the warrior type," Christopher said looking at Ralph and Stan confusingly.

"Don't worry, this is all new to them but they will do terrific in battle," Kyle said trying not to lose his nerve.

"Good. Now until that day comes, what you guys are to do is to try to recruit more 2D characters to join ya and make sure the 3D characters don't find out about this," Christopher demanded.

"And if they do?" Kyle inquired.

Christopher just gave Kyle a blank stare and whispered to him, "Then take care of them."

Upon hearing Christopher's final words, Kyle began to pick his friends up and carry them out the door. Carlos though stayed behind and continued to talk to Christopher face to face.

"You know man, you're so lucky to have a human like that for a girlfriend, what's your secret. I really want to know because you know I'm a ladies' man myself. I've got charm and class…"

Kyle rushed back into the office and viciously grabbed Carlos away from Christopher.

"What can I say? Some cartoons just don't know when to shut up," Kyle laughed embarrassed as he left the office.

"Too bad. He needs to put a muzzle on that beak of his," Christopher said as he put out his cigarette.

"That's why I like them, they're classical and unforgettable," Brittany chuckled.

"You've got it good both ways baby," Christopher smiled. "For one I'm 2D and you get to be with one of the most feared gangsters in town."

"Too bad folks don't take you seriously when they first meet you," Brittany pointed out.

Chapter 8: The New Offer

"Don't worry," Christopher laughed. "I like it when folks don't take me seriously because in the end, I'm always the one who has the last laugh."

"Precisely how many assassinations are you talking about?" Brittany asked.

"Not on my kind I hope," Christopher said as he hopped on Brittany's lap. "It just won't look pretty for any of us once this thing starts."

"When you say us does that mean you're going to be participating in the battle too?" she asked with concern.

"Of course my dear. You know I never like sitting back on the sidelines letting my people do my job for me. I always take part in my profession no matter how hazardous the situation is."

"A tiny squirrel like you wouldn't last a minute."

"Now don't put me down Britt," Christopher groaned. "You know one of the reasons why I participate in my line of work is because I'm a squirrel. I need to prove myself to others that I'm just a tough as they are."

"You don't need to prove anything to me Chris," Brittany said. "I love you just as you are."

"I know you do but I need to prove it to the rest of the scum out there," Christopher pouted.

"Don't get yourself so worked up baby. How about you and I have a little alone time together," Brittany said as she stroked Christopher on the head down to his tail.

"I was thinking the same thing my dear," he said smiling up at her.

CHAPTER NINE

THE SET UP

Around the same time Kyle and his friends left Christopher's hideout, Ryan, Fangs, and Grace were on their way to Kyle's residence. Ryan felt the need to ask his friend what was going on; after all, he was one of the characters who quit their job at Cartoon Studios so he recognized that his 2D friend knew something. Kyle lived in a huge, attractive and fancy house which was uncommon for most 2D characters. It even amazed Fangs and Grace when they approached it.

"His house is so much bigger than mine," Fangs complained miserably. "How did he get so lucky?"

"Investment," Ryan simply commented.

"I admire him, not many 2D characters have a place this expensive anymore due to our poor reputation," Grace mentioned.

"Tell me Grace—what do you admire out of a man?" Fangs asked.

"They're cute but men don't go with my species," she commented.

"Oh no, I meant being with your special soul mate."

"Are you serious?!" Grace replied. "Why are you so interested?"

"Just curious, I guess." Fangs responded sadly.

As Ryan approached the front door the three suddenly heard a dog barking in the backyard of Kyle's house.

"Kyle owns a dog?" Grace said surprised.

"He lives alone so I guess the dog is the only company he has," Ryan commented.

Chapter 9: The Set Up

First Ryan knocked on the door, but after he didn't hear a response he took a deep breath and started looking for the key.

"Kyle told you where he put the key?" Fangs asked surprised.

"Of course, we're best friends. He trusts me," Ryan answered.

In no time Ryan found Kyle's key underneath a flower pot that was placed on the front porch.

"Well I hope you're right," Fangs said feeling unsure.

Ryan unlocked the door and began to enter the house with Fangs and Grace following closely behind him. They didn't see any sign of Kyle anywhere so Ryan started to walk further into the living room.

"Kyle! Kyle are you home?" he shouted.

Grace walked down the hallway and noticed movie posters of Kyle and Ryan starring in their television series together.

"That's pretty neat. It sure does seem like you and Kyle go back a long way, you made a lot of stuff together huh," she stated.

Ryan walked up near the hallway and noticed the movie posters himself. He smiled because looking at them brought him back to the good old times when he and Kyle became friends. It brought a sense of warmth to his heart.

"Oh yeah, we worked on a lot of projects, though Kyle got annoyed with it, he was still fun to work with."

"Hmmm—maybe I should get a job at Cartoon Studios," Grace thought. "It certainly would be better than driving those bloody Ubers all the time."

"Joseph would be happy to have you work at his studio. He's not turned down a 2D character yet," Ryan said.

"That's fantastic," she cried with happiness. "As long as I can start acting again."

When Ryan looked around he suddenly noticed Fangs wasn't with them.

"Wait a minute, where's Fangs?" Ryan asked Grace.

"I don't know—I thought he was right behind me," she replied.

"Hey Fangs! Where are you! Stop playing hide and seek; this is no time for games!"

Ryan and Grace suddenly heard noises coming from the kitchen. They walked into the kitchen to find Fangs eating food like crazy out of Kyle's refrigerator making an outrageous mess.

"Fangs?!"

He brought his head out of the refrigerator with an ashamed look on his face but with a lot of food piled in his mouth.

"That's Kyle's food you idiot! Get out of there!" Ryan yelled.

"Sorry, I got a little hungry," Fangs cried, dropping his head in shame.

Next to the kitchen was a window screen that led to the backyard. Kyle's dog was chained up but was barking like crazy at the intruders.

"He owns a real dog?" said Grace. "I thought it would be an animated dog."

"He's fine, that's just Pugsy," Ryan stated. "An American Staffordshire Terrier, a very good watchdog."

Unexpectedly, Kyle and his friends came through the front door and caught sight of Ryan with his friends inside his kitchen, it was an awkward moment.

"What the fudge sickles is going on around here!?" Kyle shouted with anger.

"Oh hi Kyle, I'm sorry, uh—Fangs just got a little carried away."

"What are you doing in my house!?" Kyle demanded.

"You told me where you put the key, besides I need to talk to you."

"You know what this looks like—breaking and entering to me," Carlos snickered with glee.

"What?! What are you crazy?!" Ryan cried.

"Remember what the boss said Kyle, if any 3D characters get in the way, take care of them!" Carlos reminded.

"Boss? What boss?" Ryan questioned. "Kyle, who is that new bird, a friend of yours?"

"Don't listen to the babblings of a crazy idiot," said Kyle, he then turned to Carlos and shouted, "Shut up you loud mouth! You're going to ruin everything!"

Chapter 9: The Set Up

Ryan looked at his friend with much trepidation. He couldn't believe he was hiding something from him. Kyle and Ryan were as close as brothers and he was always able to tell him anything.

"Kyle, what is going on? First, you quit your job at Cartoon Studios and now you're getting involved with something really serious. You have to tell me what is going on?"

"I-I-I'm sorry Ryan—I can't tell you anything," Kyle said with guilt written on his face.

"You can't? Come on Kyle I'm your friend, you can tell me anything."

Ralph and Stan didn't want to see Kyle go through with Christopher's plan. They knew the tight bond between friendships and couldn't endure it if they had to stand by watching Kyle destroy his relationship with Ryan.

"Kyle, remember you said you would make sure he wouldn't get hurt," Ralph reminded.

"Yeah, please don't harm him, he's your best friend for crying out loud," Stan pleaded.

Still looking guilty, Kyle slowly brought his head up and looked at his friend with a depressive look. "I'm really sorry Ryan," he said with remorse.

The next thing Ryan and his friends knew they were sitting behind prison bars after Kyle called the cops on them. To Ryan, it seemed like he had lost one of his best friends. Ryan couldn't understand what had happened to tarnish their friendship so rapidly. But Kyle called the police to arrest Ryan and his friends to assure their safety. Apparently, Maya was still in charge of the whole police department so she was keeping them in her custody.

"Yep, some friend you have indeed," Fangs said not looking the least bit surprised.

"I just don't understand it, has the world gone crazy?" Ryan shrieked. "First my old childhood friend nearly kills me today and now my best friend calls the cops and has me arrested!"

"Oh well, I guess I can kiss that Uber company good-bye," Grace admitted. "I never liked that job anyway."

"Hey out there!" Ryan shouted. "I demand to speak to my lawyer!"

"Maybe I shouldn't have eaten the food out of his refrigerator after all, if only I had known he was going to react like that," Fangs confessed. "Ryan maybe you should take that cup on the floor and ram it against the bars screaming."

"That cliché is old Fangs. So what's your brilliant plan now Ryan?" Grace asked sarcastically.

"Like it's that easy," said Ryan angrily. "I thought I could trust Kyle but I guess I was wrong. Once we find a way out of this it's just us three."

"Why don't I just blow fire and melt the bars away?" Fangs suggested. "We could easily get out of here with my dragon breath."

"You'll only make it worse," Ryan stated. "We'll just be fugitives on the run. They'll probably have us hunted down and it'll only delay us from discovering what's really happening with the 2D characters."

"But what about your wife?" Fangs asked.

The thought of Jewel entering Ryan's mind was enough to make him go along with any plan. He didn't know what would happen to her if he stayed in prison. He had to find a way to get back to her no matter what.

"On second thought, blow the bars away!" he insisted.

Fangs looked at Grace and tried to impress her as he puffed his chest out.

"Prepare yourself baby, you're about to see the most powerful dragon breath ever!"

Before Fangs could blast the bars down, Maya and Roberto abruptly showed up. Fangs immediately swallowed his fire breath, in the process it felt like an explosion went off inside of his belly. He wearily fell to the ground with smoke coming out of his mouth feeling weak and dizzy.

"We wouldn't be trying anything stupid now would we?" Maya said looking quite amused.

"No, no of course not," Ryan claimed.

"Good because you and your friends are going to be here for a very long time," she said.

"That's not fair," Ryan cried. "We didn't even do anything wrong! Kyle is my best friend and he's always allowed me to enter his house. We didn't break inside!"

Chapter 9: The Set Up

"That's not what he told me," Maya claimed. "Besides, you 3D think you could get away with anything you want, tormenting us 2D characters in every way imaginable. I would trust a 2D character over you guys any day."

"Then how about me," Grace requested. "I'm 2D and I say we're innocent. Ryan's right, everything was a misunderstanding."

"Not so fast Miss Gator," Maya mocked cheerfully. "I already noticed you were 2D but you were assisting the 3D characters. I'm afraid you're caught up in this mess too. Maybe you should've thought of whose side you were really on. It's sad that you betray your own kind just to be with them."

Maya then walked away but Roberto didn't move from his spot feeling guilty about the whole situation. She noticed he wasn't following her, so she yelled at the timid octopus to get his attention. "Roberto! Come on!"

Defeated, Roberto took one last look at Ryan and his friends and then slithered away. After what Maya said to her, Grace was so full of anger.

"I'm going to kill that little rat when I get my teeth on her!"

"I don't blame ya," Ryan agreed. "What she said is enough to make anybody angry."

"She called me Miss Gator!" Grace shrieked.

"What?" Ryan said surprisingly.

"I hate being called Miss Gator! That's a complete insult to my character. I'm going to kill her!"

Before Grace could continue with her temper tantrum, she suddenly noticed Fangs was still on the floor coughing up smoke from his mouth. She ran to his aid and tried lifting him by the neck.

"Are you okay Fangs?" she asked.

"I've seen better days," he coughed helplessly.

"The next time you see that chipmunk, I want you to use your fire breath on her," she said spitefully. "Besides, I thought that was really sweet of you, considering your friend's well-being just to get us out of here."

"Really?" Fangs said feeling a little better. Earning some respect from Grace was enough to make him satisfied. He gently wrapped his wing around her for comfort. Watching Grace and Fangs together made Ryan wish he was back with Jewel. He missed her more than anything. Being separated from her all this time was like a sickness to him. He desperately couldn't shake the thought out of his head that the baby could come anytime soon. His agitated mood was building as undertones of fear quietly began to surface.

Back at Ryan's house, it was around 4:30 a.m. but Jewel couldn't sleep so she decided to watch some TV, unaware of everything that was happening. As she laid her paw across her belly, she could feel the baby kicking softly.

"You certainly are a little champ, I'm sure it's going to be a boy. Just don't come too soon, your father is already worried enough as it is."

Unexpectedly, Jewel heard someone knocking at the door. It was uncommon since it was so early and whoever it was, they were knocking insistently. She suspected it was Ryan but when she opened the door it was only Rex.

"Rex? I thought you were Ryan!"

"Figures," he grunted.

"Oh shut up and come in," she snapped at him as she closed the door.

"So, where's your so-called husband? Not even here to take care of you and the baby."

"He went to go and take care of some personal business, it was very urgent."

"More urgent than staying to take care of you instead?"

Jewel always had to put up with Rex's hatred towards Ryan, knowing he still didn't like him very much, but she just dealt with it.

"Rex, why are you here? It's late you know."

"There's something you should know. The real reason why Ryan left is because there is going to be a big conflict between 2D and 3D animation. William had it all planned out, the 3D characters are unaware of what's happening but most of the 2D characters already know what's going on."

"What do you mean a big conflict? How big?"

"An epic battle, there might be some casualties. It will be a lesson that the 3D characters will never forget. It's a message that will get across the world to animation and humans both."

"This is terrible! Does Ryan know anything about this?"

Chapter 9: The Set Up

"I doubt it, that's why he's off trying to find out what's going on."

"How do you know about all of this?"

"I told you, most of the 2D characters already know about this, besides I'm part of the deal. A gangster named Christopher came to me and asked me to be a part of the battle."

"Did you agree?"

"Heck yeah. I wanted to get back at 3D animation for the longest time."

"Well you're not going!" she shouted.

"But Jewel! I already agreed to it!"

"I don't care, you're my watchdog and I say you're not going. Besides if you're my true friend, then you wouldn't do this knowing how much it would hurt me."

"Killjoy," Rex muttered angrily.

"Does this mean that the 3D characters will be caught off guard?"

"I'm sure of it; it's all part of the plan."

"This means Ryan is in danger! We must find him!" she wailed.

"Good luck with that. He could be anywhere."

"It doesn't matter; you and I are going to search for him no matter what it takes!" Jewel exclaimed with determination.

"Huh? But what about the baby?"

"I'll have to take that chance, besides we're family and we look out for each other."

"Rrrrrrr! I asked you countless times why couldn't you have married a 2D character instead and now it's come down to this. I can't believe I'm going to risk my life to help your 3D worthless husband."

"Bad dog Rex! You know better than that! If you really care and want to protect me then maybe you should consider befriending Ryan. After all, the life I have growing inside of me is part of him too. Just try to remember that."

As much as Rex hated Ryan and 3D animation, he had to think about Jewel's safety and her concern for the ones she loved. Rex's only affair is to be a protective bodyguard of 2D animation even if it meant doing something he would live to regret in the process. So he took a deep big breath and had no choice but to go along with it.

"Fine, but I don't like it one bit. I'll assist you every step of the way your majesty."

"Good boy Rex but watch that smart mouth of yours. Now, where would we find Ryan?"

"How should I know?"

"Use your nose! You're a dog aren't you?"

"Great," Rex sighed feeling his self-esteem dropping lower.

Without wasting time he immediately got to work sniffing out Ryan's scent around the house and traced it, heading out the door. Jewel followed Rex as they both left the house.

"I'll never get this scent out of my nose! It makes me feel nauseous."

"Quit your complaining and continuing sniffing," she scolded. "And every time I hear a smart remark from you, I'll flick you across the nose… with a hammer."

With the sun finally rising and hours of waiting at the police station, Ryan felt like he was about to lose his mind. He couldn't handle remaining patient while stressing over his wife. The anxiety was too much for him to bear, not to mention he still wanted to find out about the 2D's absences. Fangs was lying on his back playing the harmonica on the bottom bunk bed, while Grace was on the top doing exercise push-ups.

"Please let me talk to my lawyer!" he cried out again.

"Why don't you just use your cell phone," Fangs suggested.

"Genius idea Fangs but Maya already took it from me before she locked us up!"

"Oh, my bad."

"How about you use my cell phone?" Grace mentioned.

"Hold on Grace," Ryan stuttered. "Are you telling me you had a cell phone this whole time?"

"I guess," Grace admitted. "It's not a very fancy one but…"

"Give it to me!" Ryan yelled, aggressively snatching her cell phone away.

Chapter 9: The Set Up

"Calm down Ryan," Grace said. "This wife of yours must have a really strong hold on you."

"Your cell phone is out of service," Ryan groaned irritated.

"Oh sorry, I guess I forgot to charge it," she confessed.

Ryan dropped Grace's cell phone along with himself to the floor full of depression. Then to Ryan's amazement, Roberto actually came back slithering down the hallway. In three of his tentacle arms, he had three cups of hot cocoa for Ryan and his friends.

"I'm sorry to keep you guys in here like this, I'm not supposed to be here but I thought you all could use a drink," he said respectfully.

"Oh thank you, thank you, thank you, thank you!" Ryan cried as he quickly grabbed one of the cups and drank it as fast as he could.

"Be careful, it's hot," Roberto warned.

Already swallowing it down, Ryan's eyes began to swell up with water. He could feel the steaming hot cocoa boiling his tongue instantly. As soon as he consumed it, he cried out loud trying to cool his mouth down.

"AHHHHHH!" he cried helplessly.

"I told you it was hot," Roberto confirmed.

Fangs and Grace took their cups too but blew on it first.

"Thanks buddy. By the way, what do you mean you shouldn't be here?" Fangs asked.

"If Maya caught me here, she would kill me," Roberto cried.

"Maya?" said Grace.

"She's my partner," Roberto said. "I hate to say, she's the one who's calling the shots around here now."

"Is she in charge?" Grace asked.

"No but uh…"

"Well if she's not in charge how can she call the shots around here?" Grace complained.

"Shhhhhhh! You don't seem to understand," Roberto whispered. "The Lieutenant won't be back until later on today and Maya has completely taken over. If I say or do anything, it'll cost me my job."

"Oh I see, she's blackmailing you," Grace said.

"I'm afraid so," Roberto admitted.

"Well I can't say that I blame ya," Fangs said. "We haven't been having a good day ourselves."

After Ryan cooled his tongue down and got better he immediately asked, "Hey listen pal, what's your name?"

"My name's Roberto."

"Listen Roberto, you seem like a generous guy. My friends and I don't belong here, something big is about to happen and we need to get out of here. Besides I need to hurry up and get back to my wife, she's pregnant and I need to be there for her. Will you please help us?"

"I would love to but I can't let you out. If Maya found out, I would be done for."

"Fine, instead could you let me use the telephone? I'll call my lawyer and she'll straighten everything out. Please!!! I'll be more than grateful. I must get out of here!"

Roberto squirmed with a worried look on his face. He felt uneasy about the whole situation but he couldn't ignore Ryan's plea for help. He was thinking about it for a long time and whether or not he should go through with it. Without saying a word Roberto just turned away and left the room. With no response from him, Ryan and his friends figured he wasn't going to help them at all.

"You just can't trust anybody these days," Fangs said angrily.

"Wait Roberto, come back! At least give me a yes or a no!" Ryan begged.

The clock was ticking slowly and the answer was becoming far too evident.

"I guess that's your typical law enforcement for ya," Grace commented. "On the other hand, I like him better than that Maya rat. He was kind enough to give us some hot cocoa."

"Jewel's probably worried about me as much as I'm worried about her! I don't even know how I'm going to get out of this dilemma!"

But to everyone's surprise, Roberto came back and handed Ryan a cell phone through the bars of the prison chamber.

"Here, use my cell phone," he whispered.

Chapter 9: The Set Up

Ryan and his friends slowly gazed at Roberto with cheerfulness and admiration. Ryan was grateful for his kindness.

"Thank you," he said gratefully.

"If only there were more cops as generous as you, my friend," Fangs said with appreciation.

CHAPTER TEN

THE SEARCH

Thirty minutes later Maya came back to the prison cell to torment Ryan and his friends with more of her irritation. As usual, Roberto followed closely behind her, his frame of mind is constantly subdued.

"Well, well, well. How are we enjoying prison life so far?" Maya snickered.

"I swear when I get my claws on you, you'll wish you were never a cop!" Grace yelled furiously.

"Is that a threat?" Maya demanded.

"Trust me, you'll know when I'm threatening you," Grace replied. "By the way, what's a penny made out of? Copper!"

"Seems to me like you need more discipline," Maya stated. "How about if I lock you up in solitary confinement?"

"I hate cops," Grace groaned angrily. "Especially ones that look like you."

"Hey, what about our phone call?" Fangs mentioned. "We should at least get a phone call!"

"Not while I'm in charge," said Maya. "You 2D and 3D characters think you can always get away with crimes because you're cartoons but there's a penalty for anyone who disobeys the law, including you!"

Unexpectedly, Ryan's lawyer, Alexandria, came strolling down the hallway, as usual, she was on her cell phone but it was a relief for Ryan and

Chapter 10: The Search

his friends to actually see her. Of course, Maya was more than surprised herself.

"Excuse me but are you lost?" she asked.

"I wouldn't be here if I thought I was lost," said Alexandria as she got off her cell phone. "Are you in charge here?"

"That's confidential," Maya said. "What do you want?"

"I'm here to get Ryan and his friends out," Alexandria declared.

"Now wait just a minute…"

"I'm Alexandria Anderson; Ryan's lawyer. I got a call they were being held against their will and you wouldn't even let them talk to an attorney."

"I didn't think animated characters needed an attorney."

"Well in this case, they do."

"Who called you anyway?"

"I'm afraid that's confidential. Now will you please let Ryan and his friends out of here right now or I'll call your superior about this and report you for misconduct."

Defeated by Alexandria, Maya wouldn't dare cross her any further. Her sudden power for control was now crushed and vanquished. Slowly she pulled the prison keys out from behind her back and climbed the rails to open the gate. Once Ryan and his friends were finally free from prison, Grace happily swung her tail against the gate which made Maya fall off and land into their cell.

"Man that felt good," Grace laughed. "That cell is a perfect fit for you. Be sure to pack a lot of nuts, you're going to need it."

Maya got up after her fall and stared at Grace angrily. "I'll remember your face!"

"Ditto."

Before Ryan and his friends left, he looked back at Roberto with a satisfactory smile and shook one of his tentacles.

"Thanks again," he whispered softly.

Roberto just nodded his head politely then after one last glimpse Ryan never looked back. Maya watched Roberto with a suspicious look. She angrily got up from the prison chamber and hopped on one of his tentacles.

"Roberto! You wouldn't happen to know anything about this, would you?"

Roberto started to sweat anxiously. Maya was vibrating on his tentacle because of his constant trembling from fear. He tried to hold her steadily already knowing that she found out what he did. "Uhhhh… I don't know what you're talking about? I don't know how that lawyer got here?"

Maya didn't say anything; she just glared at Roberto with a firm look that was enough to make him wet himself. Roberto couldn't stand the suspense any longer and decided to break away from the predicament. "What do you know, it's my lunch break. Gotta go! Don't want to miss it!"

In a quick flash, Roberto dashed out of the room and left Maya to fall on the floor. Before Maya could run after him, she slipped on black ink that Roberto left behind. The more she ran, the more she continued slipping, ending up looking like a black chipmunk. "ROBERTO!!" she screamed furiously.

Once Ryan and the others stepped outside of the police station they felt relieved and free from the bizarre web of circumstances. They didn't think they were going to see the light of day again. Grace even took a deep breath and exhaled with liberation.

"Free at last! Free at last! Thank God Almighty, free at last!" she cried.

"I know what you mean," Fangs said. "It felt like we were in there for days. That was not the right cell for me either, too cramped and too small."

Fangs turned to crack his back for a minute but it suddenly made him feel like an old man. "Ouch! I think I'm getting out of shape. I need to exercise more."

Ryan focused his immediate attention on Alexandria to thank her. "Thanks Anderson, I thought you'd never get here. You wouldn't believe how hard it was just to get a hold of you."

"Bloody law enforcement," she complained. "Think they own everything. She was just lucky I didn't threaten her by taking it to court. But I'll be sure to inform her boss anyway."

"Still I appreciate it, Anderson. My friend and I had a little misunderstanding it seems. When I get my hands on him, he's going to have a lot of explaining to do!"

Chapter 10: The Search

"What friend would that happen to be?"

"Kyle, apparently, and I also need to get back to my wife!"

"Did you have her sign those documents yet, I need them back."

"Anderson! Show me some consideration, will ya! My wife is pre…"

Before Ryan could continue, Alexandria's cell phone went off again and she answered it. Ryan just sighed with frustration. She might have been a demanding woman; nevertheless, she was a lot of help to him when he needed her. After she was done, Alexandria focused her attention back on Ryan.

"Tell me something Ryan, would this Kyle friend of yours happen to look like a 2D pterodactyl?"

"Yes! Yes he is! You saw him?"

"As a matter of fact, I did. Before you called me, I saw him and his friends on their way to the mall."

"What mall was it?"

"It was the Daylight Savings Mall. I was there earlier getting supplies and meeting a client I had a case with later on this week. On my way out, I noticed Kyle with some other friends."

"What in the world are they doing at the mall?"

"How should I know? I didn't bother to stop and ask them. I only noticed that he's your co-star when I sometimes watch your TV shows on my short breaks."

"Well, that's good enough. At least we know where to find them, thanks again Anderson. We couldn't have gotten through any of this without you."

"No problem, just give me those documents when you're ready and please don't get into any more trouble." Alexandria eventually left talking on her cell phone yet again as she headed to her car.

"Listen you guys," Ryan told Fangs and Grace. "We need to go to the Daylight Savings Mall right away!"

"Great, I need to catch up with my shopping," Grace said delightfully.

"We're not going there to shop!" Ryan shrieked. "Kyle and his friends are there. It's our chance to confront them and find out what's going on. Besides, I want to get back at Kyle for putting us in prison to begin with!"

"I couldn't agree more," Fangs concurred. "So how are we going to get there?"

Ryan didn't say anything; he just smiled at Fangs with a devious look. Fangs didn't know what Ryan was thinking, but when he finally realized it he took a big gulp. The next thing he knew, Ryan and Grace were riding on top of his back as he flew them high into the air. Although Ryan and Grace were enjoying the flight, Fangs felt miserable. His back was still hurting and this only made matters worse. However, Grace was enjoying the flight more than Ryan. Watching the city from below her was a beautiful sight, it started making her care for Fangs even more.

"You're so lucky Fangs, to have wings that could take you anywhere you want to go," she said. "I always wanted to fly; this is almost like a dream come true."

This brought more warmth to Fangs' heart. He could see his patience was paying off in earning her affection. It was even making him forget about the pain in his back.

"I'll always be your transportation baby," he happily replied.

"Let's stay focused on the mission instead," Ryan responded. "Just head to the Daylight Savings Mall as soon as possible."

"Then hang on tight!" Fangs advised. "This is going to be a bumpy ride."

Fangs swept and looped through the air which made Ryan and Grace feel like they were on a rollercoaster. He continued soaring through the air and started passing by big buildings like a game of chicken. Ryan got scared for the moment; however, Grace was having too much fun. She raised her arms in the air excitingly.

"I haven't had this much fun in years!" she cried delightfully. "Go faster Fangs!"

"I'm going to live to regret this," Ryan whimpered helplessly.

Meanwhile, Rex and Jewel continued their search for Ryan. Rex constantly sniffed the ground tracking him and it eventually led to Kyle's house. Rex stopped sniffing and he lifted his head.

"It seems Ryan was here earlier," Rex assured Jewel.

"Kyle's house?" she asked as she approached the front porch.

Chapter 10: The Search

"It's probably obvious that Kyle is also a part of the plan. Ryan must have come here to ask him about it?"

Jewel knocked on the door but there was no answer. When she knocked again the door swung open. Jewel steadily looked inside to see if anyone was home. Rex rapidly jumped into Jewel's path.

"Let me go first!" he demanded

He put his nose to the floor again and started sniffing excessively. He scanned through most of the house and didn't find anyone. Jewel entered the house and walked inside the living room. Near the telephone table, she noticed a picture of Kyle and Ryan together. On the side of the picture was a signature from Ryan that read, *"Best friends forever, from your good friend Ryan."* Jewel felt sad for a moment. She was suddenly wishing that she listened to Ryan's judgment about staying with her. She was also hoping Kyle wouldn't have done anything bad to Ryan because he was his best friend. She set the photo back on the telephone table when she saw Rex enter the living room.

"No one's here," he declared.

"If Ryan was here, where would he go to next?"

The two randomly heard Kyle's dog barking from the backyard.

"He would know," said Rex as he walked into the kitchen. Jewel followed as she watched Rex approach the screen door with Pugsy barking from outside.

"Are you sure that's wise?" Jewel asked watching Rex open the screen door.

"Don't worry honey, it's just dog talk," he said.

Once Rex opened the door, he met Pugsy face to face outside then let him off the chain. Pugsy became excited by waging his tail then sniffed Rex on his butt.

"Alright, alright," Rex sighed annoyingly, "we've been properly introduced now if you're finished we need some information from you."

Pugsy barked in response.

"No I assure you we're cool," said Rex. "We're good friends of Kyle. We just need to know if some friends of his were here earlier?"

Pugsy barked again. Some things that Jewel could somewhat make out but her understanding dog language was a bit rusty.

"He says Ryan and his friends came in the house first going through Kyle's refrigerator then Kyle and his friends came in and got into an argument," Rex described from Pugsy. "After that, the cops came and had them arrested."

"Kyle called the cops on his friends?" Jewel said in shock.

"That's what Pugsy here observed," said Rex.

"I never should've let him go, he was right. I just hope he's okay."

"Give me a violin," Rex groaned miserably.

"Oh shut up Rex. I guess we have no choice but to go down to the police station."

"Not a good idea. Law enforcement is just going to get in the way of things. Besides, if they found out about the 2D and 3D battle they could put us away for getting involved."

"Alright, then where do we go to next?"

Pugsy barked to Rex again as if he were answering their questions.

"Did he say stage?" Jewel asked confusingly.

"The stadium," Rex clarified.

"The stadium? What stadium?" Jewel asked.

"Pugsy said he overheard Kyle and his friends talk about heading to the stadium. It's where the battle will take place. If Ryan is still searching for them then that's where he'll be."

"Then let's get going," Jewel announced.

"It's a long way off. Are you sure you want to travel that far?"

"I have to Rex and you know it."

"Here we go again. You're determined to drag me there."

"Besides, you'll carry me most of the way. I am pregnant after all," she snickered.

"Oh that's just great!" Rex complained.

Before the two left they watched Pugsy go into the living room as he happily jumped on the couch rolling all over himself then flicked the remote to the television on with his paw.

Chapter 10: The Search

"I think we'll leave him unchained," Rex commented. "Kyle is going to be gone for a while and his dog needs all the relaxation he can get."

"Fair enough," said Jewel as she walked out the door. "I just hope he's housebroken."

Jewel's words were answered when Rex noticed Pugsy lift his leg on the living room couch.

"Yep, perfectly housebroken," he said as he closed the door from behind him.

CHAPTER ELEVEN

THE CHASE

Shortly a little while later, Ryan and his friends made it to the Daylight Savings Mall as Fangs landed in the parking lot area. Grace leaped off of Fangs with exhilaration, jumping up and down with such enthusiasm.

"Waaa Hooo! Let's do that again! That was electrifying!"

"You really liked it, buttercup?"

"Buttercup?"

Fangs blushed in humiliation. "I'm sorry I mean…"

"I like it!" Grace rejoiced.

"Huh? Really—you like buttercup?"

"I like being called that name. It makes me feel so fuzzy and warm inside. It almost makes me feel like, like…"

"Li-i-i-i-i-ke?"

"Like I'm in love," Grace said hugging herself.

"Really?" Fangs asked amazingly. He began to feel weak at the knees, while his heart felt as though it would burst through his chest and started panting like a dog. In the meantime, Ryan's body finally fell out onto the parking lot. He was genuinely sick from the flight and couldn't handle it. He held his mouth to keep himself from vomiting. His head turned green as he began walking in circles trying to get rid of the queasiness.

"Are we there yet?" he asked nauseously.

"Just take a good look," Grace said.

Chapter 11: The Chase

Ryan could see the mall in double vision from his perspective but his head cleared and came back to normal. He saw the Daylight Savings Mall clear as day right before him. Citizens were entering and leaving it simultaneously. The mall was pretty packed; so finding Kyle would be like hunting for a needle in a haystack, however, Ryan was determined to get this finished.

"Alright guys, what we're going to do is to look for Kyle and his friends. Let's not try to start a ruckus that could have us thrown back in prison again."

"Gotcha," Grace replied.

The Daylight Savings Mall was a big and spacious complex. It was a popular mall enclosed with plenty of stores, food plazas, and even a movie theater. It had its abundance of humans mostly instead of cartoon characters, although a few of them do roam the mall from time to time. When Ryan and his friends entered the mall, they already knew this was going to take them a while.

"Why don't I just fly around the whole mall until I find them," Fangs suggested.

"When's the last time you saw a big 3D dragon flying around the Daylight Savings Mall," Ryan requested. "That could start something and scare people especially the small children. We need to be calm and less suspicious. Just act like we're here to shop or to have a good time."

"Even if this is a mission, I'm already having a good time," Grace claimed. "I always enjoy coming to the mall."

Ryan, Grace, and Fangs walked around the first floor then took the escalator to the second. Once the escalator led them to the next floor, Grace noticed a perfume fragrance store. She smiled enthusiastically then quickly ran to the store almost knocking Ryan over.

"What are you doing?" Ryan bellowed.

"I'm behind schedule with my shopping and this is the perfect opportunity to start."

"Grace, remember the mission. We must find Kyle and the others, right Fangs?"

But when Ryan looked for Fangs, he was already by Grace's side.

"I'll buy anything you want… buttercup."

"You sure do know how to capture a woman's heart," Grace said as she scratched Fangs underneath the chin. He just waged his tail happily like a dog.

"Great, looks like I'm on my own," Ryan complained dejectedly.

He continued traveling around the whole mall constantly muttering to himself angrily. He knew Fangs and Grace were in love with each other but he desperately wanted to get back to his wife. He needed their help to get this case over with, the more he thought about it the angrier he got at Kyle. If he hadn't called the cops on them then he wouldn't have wasted all those hours in prison and probably could've been home by now. He was going to kill him once he got his paws on him. While Ryan continued searching on his own, he observed a beach store nearby. Nothing unusual, but what caught his attention was a 3D dolphin character. This dolphin was named Silver, because of his visual attributes of blue and silver. His body always seemed glossy and polished which made him glow beautifully. He was good-natured and almost constantly cheerful. The beach store was the perfect place for someone like him to go shopping. Frequently he was flipping in circles like a regular dolphin would do if he were in the ocean. He was practicing on a lifeboat that was left out on display in front of the store. Ryan couldn't help but ask for his assistance.

"Excuse me sir but—uh… could you help me?"

"Well hello Vulpes fulva," Silver replied.

"Vulpix—what?" Ryan said confusingly.

"The scientific classification of a Red fox is called a Vulpes fulva."

"Oh really—I—didn't know that."

"Did you also know that the scientific classification of a bat-eared fox is called an Otocycon megalotis. The gray fox is Urocyon cinereoargenteus, the kit fox is Vulpes velox and because you're part of the dog family, the maned wolf is a Chrysocyon brachyurus. Not to mention the raccoon dog is a Nyctereutes procyonoides."

Ryan was speechless. He never met such a cartoon character so knowledgeable. "I—I don't know what to say."

Chapter 11: The Chase

"It's okay Vulpes. You just probably didn't know that the dolphin was the smartest animal in the world."

"Oh right—I always thought it was the dog or the monkey?"

"The dolphin is first, then the monkey, and last the dog but it's scientifically known that the pig and rat are more intelligent than the dog itself. So Vulpes, what's your real name?"

"Ryan, the name is Ryan. What's yours?"

"You can just call me Silver my good friend. So when you first came here, you were asking me for help, correct?"

"Yes, yes I was. You see, I'm looking for a friend of mine. His name is Kyle and he's here with his friends. He's a 2D pterodactyl by the way."

"Specifically, I did see him, approximately one hour, twenty-five minutes, and fourteen seconds ago. He and his friends headed to the third floor."

"That's fantastic. If only I knew where to find them on the third floor."

"That won't be necessary."

"Why not?"

"They're standing approximately 3.7 feet from your left."

Incredibly, Ryan turned his head to the left side and spotted Kyle and his friends. They were heading in his direction but didn't notice him. That was until Carlos opened up his big mouth.

"Say Kyle, is that your fox friend?" he shouted.

When the others suddenly noticed Ryan, Kyle never thought he would feel so scared in his whole life with a twisted note of surprise; he didn't expect Ryan to be out of prison standing just a few feet from him. He could probably imagine the horrible things Ryan thought of him after what he did. Kyle remained still like a statue. Ryan just glared at him furiously and started to snarl like a dog with claws rapidly coming out of his paws.

"I think he's mad at you," Stan said to Kyle.

"Who wouldn't be after what you did," Carlos snickered.

"Now come on you guys, you know why he did it; to protect him because he didn't want his friend getting involved in this battle," Ralph mentioned.

"Well it looks like he's involved now," Carlos acknowledged. "And you're right Stan, he's pretty angry. In fact, it looks like he's ready to attack you."

But Kyle remained silent and frozen with fear. Carlos began jumping on top of Kyle's head to snap him out of it.

"I think he's out of order."

Stan had to heave one of his horns into Kyle's butt to wake him up.

"OWWW!" he screamed. "What did you do that for?"

"Quit staring and start running!" Stan yelled.

"Yeah, if you still want to keep him out of it!" Ralph shouted.

"I can't argue with that!" Kyle agreed as he began to thrust his wings out.

Kyle and his friends began to run away from Ryan's direction. This made Ryan even more furious, why was his friend desperately avoiding him? It was like he didn't even know him anymore.

"KYLE!!" he screamed.

Ryan wasted no time running after them; he was hot on their tails but not close enough. Silver watched everything and wanted to be a part of the action. He quickly ran inside the beach store and grabbed a surfboard. "Surfs Up!" he called.

He threw the surfboard on the floor and incredibly started riding it as though he were surfing on the beach. He was using the surfboard like a skateboard and he was pretty good at it. While Ryan was still running, he unexpectedly saw Silver roaming by his side.

"Silver?" he said surprised.

"Foxes are fast but you'll never catch them at this rate Vulpes. Hop on."

The cheerful dolphin quickly grabbed a hold of Ryan and threw him across his shoulder. Ryan held on tightly preparing for anything, while Silver avoided citizens who were in the way or just strolling by. As Kyle and his friends continued running, Ralph turned his head and saw Ryan gaining on them.

"Whoa! Ryan's got backup! He's riding with a dolphin on a—surfboard!?" Ralph cried.

Chapter 11: The Chase

When Kyle and the others turned their heads to see for themselves they became uneasy.

"That's just great! He's going to catch us!" Kyle shouted.

"Not by a long shot! Everyone hop on top of Kyle! He'll fly us out of here!" Carlos declared.

"WHAT?!" Kyle cried. "You know I can't carry all of…"

But without listening to Kyle, Ralph and Stan immediately hopped on top of him, including Carlos who relaxed on his head. With all of his strength, Kyle lifted everyone. It seemed entirely impossible with carrying Ralph let alone Stan who were much bigger than he was, however, he managed to lift them into mid-air away from Ryan and Silver. He was sweating heavily and whimpering like crazy, fluttering like a dying housefly. Stan and Ralph held on to him tightly not wanting to fall.

"Please don't fall Kyle," Stan begged.

"Yeah, we're right above the whole mall," Ralph whined.

"Don't worry, this bird is a natural. It's in our blood to never fall," Carlos said with no worry.

Kyle had his eyes closed the entire time; he was completely out of breath and couldn't handle the pressure anymore. After a few seconds, Kyle stopped flapping his wings and his body gave out. As they started to fall, Ralph and Stan looked at Carlos irritably.

"Well… almost never," Carlos admitted.

With that, the whole gang fell, including Carlos because Ralph snatched him. Silver stopped the surfboard in observation with many on-lookers as they watched Kyle and his friends fall screaming from the height. Once they hit the bottom with a loud thud, people began laughing and cheering. It was always amusing to them seeing cartoon characters get hurt but everyone went back to their normal business as usual. From the upper level, Silver and Ryan tried to see if they could spot Kyle and the others after their fall.

"We're not going to be able to see them from up here, we have to go downstairs," Silver pointed out.

"You're right let's go," Ryan confirmed as he hopped off of Silver's back.

He and Silver quickly took the escalator downstairs but by the time they got there, Kyle and his friends were already gone.

"Where could they go that fast?" Ryan asked anxiously.

"The only solution is that they quickly ran into one of the nearest stores for cover," Silver suggested.

"What store would that be?" Ryan demanded.

Silver glanced around for a minute until he caught sight of the movie theater right next to them.

"They're in there," Silver revealed.

"Are you sure?" Ryan asked.

"Predicting the irony of the situation, my calculations say it's an 87% possibility," Silver assured him.

"Good enough, let's go," Ryan ordered.

Ryan and Silver quickly headed inside of the matinee and began to scan the area.

"So tell me Vulpes, why do you have a beef with this guy?"

"Kyle is supposed to be my best friend but he's hiding something from me, something extremely important that he doesn't want me to know about."

"If he's your best friend, maybe he's only trying to protect you."

"Protect me? Why? Why would he want to protect me? I don't need any protection. I just need to find out what's going on so I can get back to my wife."

"Wife huh? She's pregnant isn't she?"

"How did you know that?"

"Your facial expressions, anxiety, and constant frantic behavior gave me the idea."

"You're really good. Say Silver, your brilliant mind could be a lot of use to me for solving this mystery. Would you be willing to come with me and my friends? We're trying to unravel this case and we're not making much progress so far. I need all the help I can get."

"Certainly, I've got nothing better to do anyway."

"Thanks Silver, brains like yours are hard to find. So—where would Kyle and his friends be hiding?"

Chapter 11: The Chase

Silver browsed around the matinee for a minute and pointed to one of the theaters; he suspected they were hiding in there.

"This one?" Ryan asked confusingly.

"Estimating the time and meters of the tracks taken to approach this specific room to avoid you, this is the exact calculations for them to enter here," Silver assured.

"Oh—okay," Ryan said softly.

By the time Ryan and Silver entered the room, the motion picture had already started. Ryan scanned through the audience and aisles but didn't see Kyle or his friends.

"They're in disguise Vulpes," Silver confirmed.

Ryan cautiously and quietly walked through the aisles and crawled underneath the seats to avoid being seen or distracting anyone from their show. After checking a few aisles, Ryan spotted three suspicious-looking characters sitting in the fourth aisle. They wore big hats to cover their heads and full-sized jackets to cover their bodies. Kyle and his friends desperately tried to blend in by eating popcorn and remaining completely silent. Ralph slowly turned his head around and spotted Ryan a few feet from him.

"He's in here," Ralph whispered.

"That's just great," Kyle spoke softly.

"I can't run anymore. I feel like I broke my back when we collapsed on the ground," Stan cried.

"Broke your back! I'm the one who had to carry all of ya!" Kyle quietly shrieked.

"Shut up you guys," Carlos said as he stuffed his face with popcorn. "This movie is just getting to the good part."

"We're not here to enjoy the movie you idiot! We're here to hide!" Kyle complained.

Before they knew it, Ryan was a few inches behind them. They could hear him approaching and getting closer by the minute.

"Time to make another run for it boys!" Kyle ordered his friends.

Right before Ryan could check them out, Kyle and the others quickly made a run for it. They jumped frantically out of their disguises and desperately ran through the aisles. Popcorn and drinks were being scattered everywhere. The audience started complaining and yelling at Kyle, Ralph, Stan, and Carlos who got in their way. Ryan tried to catch up with them by hopping aisle to aisle but it was difficult with all of the food and drinks hitting him. After most of the chaos was over, Kyle and his friends exited out of the theater but Ryan fell to the floor after slipping on a drink. Silver came to his aid and helped him up.

"Shhhhhh! Silence is golden," Silver reminded.

"Where are they?" asked Ryan sluggishly.

"I'm afraid they're gone again," Silver admitted. "The thing about 2D characters, they're a little quicker than us 3D. They can easily disappear like a puff of smoke. I guess we can too but it really depends on the specific animation genre."

"We can't let them get away again!" Ryan cried. "Let's go!"

Ryan anxiously ran out of the matinee and caught sight of Kyle heading up the escalator along with his friends.

"Oh no you don't!" Ryan yelled in a fit of rage.

With Ryan heading after them much closer this time, Kyle and the others decided to make their exit on the second floor.

"I regret eating at EATS or I wouldn't be in this situation!" Stan cried.

"I agree!" Ralph concurred. "It all started from that place!"

"Just shut up and run!" Kyle ordered.

"I've still got plenty of popcorn left," Carlos announced, happily holding a bag of it by his feet.

Running, they quickly came across a pet shop. Carlos immediately spotted a beautiful bird inside a birdcage hanging on display with many of the other pets for sale. He wasted no time zipping towards the bird landing inside the cage with her. He perked his chest up trying to impress the bewildered animal.

"Hey there sexy," Carlos chirped. "I can make a deal with the shop owner and you and I could leave this so-called dump and crash at my crib. You're the most gorgeous thing I have ever laid eyes on. I'm Carlos by the way. What's your name sexy?"

Chapter 11: The Chase

The bird just chirped in response as if she didn't understand a thing this crazy cartoon character was saying.

"Popcorn," he said handing her a piece.

Carlos was then snatched away by Kyle in the blink of an eye.

"This habit of you hitting on every woman you come across is getting pretty old," Kyle shrieked as he kept on running. "I would like for you to remain civilized for once."

"There's no such thing as being civilized with cartoon characters, besides, do you think she found me hot?" asked Carlos.

"The mission, remember the mission," Kyle cried.

Carlos glanced back at the bird in the pet shop and remarked, "Call me!"

Ryan's friends were still on the second floor inside the perfume store. Grace was trying on different types of fragrances while Fangs was buying them for her.

"I'll take this one too," Grace said, as she looked at the bottle. "This one will go good with my collection."

"Anything you want, my buttercup," Fangs chuckled happily.

"You're really making me weak in the knees every time you call me that."

"I sure hope so."

Suddenly, Fangs and Grace caught sight of Kyle and his friends scurrying past them as they headed to the exit. Abruptly, Ryan ran in front of Fangs and Grace.

"Are you finished shopping?! Can we please get back to business?!" he yelled.

"Oh yeah, sorry," Fangs said sympathetically.

Ryan and Grace both hopped on top of Fangs' back. He quickly thrust his wings out and headed out of the exit following Kyle and the others. Outside Kyle and his friends ran through the parking lot while Fangs watched them as he glided high from above.

"Keep running and they won't catch us!" Carlos advised. "I smell the taste of victory, I just know it!"

Before Kyle and the others knew it, Fangs landed directly on top of them. He easily held them down, keeping them from escaping his big claws. Kyle tried to squirm away but it was useless. Stan and Ralph eventually gave up, without fighting any longer; they fell unconscious under Fangs' claws. Carlos was pinned down right beside Kyle feeling dumbfounded by the sudden situation.

"Don't you say another word," Kyle groaned angrily at Carlos.

Finally relieved and satisfied that he captured Kyle, Ryan felt he could relax a little. He glared down at Kyle while he was on top of Fangs' head.

"No more running Kyle," Ryan explained. "Now's the time for answers."

"You've got nothing on me," Kyle cried. "I swear I'm not hiding anything."

"Then why did you run? Why are you sending me on this wild goose chase?"

"You chased me."

"Why did you call the cops on me and my friends?"

"Uh—you broke in my house."

"You're going to have to do better than that. Tell me what is really going on Kyle!"

As much as Kyle wanted to tell his friend, he just couldn't get him involved, knowing Christopher told him to get rid of any 3D characters that got in the way; he could never do that to Ryan. Over the past few years, Ryan had become like a brother to him, he just couldn't bear the thought of him getting hurt, so Kyle remained silent. Then unexpectedly, a limousine arrived and rammed itself right into Fangs, knocking him, along with Ryan and Grace out of the way. The three of them fell up against some nearby cars but luckily didn't break any windows. Kyle and Carlos looked on with amazement not realizing what happened. The limousine pulled up to Kyle and the others, revealing Jackson who poked his head out the window.

"Jackson?" Kyle said surprised.

"Get in the limo you fools!" Jackson growled fully annoyed.

Chapter 11: The Chase

"I told you I smelled the taste of victory," Carlos cried happily. "You should start listening to me more often."

Ignoring Carlos, Kyle dragged Ralph and Stan's unconscious bodies and threw them into the limo then hopped inside himself. After that Jackson started the limo and drove off leaving nothing else behind except for smoke and dust. Ryan and the others woke up from the impact and realized it was too late to catch up with them, leaving the infuriated fox upset again. Will he ever get through this terrible dilemma? It was starting to drive him crazy. Grace got up and began to help Fangs get on his feet.

"Are you okay Fangs?" she asked.

"It's no big deal," he assured her. "I've been hit with worse things than a limo; it just caught me off guard, that's all."

"Poor thing," Grace said. "Filmmakers shouldn't work you so hard."

"Thank you for caring—buttercup."

Grace blushed shyly as she held on to her tail.

"What are we going to do now you guys?" Ryan complained pulling his fur out. "Kyle's gone again and this time we don't even know where he's going."

"Maybe I could find out," said Silver.

Ryan, Fangs, and Grace turned their heads noticing Silver standing behind them.

"Silver!" Ryan cried with joy.

"Silver? A new friend of yours?" Grace asked.

"While you two were busy shopping, he helped me find Kyle with his brilliant brainpower," Ryan informed them. "Are you able to find out where they're going Silver?"

"Sure can, if you just follow me, we can piece this puzzle together."

CHAPTER TWELVE

KYLE'S REGRET

Kyle and his friends tried to settle down in the backseat of the limo while Jackson continued driving. Ralph and Stan were still out cold on the floor but Carlos was flying around the limo with much enthusiasm.

"YEAH!! We beat those 3D scum! They thought they had us, but we escaped them once more!"

"They would've had you if it wasn't for me," Jackson commented.

"Sorry boss, we tried to stop them but they just kept on coming," Kyle remarked.

"What were you doing at the mall in the first place?" Jackson asked.

"Shopping for weapons," Kyle stated. "We just wanted to prepare ourselves for the battle."

"I don't need any weapons," Carlos remarked. "With this beautiful body, I can take on anything."

"Yeah, with a body like that, you won't last two seconds," Kyle complained.

"Christopher doesn't want you guys causing any more attention," Jackson ordered. "He wants me to take you all to the stadium right now."

"NOW!!" Kyle said flabbergasted. "You mean the battle is going to happen today?"

"It's gotta be done now!" Jackson remarked. "William is preparing the 3D characters to meet him at the stadium as we speak and the people are also gathering. Besides all the talk of 2D characters leaving their job has

Chapter 12 Kyle's Regret

been raising too much suspicion and this needs to take place the sooner the better."

"This will be a fight I wouldn't want to miss!" cried Carlos with excitement. "Take us to the stadium, my good friend. I'm looking forward to 3D seeing their last day."

Kyle didn't say anything this time. Suddenly he started regretting the whole thing, especially after Ryan pursuing him. Ryan made him realize how determined he was to find out the truth. He truly was his trustworthy and loyal friend, even if he was 3D. Kyle hated being treated as the underdog for so long, he desperately wanted to pay all the 3D characters back for their fame and fortune; nonetheless, he suddenly realized everything wasn't about him anymore. It was about the lives of the 2D and 3D characters that would be caught up in the commotion. Christopher even said there would be some casualties and it would be an epic battle. Something this enormous could only lead to a blood bath. William obviously didn't care about the cartoon characters; all he cared about was capitalizing on them. The 2D and the 3D were so blinded by their hatred for each other; they didn't care if William was only using them for his own achievements. Kyle's repugnance was finally surfacing and making him see the light at last. Reflecting on this, Kyle's mind instantly went to a flashback which happened two years ago at Cartoon Studios. This was the first time Kyle met Ryan when they were getting ready to make their first cartoon series. Kyle walked onto the Hollywood set beside Charles with the script in his hands. He was reading over it and thought it was pretty good, assuming he was going to be working with a 2D fox.

"I like this script boss but what kind of television series has a pterodactyl and a fox as best friends?" Kyle asked confused.

"A stupid one," Charles replied. "Besides, cartoons don't make any sense, that's too apparent."

"Whatever you say boss, but I just want to let you know it's an honor working in the movies again. I thought we 2D characters couldn't find jobs acting anymore but it's literally like a dream come true. I guarantee you that'll I'll do a perfect job and I won't let you down."

Charles just rolled his eyes impatiently at Kyle's lecture. He didn't care much for 2D animation because for him it was just a tiring cycle he dealt with years ago. Still, he had respect for them which only ascended from his interior while his exterior was more of a hard, ruthless man.

"So where's this so-called fox I'm going to be working with?" Kyle asked excitedly.

Charles smiled devilishly at Kyle suspecting he probably didn't know. "Why he's right here," Charles replied. "Ryan, come on out and meet your new partner."

Ryan left his powder room and walked out onto the movie set where he sat down in front of Charles and Kyle respectfully. No doubt Kyle was flabbergasted and disgusted at the same time, suddenly wondering what had he gotten himself into.

"Nice to meet you Kyle, I'm Ryan your new partner."

But Kyle didn't respond to Ryan or shake his paw when he brought it out to him. He slowly stepped away from him and looked up at Charles with anger.

"Um, boss excuse me, there must be some kind of mistake here. I didn't think I was going to be working with a 3D character."

"There's no mistake," Charles declared. "Whether you like it or not, you and Ryan are going to be starring in these television series together. So you better get used to it and put your racism aside."

"I won't work with a CGI freak!"

"Then find another job."

Kyle realized he was stuck in this circumstance. He agreed to be a part of it before he found out that Ryan was a 3D character; if he didn't go through with it then he would easily get fired. He'd want to work at a studio more than anything, especially compared to being a janitor at the movies from his previous job. He found cleaning up popcorn and drinks from the floor a humiliation he could only find tolerable, by sneaking glimpses at the films on the big screen, daydreaming of being part of the motion pictures again. Now that he had the chance he couldn't blow it and had to suck up working with a 3D character. Kyle's face started to turn red and fuming with anger as he grumbled curse words under his breath. After

Chapter 12 Kyle's Regret

he was done releasing his rage, he gradually calmed down but he was sweating and wore a troubled look on his face.

"Okay boss—you win," he cried shamefully.

"Good, now bury those emotions and get ready for your first filming," Charles demanded. "We've got a lot of work to do today and I don't appreciate any slackers."

"This is going to be a long and painful acquaintance," Kyle commented.

"You're telling me," Ryan agreed.

Ryan and Kyle started out making their first episode where they traveled in Transylvania. Kyle of course was being torn to pieces by all the monsters he came into contact with while Ryan was making a noble escape. Charles yelled from his bull horn once the whole episode was completed.

"And cut! Perfect, Ryan and Kyle, good take but Kyle next time let the werewolves take a bite out of you just like the vampires did. Alright everybody, pack it up for the day. I need to go home and get away from this cartoon madness."

While everyone gathered up their belongings, Ryan, stopped by to check on Kyle who was mangled on the ground.

"You okay?"

"I-I can feel my blood running cold," Kyle quivered. Suddenly his body began cracking itself awkwardly. Then miraculously sharp fangs appeared from his mouth, in addition to having bat wings and a black cape behind his back. "Oh this is just great! Being bitten by so many vampires has turned me into one. Someone get me an antidote! I can't go home to Pugsy looking like this."

"Would garlic or a stake through the heart be your remedy?" Ryan asked.

"Back off before I suck your blood!" Kyle threatened as he hissed at him.

Ryan submissively backed away as Kyle took flight heading out of the studio. Minutes later Kyle was back in his true form, walking down the street of the big city.

"I gotta get myself a lawyer," he complained. "This is cruel and inhumane the way they treat me. Blackmailing me into working with a 3D character."

Kyle continued his ranting as he crossed the street when the light turned red. If he was paying attention he would've noticed a random speeder that was making his way towards him. Kyle didn't see until it was too late. Before the car could hit him he was swiftly thrown out of the way. He and his rescuer were rolling on top of each other until they made it safely on the other side of the street. The car just drove off almost making the accident a hit and run. As Kyle stood himself up he realized Ryan was the one who just saved him.

"You?" he asked surprised.

"I'd be more careful next time if I were you," Ryan said dusting himself off.

"You rotten dirtbag!" Kyle yelled at the driver who was already gone from sight. "If I so much as see you again you'll be sorry." Kyle then turned his attention back on Ryan. "Uh—thanks for saving my butt."

"No problem," said Ryan. "We were both going the same way but when I saw that car heading towards you I had to do something."

"You're a very reasonable guy, sticking out your neck for a 2D character you hardly know."

"Let's just say, I have a decent heart for everyone."

Kyle looked away ashamed. He still didn't know Ryan that well but after what he had done he should've at least give him a chance. "I generally don't like hanging out with 3D characters—but since you helped me—I'll give you a chance."

"I hope that means you'll give more 3D characters a chance down the line. Not all of us are the same. By the way, I've asked Charles to cut you some slack. Tomorrow he says you don't have to do the stunt doubles."

"Really?" Kyle said feeling blissful. "Gee thanks, you didn't have to do that for me."

"Hey you're new," said Ryan. "I feel newcomers should be given a little break."

"You know Ryan, I've really misunderstood you. You might be alright after all. Would you like to go and get something to eat?"

"Sure, but who's buying it?"

"You are of course," Kyle grinned.

"Obviously," Ryan sighed.

Kyle's flashback ended with Ryan's words still echoing in his head. "Let's just say, I have a decent heart for everyone." His first intention was just to make sure Ryan wouldn't get hurt, however; now he was beginning to realize if others did get hurt, what kind of friend would that make him. Kyle wouldn't be much of a good friend if he fought Ryan's 3D family. If it were the other way around, Kyle wouldn't like it if Ryan was going to fight any of his family members either. Ryan sacrificed so much to help Kyle in the past and this is how he was going to thank him. Kyle felt lower than dirt and didn't want anything to do with the battle anymore but he knew there was no way of escaping it because he was already in way too deep.

"What have I done?" he said to himself.

"Kyle, are you alright?" Carlos asked.

"I-I-I'm alright, I just need to think this through very carefully."

"What is there to think about? We're going into combat!"

"Shut up!"

Kyle checked Jackson to see if he was eavesdropping on their conversation. Although it didn't seem like it, Kyle didn't want to take that chance.

"Listen we'll talk about this later," he whispered.

"Sure, whatever you say my brother," Carlos replied.

CHAPTER THIRTEEN

THE DOLPHIN CLUB

Meanwhile Silver led Ryan, Grace, and Fangs to the beach. It was 11:37 a.m. and the beach was pretty active due to the nice weather. Most of the citizens were relaxing in the sun; others were surfboarding on the durable waves, while others were eating at concession food stands and playing video games in the arcade area. It was pretty strange for Ryan and his friends going to a place like the beach, they didn't know exactly what Silver had in mind for them; however, Ryan trusted Silver's judgment because he was the brains of the operation. He slowly guided them further along the shores as they got closer to their destination.

"It's pretty obvious you would take us to the beach," Fangs stated. "It's the best place for dolphins."

"Don't knock it until you try it," Silver remarked. "Besides, I have a good reason for bringing you guys here."

"What—to take us for a swim?" Fangs asked sarcastically.

"Don't challenge him Fangs," Ryan declared. "He's smarter than all of us put together."

"Oh really, then what's 148,956 x 7,589,362?" Fangs asked him.

"1,130,481,006,072," Silver answered quickly.

"Uh… is it?" Fangs asked Grace.

"I don't know," Grace responded.

"Okay, then answer me this," Fangs said. "What is Grace? Is she an alligator or a crocodile?"

Chapter 13: The Dolphin Club

"Oh please," Grace groaned.

"It's evident that she's an alligator," Silver said without hesitation. "Alligators are often mistaken for crocodiles but are different from them in some ways. The fourth tooth of the alligator's lower jaw fits into a pocket of the upper jaw. The same tooth in the crocodile fits into a groove in the side of the upper jaw, making it visible when the animal's mouth is closed. Alligators also have a much broader snout and are much less aggressive and active than crocodiles."

"Uh…. okay, what's the meaning of life?"

"Life has no meaning. It's just the state of existence."

"Uh… uh… how big is my I.Q?"

"I prefer not to answer that one," Silver retorted.

"And, why not?" Fangs demanded.

"Because I don't want to embarrass you in front of your friends."

Fangs stood humiliated, wishing that he had just kept his mouth shut. "Alright I'll keep my mouth shut," he said frustratingly.

"So Silver, where are you taking us anyway?" Ryan asked.

"Here we are!" Silver shouted excited.

When Ryan and his friends looked in front of them, they witnessed a huge Uberin placed right on the beach sand called The Dolphin Club.

"The Dolphin Club?" Ryan asked.

"You have your own club?" inquired Grace.

"It's not just my club," Silver replied. "It's a club for all of my comrades which are dolphins. Come on in and meet my family."

"You guys aren't racists are ya?" Grace asked with much concern. "After all, I'm the only 2D character around here."

"We're not racist, we like everybody no matter what you are!" Silver claimed merrily. "That's something that everyone should consider. Now come right this way."

The cheerful, blissful warm-blooded mammal led Ryan and his friends inside the club. Once indoors, the whole club was filled with nothing but 3D dolphins, however, there were many different types of them, like a Dall's porpoise, the common porpoise, the bottle-nosed dolphin (Silver's type), the white-sided dolphin, the common dolphin, and even killer whales. They were all part of the same family so they treated each other as one. They were always good-natured, constantly laughing, and communicating with one another, making a wide variety of sounds. There was a medium-sized swimming pool in the club, a pool game, plus a tavern, and a large television which premiered an animal documentary of real dolphins. The room went into complete silence when they saw Silver, Ryan, Fangs, and Grace enter the club. They stared at them with astonishment which made, Grace and Fangs, feel uneasy at first.

"Maybe this wasn't a good idea," Grace cried feeling entirely uncomfortable.

But immediately all of the dolphins in the club cheered with excitement. "Visitors!" a Dall's porpoise shouted as the rest of them greeted Ryan and his friends with a warm welcome. They picked them up and carried them across the room. They set them down near the tavern for a drink. The bartender dolphin quickly made three drinks for Ryan and his friends.

"Saltwater on the house," said the bartender dolphin.

"Uh—thanks but I don't drink salt water," Ryan said.

"I never got this kind of welcome from 3D characters before," Grace admitted. "I really like the atmosphere. I think I can enjoy 3D animation after all."

Silver clapped his flippers together and got everybody's attention. "Listen up my brothers, these are my new friends; Ryan, Fangs, and Grace!" he announced. "They're struggling to decipher a serious circumstance and need our assistance to unravel it!"

The whole club cheered with a loud uproar. Dolphins loved solving cases or basically anything because of their high intelligence; it was always fun and entertaining to them. The dolphins continued chortling with their constant sounds that was sort of making Fangs nervous; he'd never been around anything like this before.

"Surrounded by Albert Einsteins," he said to himself. "Now I really feel below the average intelligence."

"We're more than delighted to assist you!" said a common porpoise.

Chapter 13: The Dolphin Club

"We're also delighted to get visitors different from ourselves for once," said a common dolphin.

"Say, Grace would you like to go for a swim?" said a killer whale who kindly tapping Grace on the shoulder.

"Now wait a minute…" Fangs interrupted.

"Why sure," Grace accepted.

"Huh?" Fangs said surprised.

Grace strolled over to the swimming pool area and jumped inside with the other dolphins. She leaped a professional diver that had all the dolphins cheering and applauding her.

"What a natural," one dolphin congratulated. "An individual admirably suited for some purpose and destined for success."

"A real skillful expert," another one commented. "Identified with exclusively natural desires and ambitions."

All Fangs could do was look in utter torment. "Hey don't any of you guys touch my woman," he declared awkwardly. "Uh, buttercup—wouldn't you rather be over here with me."

"Fangs!" Ryan yelled as he kicked him on the foot. "Will you stop acting like a jealous boyfriend and focus on the mission."

"Oh yes, the mission," said a Dall's porpoise. "Tell us, without vacillating and being indecisive, but be very meticulous, fastidious, and punctilious in explaining the trenchant condition, actuality, and occurrence which resulted in your current circumstances."

"Uh…" Ryan stuttered not understanding what the Dall's porpoise just said.

"Sorry," he apologized. "We're so used to exercising our mental proclivities to grasp the significant factors of a convoluted predicament or exceptional situation; we neglect to remember to communicate compassionately with the average intelligence. What I mean to say is, how did all of this start for you and your friends?"

"Well—it all started yesterday when all of the 2D characters quit their job," Ryan started. "Including my best friend Kyle, who has been avoiding me all day. To make matters worse he even had us put in the slammer!"

"Mmmm—seems to me like he wants to keep you out of trouble," the Dall's porpoise replied.

"I am in concurrence with the veracity and validity of that statement. I also insinuated that the existing tribulation was the forerunner of that conclusion," Silver confirmed.

"What!?" said Ryan, befuddled.

"I mean I also suggested that information to you before," Silver clarified.

"But why?" Ryan asked.

"It seems like the 2D characters are planning something they don't want you 3D characters to know about," a white-sided dolphin chimed in.

"But what is it that they are planning?" Ryan asked again with much apprehension.

"Mmmm—putting everything together—with all of the 2D characters quitting their jobs and 3D characters unaware of the situation," the Dall's porpoise contemplated, "it could be… that the 2D characters are planning a confrontation, a melee, a fracas, a skirmish, …I mean a battle against the 3D."

"WHAT?" Ryan cried.

"I wouldn't doubt it," the porpoise replied. "After all, there was a breaking point sooner or later. The 2D has been treated like ancient history and disrespected for all these years since 3D came on the scene. They would do anything to get revenge. This could be what they're planning to do."

"B-but how could my friend Kyle be a part of this?" Ryan questioned.

"Was Kyle ever treated as second place?" asked Silver.

Recalling the countless times Kyle talked about, it would be too obvious that he would want to join the battle.

"Of course he was," Ryan admitted with shame.

"The main reason he had you put in the slammer is so you won't be a part of the battle," the white-sided dolphin pointed out. "He probably did it because he cares for you."

Everything was finally making sense to Ryan. He still might have been a little angry with Kyle but he understood his reasons more clearly now.

Chapter 13: The Dolphin Club

The horrible thought of his friend getting killed in the battle was too much to stomach and if others were going to be involved, he had to find a way to stop this catastrophe.

"Alright, if this is all true… then where would the battle be located?" Ryan asked.

"Could you give us more information?" Silver requested.

Ryan tried to think hard for a minute. "Ummm—I—uh… oh yeah! My boss Joseph said that William might be involved," Ryan remembered.

"William? Is that the famous William who plays miniature golf every Saturday morning or is that big-time bookie William who makes wagers on everything and has a polar bear as a partner?" Silver pondered.

"I wasn't aware there were even two Williams," Ryan reflected.

"No doubt about it, it's the gambler William. He has a readiness for gambling, like a mother bear to protect her cubs," a killer whale added.

"But what would William want with the 2D characters?" Fangs asked.

"For the battle of course," said a common porpoise. "He invests in many things. One of them happens to be a stadium."

"Stadium? What stadium?" Ryan demanded.

"Six months ago, we heard rumors of William investing in an enormous stadium," Silver said. "No one was supposed to know about it but nothing escapes the attention of us dolphins."

"Tell me more about the stadium!" Ryan insisted.

"This stadium is supposed to be the most substantial structure in the whole area," said the killer whale. "It's even larger than a baseball stadium; it has enough seats for thousands of spectators. William will make enough money for a lifetime."

"So six months ago William invested in a stadium, conned the 2D characters into quitting their jobs, and planned to catch the 3D characters off guard with a deadly encounter just to profit off the whole thing," Ryan concluded.

"There you have it," said the killer whale.

"I can't believe this!" Ryan cried. "Don't the 2D characters know that William is only using them?"

"They don't care as long as they can get vengeance on 3D animation," Silver said. "You see, when you're blinded by so much hatred for too long, it's difficult to see the truth anymore."

"Like your friend Russell," Fangs reminded him.

Ryan knew this bickering and conflict was going to have a breaking point sooner or later, nevertheless, this fight wasn't going to solve anything. The anger would just build up until it fully consumed them and William who was behind everything, would just eliminate them once he made what he needed.

"We've got to find that stadium!" Ryan insisted.

"Now wait a minute Ryan!" Fangs objected. "I didn't expect to be walking into an ugly battle. Who knows what is going to happen? Cartoon characters killing each other left and right; and who knows what else William might have in store for them. It's suicidal! I did want to help you solve this mystery but after finding out what we're really dealing with; I want nothing else to do with it. It's insane, I tell you! Just insane!"

"I think it's a good idea Ryan, I'm in," Grace said coming back to Ryan's side.

"So am I," Fangs said quickly changing his mind.

"Typical, I knew he would jump to her side," Ryan criticized.

All of the dolphins in the club began applauding once more excited. They laughed with their dolphin chortle which was making Fangs feel uncomfortable.

"Must they keep on doing that," he complained.

"It's what they do Fangs," Ryan stated.

"Don't worry Vulpes," Silver reassured Ryan. "I'll be happy to guide you to the stadium. My comrades and I are the only ones who know where it is and I'll go with ya to show you the way."

"You're a lifesaver Silver!" cried Ryan. "I couldn't have done any of this without you or your friend's help."

"Yeah, we should come here more often," Grace commented. "I like spending time with you dolphins, you really make me feel like I'm wanted."

"No problem young lady," one dolphin replied. "Our doors are always open to visitors."

Chapter 13: The Dolphin Club

"We're friends with everyone and love companionship!" another one declared.

"Come back any time and we can play games like Jeopardy, Family Feud, Wheel of Fortune, and Who Wants to Be a Millionaire!" a common porpoise cheered happily.

"Great, intelligent games," Fangs said less enthusiastic. "My brain hurts already."

"Before you guys leave, how about a toast to wish you guys good luck on your mission," said a killer whale.

The waitress dolphin handed Ryan, Fangs, Grace, and Silver four cups of saltwater to drink; every single dolphin in the club also had their own cups.

"Let's wish Ryan and his friends the best of luck and hope they succeed!" the killer whale announced.

At that moment, all of the dolphins cheered once again and then drank their water. Grace didn't mind drinking saltwater since she was an aquatic type but Ryan and Fangs on the other hand felt apprehensive about drinking it. They curled up their faces preparing for the worst then in a quick flash, Ryan and Fangs drank the saltwater which made them feel like they had to barf. Fangs held his mouth thinking he couldn't hold it down, while Ryan tried to gain his composure by pumping his hand against his chest and coughing at the same time.

"Th-th-thanks again—you—guys," Ryan stuttered. "I-I'm forever grateful to all of ya. Yuck!"

CHAPTER FOURTEEN

THE STADIUM

William confidently fixed his best suit and tie with great confidence, as he watched himself in the mirror with satisfaction knowing his plan was going to work. Christopher and Brittany sat in a chair right behind him. They stayed in a full-sized office that was on the top floor of the stadium.

"All the 2D characters are on their way here," Christopher confirmed, "and I'm sure you have all of the 3D characters on their way too?"

"Of course, as well as our general public," William declared. "I've been looking forward to this for a very long time. I'll become a wealthy man overnight."

Christopher annoyed, coughed at William to make sure he wasn't leaving him out of the picture.

"Oh yes—I didn't forget about you Chris," said William. "Don't worry you'll get your full share, fifty-fifty."

"By the way, where's your polar bear assistant Miriam?" Christopher questioned. "I haven't seen her since you arrived."

"Let's just say I fired her," he happily claimed. "Once this whole battle takes place, I won't need any more assistants."

"Harsh, if you ask me," Christopher scoffed.

"Let's just hope for the sake of the cartoon characters, this will turn out to everyone's benefit," Brittany said. "I'm going to feel sorry for the ones who won't live through this."

Chapter 14: The Stadium

"A minor tragedy," William commented. "That's what you get from disasters."

"Watch your mouth William," Christopher angrily remarked. "Those will be my people down there in battle, risking their necks for you."

"I have no doubts about that my friend but this is what the spectators are going to be hoping for," William replied. "Some will bet on 2D while others will bet on 3D. Throughout the battle, some will get their wishes and others will just have to accept the possibility of disappointment."

"William, just how long is this battle going to take?" Brittany asked.

"You shall soon see my dear," William answered. "You shall soon see. Christopher, will you be a good old chap and check on the new arrival?"

"I'd usually ask Jackson to do that for me but since he's not here—oh I guess I suppose I better go check," Christopher grumbled. "And while I'm gone William, don't touch my girl!"

Christopher angrily left the office, causing William to be quite amused by his last comment.

"So what if I did, what's he going to do—beat me to a pulp? Hmmm—tell me Brittany, why do you hang out with someone like that?"

"First of all, he treats me far better than any man ever has done and that's respect. What's the matter William? Still jealous because I turned you down a few years ago."

"Trust me honey, that's water under the bridge. However, if you're still up for that offer, you know I'm about to be the richest man in the world and I could buy you whatever you want."

"Money doesn't mean anything to me William. That's what you failed to realize about me. I'm not a gold digger."

"Still a beautiful woman like you shouldn't waste your life with that 2D rat. I can give you so much more than he can."

"I understand your choice of words, but I already have everything I need with Christopher."

"Poor girl, Christopher has poisoned your mind to the point where you don't know the difference between reality and fiction anymore."

"I'm just as rational as you; it just disappoints you that I'd rather be with someone like Christopher than with someone like you."

"You've got a smart mouth that can get you into a lot of trouble."

"Truth hurts, doesn't it?"

"Oh well, no matter. Before this day is over, I will have everything I ever wanted."

"You're hiding something William. What else do you have up your sleeve?"

"Hey, I'm giving the 2D animation everything they ever wanted. All they ever cared about was getting vengeance on 3D animation and to be heard from again, now this is their chance. Before the day is over, you'll see it for yourself."

From outside the office, the stadium was finally being prepared for its upcoming visitors. Just as the dolphins described it, the stadium was a large modern structure, the biggest building in the whole district. Everyone was invited except for children. Due to the extreme violence of the show kids were not allowed, however, teenagers and other viewers were permitted. Crowds of people were waiting patiently outside, as the front doors to the stadium begin to gradually open. Everyone cheered with excitement as though they were entering an amusement park. The visitors leisurely strolled in marveling at the site of the large stadium, some took pictures while others tried to find their seats. In the center of the stadium, the scenery was designed as a battlefield. Two sections were divided off for 2D and 3D characters alike. Back inside William's office, he happily watched the people arriving from his window then pulled out a large microphone from his desk that was attached to all of the speakers in the stadium.

"Welcome my friends!" he spoke through the microphone. "Thank you for coming! Please just make yourselves comfortable for now. There will be plenty of food and drinks but the fight will not begin for another two hours. So for now, just relax, take pictures and most of all… make your bet. Advertisements of 2D and 3D cartoons will play on the television screens for your enjoyment. They will also help you decide which character you would like to choose for your bet!"

The audience roared with excitement after William's speech, following his instructions some began to place their bets, grab food and drinks from the food concession, while others took their seats. The remainder of the

Chapter 14: The Stadium

audience watched cartoon advertisements on a large motion-picture projector that advertised commercials, cartoon series, and upcoming movies of both 2D and 3D.

William turned off the microphone then turned to Brittany. "Christopher should be checking on the 2D arrivals on the left side of the building. I will go and accompany the 3D characters. We wouldn't want them to run into each other and spoil everything, now would we?"

William left the office and closed the door behind him.

"Sure, I'll just wait right here," Brittany said annoyed.

A few blocks away from the stadium, Russell and a whole gang of 3D characters were traveling up the street. Unaware of what was about to happen to them, they had received an invitation from William. Russell felt this was a perfect opportunity just to get away from the 2D animation. Flauntingly, Russell led the parade while all the others behind him began chanting and reciting a song they created. "Who are we? 3D! Destiny to overthrow 2D! CGI is the force of the new time, listen to our rhyme. Technology at this rate will become our permanent state. Haha, 2D too late, you won't escape your fate, our public thinks we're great. Who are we? 3D! All hail to CGI, 2D we will make you cry!" Among the gang was Miriam, who suddenly jumped in Russell's path.

"What do you think you're doing?" Russell asked. "Get out of my way!"

"Hold on Russell, this is a trap. William has been planning this for a long time and I highly recommend that all of you don't go to that stadium."

"Hey, you're that polar bear assistant of his," said Rascal who was also in the crowd recognizing her.

"Not anymore. He fired me," she confirmed. "Trust me on this one guys. Please don't go to that stadium!"

"She might have a point," Rascal said. "Why would William want to invite all of us to meet him in a big stadium so unexpectedly?"

"Who cares, he said that he would make it worth our while. Besides I'm sick and tired of being around those 2D low lives. Anything just to get away from them."

"I don't blame ya but what if it is a trap!" Rascal declared.

Another character in the group was a 3D Meerkat named Meeko who preferred staying out of conversations but if it didn't seem right to him then he would always modify his opinion. Furthermore, he liked being a nuisance, almost like a second Carlos. He swiftly ran in between Russell and Rascal.

"Now, now, now you guys," he spoke calmly. "This isn't anything to work ourselves up over. Even if it is or isn't a trap, I'm sure we'll get some entertainment out of it. It's like my mother always told me; expect the unexpected… whatever that means."

"The rat's right," Russell commented. "The more time we waste talking here, the bigger the chance we're going to miss something really big."

"Hey I'm not a rat! I'm a meerkat! And my name is Meeko."

"Okay Meeko kat, maybe you don't fully understand the reality of the situation," Rascal argued, "but I don't like surprises. Besides, Miriam here says that William is planning something and I don't want to be around to see it."

"Listen dog, you stay and sit," Russell responded angrily. "If you have a problem with it so much then why don't you stay behind and dwell amongst the 2D garbage."

Russell turned to all of the 3D characters and told them, "Any 3D character who wants to stay behind is known as a traitor because you'll have no choice but to go back to them! I'd rather die than to be with one of them. We're doing this for us! We 3D characters have to stick together no matter what the cause is. If it is a trap then I'm ready for it. I will go to the end if I have to for humanity and for us!"

All of the 3D characters shouted their approval in agreement with Russell's announcement. They didn't know what was in store for them, however, they were ready for it. Russell then glared back at Rascal who had his tail tucked between his legs and his ears dropped down.

"Are you in—or are you out?" he asked him.

Rascal wouldn't dare to try and come up against Russell, especially with his large size, so ultimately he just took a deep breath and nodded his head.

Chapter 14: The Stadium

Russell then proudly puffed up his chest saying, "That's what I thought."

After that little intimidation tactic, all the 3D characters marched forward. The only ones who stayed behind were Rascal, Miriam, and Meeko.

"Males always act without thinking first," Miriam angrily remarked.

"Well shouldn't we, I mean how else are we going to find out what's happening?" Rascal answered.

"Anyone who jumps to conclusions is a fool," she said. "But trust me when I say this, no one knows William better than I do. He's been planning this strategy for months and his only intention is to get rich off of it without the wellbeing of our kind and 2D alike. I couldn't stand by any longer while he planned this and he eventually fired me. Good riddance anyway because I was quite sick and tired of working for that idiot."

"Hmmm—suppose you're right," Meeko agreed.

"What else could you tell us that would indicate William is planning something far more dangerous than the 2D and 3D going into battle?" Rascal questioned.

"Well a few months ago, when he started investing all of his money in that stadium, I knew he was planning something huge. He didn't want anyone to know anything about it, including me. One night when he was working alone, I decided to eavesdrop on him. Before I could fully gather all of his information, he severely punished me and said if I ever told anyone, no one would believe me anyway. You already saw how everyone reacted to my statement about William."

"How bad could that have been?" Meeko inquired.

"I didn't hear everything but the one thing I do remember him saying is once it's all finished, everyone is expendable."

"Expendable? Does he mean us?" Meeko presumed.

"Of course, who else," Miriam replied angrily. "Whatever he has planned for us in that stadium is only the beginning because once he's finished with us; we'll just be disposable afterwards."

"Then we shouldn't go!" Rascal suggested. "But I don't want to stay behind either and be known as a traitor."

"We don't have to stay behind to be a traitor," Miriam responded. "We can still go to the stadium but remain cautious. I advise that we wait outside the stadium instead."

"Good idea snowy," Meeko commented. "We should wait outside."

"Don't call me snowy," she said gritting her teeth.

"What about Russell and the others?" asked Rascal.

"We'll help them every way possible," Meeko said. "If something happens, we'll find some way of breaking them out of there."

"Sounds good enough to me, how about you sno… uh… I mean Miriam?" Rascal asked.

"You're just lucky I'm dealing with a class of lower intelligence," she said annoyed.

CHAPTER FIFTEEN
WE'RE GETTING CLOSE

Jackson pulled the limousine around the corner to the stadium while Kyle and his friends were waiting in the backseat. Kyle was extremely nervous but fought to remain calm. Ralph and Stan eventually awoke, not knowing what was going to happen to them. Once Jackson stopped the vehicle he turned his head to Kyle and the others.

"We're here," he moaned quietly.

"We are? So soon?" Kyle shivered.

"What do you mean so soon? It took us at least two hours to get here!" Carlos complained.

"Thank God, because I have to go to the bathroom," Stan cried.

"Let's just go and get this over with," Jackson demanded. "The sooner this is all over, the sooner I can get the four of ya off my back!"

"Oh that hurts, that really hurts," Carlos whimpered. "I was starting to like you as part of the gang. You hurt me, Jackson."

Exiting the limo the frustrated cat just hissed irritably as he grumbled under his breath and opened the back doors for Kyle and the others to get out.

"You see that entrance on the left side of the building," Jackson directed. "You guys are to go there. That's where all of the other 2D characters will be gathering."

"Aren't you going to come with us?" Carlos asked.

"What am I, your mother!?" Jackson yelled furiously. "I've already done my job with saving your butts! Just go to that entrance over there; I have to return to my boss!"

Jackson angrily left Kyle and his friends by the limo, leaving them a little stunned while Carlos just smiled.

"Don't worry about him," Carlos remarked. "He's just expressing his anger, that's all."

"He could've at least told me where the bathroom was," Stan whined as he desperately held himself between his legs. "I feel like I'm going to burst."

"So are we going to go and get this battle over with or what?" asked Carlos.

"We're not going anywhere near that building," Kyle demanded.

Carlos, Ralph, and Stan all stared at Kyle in bewilderment. They couldn't believe what they were hearing, especially Ralph and Stan.

"Are you scared?" Carlos asked him. "If you are, I completely understand. I know what it's like going into battle and being scared for your life, but don't worry Kyle. I'll hold your hand and we'll get through this toge…"

"No Carlos! I'm not scared. I just changed my mind—that's all."

"Not that I'm ungrateful you changed your mind, but why?" Ralph asked.

"Well—let's just say I've finally come to realize the truth about everything."

"The truth?" Carlos inquired confused.

"Ryan made me see myself for who I am. For so many years it's always been about me. I've become selfish and arrogant; regardless, my friend has put up with my complaints for so long, I'm surprised he stuck by me all this time. Ryan sticking by my side was trying to show me that 2D and 3D could get along. This battle won't solve anything but fuel hatred and—bring death. I've finally come to realize that and I don't want to be a part of it anymore."

"You've finally seen the light my friend," Stan said happily.

"Hallelujah!" Ralph rejoiced.

Chapter 15: We're Getting Close

"So let me get this straight Kyle," Carlos questioned. "First you hate 3D animation for all these years. Second, we get thrown in jail because of them, not to mention our own 2D family helped us get out of prison. Third, we agreed to go along with this battle. Fourth, your friend Ryan chased you all over the mall, nearly attacking us and now that we're here you just want to call the whole thing off!"

"Yep, pretty much," Kyle responded.

"Cool," Carlos reacted. "I like the way you think Kyle. We birds have the same genetics for that matter. This is going to turn out to be more exciting than I realized."

"But what about your hatred towards 3D animation?" Kyle asked.

"I'm down with whatever you decide Kyle, I've got your back bro," Carlos said enthusiastically.

"So—since we're not going into battle then what are we going to do?" Ralph asked. "What if Christopher comes looking for us if we don't show up?"

"I doubt he'll do that since he's going to have his hands full. Besides, we're not going to go inside but we'll stay outside," Kyle suggested. "That way we can stay out of the fight."

"But I have to go to the bathroom!" Stan bawled.

"For crying out loud Stan, why don't you just go in the bushes!" Kyle yelled.

"But I've always used the public bathroom," Stan blubbered. "Isn't this a little unsanitary?"

"We're animals Stan," Kyle remarked. "We're supposed to go in the bushes."

"Great, now I feel like a dog marking my territory!" Stan argued back.

A couple of feet away from the stadium, Jewel and Rex continued their search for Ryan.

"Are we there yet?" Jewel asked for the fiftieth time.

"Thank God, yeah," Rex grumbled. "This hasn't been a pleasant journey with you on my back complaining the whole way."

"The sooner I get back to Ryan the better, the more relieved I'll feel," Jewel said. "I don't want anything to happen to him."

"Even if you do find him, how are you going to stop the battle if he's in the middle of it? There are going to be hundreds of 2D and 3D characters on both sides. A fight this ugly isn't going to be easy to break up."

"That's something that you and I are going to have to figure out."

"Hold on a minute. I didn't intend on this being a rescue mission in the first place. I'm not going to risk my life for your 3D jerk… I mean your husband."

"Oh yes you are Rex. We've already come this far and you're not going to abandon me now!"

Rex barked furiously out of frustration. He'd much rather be a part of the big battle instead of rescuing Ryan from it, however, for Jewel's sake, he didn't want to start anything. He dedicated his life to protecting her even if he didn't agree with her judgment half the time. Gently, he helped Jewel off of his back placing her on the ground.

"Good boy Rex, I'd knew you'd see it my way."

"Your sarcasm doesn't amuse me."

"Lighten up Rex, we're almost there. We'll figure something out."

"The only thing I can't figure out is why you're so in love with a 3D character," Rex said walking ahead while Jewel tried to catch up.

Suddenly Jewel felt something weird. She stopped dead in her tracks and felt a terrible cramp inside of her. Quickly clutching her stomach tightly, she knelt down to the sidewalk and began to convulse. It couldn't happen now, not at a time like this. All Jewel could do at this moment was clench her teeth together and sweat uncontrollably, praying that it wouldn't happen. Trying to relax and not worry, she took a few deep breaths and exhaled with relief. Eventually, just as she had hoped, the pain slowly subsided. When Rex turned his head and witnessed Jewel kneeling on the sidewalk, he immediately ran to her aid.

"Jewel, tell me what's happening?"

"It's—it's—nothing—I…"

"Jewel, if the baby is coming, you must tell me now!"

"No, no, no Rex—I'm alright. It was just a little kick. The baby is getting a little restless."

Chapter 15: We're Getting Close

"Jewel if you're lying to me…"

"I assure you that I'm fine Rex. I promise you, I'll let you know for sure if the baby is coming. For now, let's hurry up and get to the stadium. We must find Ryan."

Jewel didn't hesitate getting back on her feet and walked ahead of Rex. The pain was gone for now, and she was hoping it wouldn't come back soon. Rex knew that Jewel was lying to him and didn't like the idea of risking her safety and the safety of her child, however, if she was determined to find Ryan and jeopardize her baby, then Rex had no choice but to support her. All it did was make Rex hate Ryan even more.

"Good for nothing husband not even here for his wife's pregnancy," he grumbled furiously.

CHAPTER SIXTEEN

THE BATTLE BEGINS

On the left side of the stadium entrance, Christopher stepped out of the building scanning the area to see if any of the 2D characters were arriving. Much to his approval, he didn't have to search long because he immediately spotted them. Christopher smiled when he witnessed a whole gang full of cartoon characters assembling. Most of them were from Cartoon Studios, while others were from around the district. A variety of cartoon characters emerged, animals, humans, and weird creatures, it was enough of them to fight against in the upcoming battle. Among them was Diana, who quit her job at EATS and was the first one to approach Christopher.

"Glad to see that you all finally made it Diana, how are you doing?" Christopher questioned.

"Christopher, are you sure this battle is worth it?" asked Diana.

"You knew the risk when I informed you guys of the situation," Christopher warned strictly. "I thought it was worth it for all of ya to finally punish the 3D animation. After all, I say it's all for a good cause."

"It still better be worth it," Diana remarked. "By the way, have you seen a small bird named Carlos arrive yet?"

"Not that I'm aware of," Christopher said.

"Well if you do, just keep him away from me! I just hope the 3D characters will take him out before I do."

A confused Christopher looked at Diana as she walked past him and then nearly got trampled on by the rest of the 2D gang. They excitedly ran

Chapter 16: The Battle Begins

towards the entrance of the stadium preparing for the battle they had been waiting for. Christopher quickly flew out of the way from the stampede breathing excessively afterwards.

"Whoa—maybe Brittany had a point," Christopher said as he got up and dusted himself off. "Someone as small as me could get killed in a split second. Oh phooey. I'll be fine. I'm just going to have to keep my head up."

Once he made sure all of the 2D characters were inside, he proceeded within the stadium and locked the door behind him. Just on the other side of the stadium, William accompanied the arrival of the 3D characters that gradually entered the stadium as well. The main room where Christopher had the 2D characters settled resembled a locker room which was spacious enough for each individual to relax or rejuvenate after the battle. The 3D characters had the same thing in their room as well. Christopher flew his way over the crowd and landed on top of a stand which was placed in front of the room. It had a microphone positioned in the center of it, which Christopher tapped on trying to test it.

"Excuse me—testing, testing. Is this thing working?"

Loud screeching noise from the microphone emitted which made everyone cover their ears. The 2D characters began to complain and get upset.

"Sorry, sorry about that, my bad," Christopher said as he fixed the device as quickly as possible. "There we go, that's better. Alright everyone, pay attention. This will be an imp…"

"Excuse me," a random rabbit called out.

"Yes," Christopher answered.

"Can I have a carrot?" the rabbit asked peacefully.

"What! Are you serious? Listen we need to…"

"I have a question," a large spider yelled.

"Yeah."

"Do you have a life insurance policy out on any of us?" the spider asked.

"Huh? Of course not! I already have all the money I could ever need, why would I…"

"Oh, oh, oh! Pick me, pick me!" a bat shouted.

"What?!"

"Can we have a party when this is all over? I like cookies and cake!" the bat stated happily.

"You guys are trying my patience!"

"I have a question too," said a horse.

"Grrrrrrrrrrrrrrrrrrrrr!"

"Comes dawn before the night. How will thy shining star see daybreak, in the midst of corruption," the horse replied.

Christopher had no idea what the horse was even talking about however, everyone's questions were driving him crazy. He couldn't believe how stupid they were acting compared to the actual combat they were about to face.

"SHUT UP!! SHUT UP!! All of you just shut up!!" he screamed from the top of his lungs.

All of the 2D characters fell silent and felt a little frightened by Christopher's aggressive tone.

"We're about to go into battle for crying out loud! Have you guys forgotten!? I know you're cartoons and your mentality is very low but please try and stay focused! Remember, we're here because we need to teach society that we can't be ignored. We're not going to stand by and be treated as yesterday's garbage by society while they support the 3D characters. We all have a purpose on this planet and ours is to entertain humans but we can no longer take that place in the spotlight while the 3D animation brings shame to our name. This battle will prove to the humans, as well as the 3D characters that we will stand and cause a revolution! This day will be remembered as the 2D characters that fought for their own rights to exist and be accepted among society, even if we have to fight to the death!"

Everyone in the room instantly shouted in an uproar after Christopher's speech. Every individual had their heads clear about what they were going to face, geared up, and ready for battle. Their extreme dislike for 3D animation was to the point where nothing was going to stop them. The uprising of 2D animation would create their chronicles for the

Chapter 16: The Battle Begins

whole world to see today, unforgettable combat that would one day make the history books as time goes on.

William gradually associated himself with the 3D characters in their room while standing on top of a stand and made his speech.

"Welcome 3D animation! Welcome all. I'm so glad you all could make it."

"Tell us why we're really here, William?" Russell asked aggressively.

"Glad you asked my friend. You see, the reason why I called you 3D characters here is because you all have something in common. You hate 2D animation!"

"Yeah!" a buffalo shouted.

"You got that right!" a cheetah exclaimed.

"Down with 2D animation!" a giraffe yelled.

The rest of the characters agreed and commented on the same subject.

"Listen up my friends," William called out. "Today is going to be an important event. Humans have gathered from everywhere just to see you in action."

"Action? What action?" Russell questioned.

"Let's just say, you all wouldn't be here if you didn't hate 2D animation. Keep that thought in mind. By the end of this day, we will all be happy."

"Don't play us for a fool William," Russell demanded. "If you're hiding something, you'll pay for it."

"On the contrary, I'm already being well paid. Your public awaits you. If you go along with what I have to show you, then you'll never see the 2D characters ever again. Not to mention, humans will give you a grand prize in the end if you pull through."

"What do you mean if we pull through?" Russell inquired.

"You'll see. Now as soon as I leave, this door right next to me will open up. It will lead you to the open stadium inside. By then, you'll see the big surprise."

William smirked at all of the unsuspecting 3D characters as he got off the stand and left the locker room. Russell grunted after William left. He wasn't sure about the situation but if it meant that they wouldn't have to see 2D animation ever again, he was willing to take that chance. "Well, we're not going to turn back now. Let's see what's in store for us and be prepared for anything," Russell ordered to the rest of the group.

The door suddenly unlocked itself and flung open for all of the 3D characters. The same thing was happening to the 2D characters at the exact same moment. A bright light flashed before all of them as they each took a deep breath and prepared for the unforeseen. One by one, all of the cartoon characters steadily walked outside into the arena. They could hear sudden applause from all around them. As the vivid light began to gradually fade away, they witnessed thousands of humans who were seated in the aisles of the stadium. The applause grew louder and louder as every single cartoon character walked out onto the battlefield. Every single one of the humans had already placed their bets knowing this was going to be an impressive and celebrated event. The scoreboard was up and everything was set. The viewers could only watch now, preparing for the event of a lifetime. The 3D characters were moved by the audience's passion for them, most waved back and showed off with their comical personalities, unaware that the 2D characters were approaching them. It didn't take long for the 3D characters to catch sight of the 2D gang. The 2D characters had a whole team of warriors prepared. Though most of them didn't look the type, they were ready to face anything. Without a doubt, the 3D characters were more than surprised, shocked, and traumatized by the sudden circumstance, however, the 2D characters were ready. This was a fight they had been looking forward to for a long time. William and Christopher quickly took their place back in the office where Brittany awaited them. Christopher gently hopped on Brittany's shoulder cuddling himself up against her while William pulled out his microphone smiling wickedly as he watched the crowd from his window.

"Ladies and gentlemen! I give you 2D animation and 3D animation!"

The audience clapped once more in an uproar.

"The battle of the century has come! Without further ado… let the fight begin!"

Right away the 2D animation charged upon the 3D characters with great intensity. The violence escalated as each character gave its opponent a

Chapter 16: The Battle Begins

slamming hard blow to any sensitive part of the body. Each 3D character was thrown back from their attack by the 2D characters which had the upper hand because they were prepared for battle. All of the 2D characters continued to combine their forces against their adversaries. A 2D sheep rammed viciously into the stomach of a 3D wolf. A 2D walrus slammed its enormous body on top of a 3D penguin like a sumo wrestler. A 2D snake slithered around the neck of a 3D giraffe and strangled him. A 2D hawk swooped down and picked up a 3D rabbit, then dropped him in mid-air and he tragically fell resembling an accordion upon impact. Every 2D character continued to brutally hammer and batter the 3D characters with no sense of remorse. Russell watched the whole fight around him as he witnessed bodies flying from left to right. He was more furious than anyone could ever imagine. As much as he despised 2D animation, he was going to make sure that he would take a few lives with him, especially since William set them up this way. At the same time, he was glad because this was his chance to annihilate them. He looked for an opponent to attack and spotted Diana who wasn't fighting anyone. He immediately charged upon her like a wild bull but Diana noticed him and turned around just in time. Before Russell could do the unthinkable, Diana quickly grabbed her utters and sprayed milk directly into his eyes. Russell hollered as he closed his eyes still running but without seeing where he was going, he jammed his horn into the enclosed wall of the stadium. He was stuck on it like glue and couldn't get off. The audience yelled with excitement throughout the whole event. Most of it seemed comical to the humans but some of it was genuinely brutal. The heavy battle continued with the 3D characters defeated and completely taken off guard by the whole thing, although they did remember Russell's statement to be prepared for anything. William observed the entire battlefield from his office window taking a drink of champagne while Christopher and Brittany observed the conflict for themselves.

"There you go Christopher, you and your kind have finally got your wish," he remarked.

"Yes, I guess we have," Christopher replied pressing his face up against the glass window. "I can see the 2D characters are actually winning. Maybe now the audience will consider giving us another chance. They probably didn't imagine we had this much power in us. This is pointless I should be down there with them."

"Then why aren't you," said William. "Too scared to do your own work."

"I convinced him to stay out of it," said Brittany. "I don't want to see my sweetheart getting hurt in battle."

"Oh how sweet," William said sarcastically. "Not the first time a tough gangster got soft over a woman."

"Don't make me hurt you," Christopher glared.

"Well I don't think we should jump ahead of ourselves anyway," William pointed out. "The only reason the 3D characters are losing is because no one informed them of this encounter. This is only the first round, let's see how the next one turns out."

With the 3D characters all wounded and feeling defeated, the 2D characters remained victorious just as the first round ended. The humans who bid on the 3D characters obviously lost and started to complain but the rest of the audience celebrated and were glad they had bet on the 2D characters. With the fight over for now, the 2D gang retired back to their locker room, although most of them weren't that badly hurt, nonetheless, some of them did have injuries. The 3D gang also retreated to their locker room, collapsing with soreness and terrible agony. Soon afterwards it started to turn evening outside and William happily tossed his glass of champagne standing up from his seat.

"I think it's time to turn on the shades," he stated.

"Shades—what shades? The sun's going down, what are you talking about?" Christopher asked anxiously.

"Just watch," William maintained.

William strolled over to a monitor that was placed near his desk and touched a particular switch. A sudden earthquake shook the entire arena and took everyone by surprise for a brief moment. The switch operated a wide shield above the stadium. It covered the whole arena, sealing it like a barrier. From this point on, no could enter or leave.

"I didn't know the stadium could do that," Christopher reacted.

Chapter 16: The Battle Begins

"And when were you planning on telling us about this?" Brittany queried.

"Nothing to worry about my dearest," William answered. "It's only to keep the 2D and 3D characters from leaving in case any of them decide to chicken out too early. Besides, it sets the mood for the people—just watch."

As William clicked on another switch, this one operated the shield to set off glowing decorations like Las Vegas city lights. It sparkled with radiance and was adorned with luminous neon lights. The audience was captivated by its beauty and applauded enthusiastically.

"See, I always think ahead," William said as he smirked at Brittany.

Christopher didn't like the way William was looking at his girl. It not only made him uncomfortable, but it made him boil with anger. He quickly got in the way by literally jumping onto William's chest and stared at him dead in the eyes.

"Hey pal, keep your eyes elsewhere! I told you countless times, she's already taken!"

"What's the matter Christopher, trying to compensate for something," William teased.

"What's that suppose to mean?" Christopher demanded.

"Figure it out when you get nuts," William groaned as he threw Christopher off of him with just one flick of his finger.

The poor squirrel took a dive across the room and embarrassingly landed in Brittany's top with only his tail and feet sticking out. Brittany groaned miserably as William looked on with amusement.

"Now that's the kind of comedy I can watch any day," William laughed. "A little too overrated for kids though."

"Your sarcasm is not the least bit humorous Will," Brittany complained as she pulled Christopher by his tail to remove him then set him down on her legs. The infuriated squirrel shook his head and looked on with rage at William.

"HOW DARE YOU!" he screamed hysterically.

"On the contrary Christopher, I wouldn't want to start anything," William replied. "But if you feel the need to fight, then maybe you should join your friends in the arena."

"That's fine by me," Christopher argued. "Just you and me, come on!"

Brittany gently grabbed him by the waist trying to settle him down. "Calm down honey," she told him peacefully. "Don't let your temper get the better of you. You know how many times that became your downfall."

"I just can't bear it when people take me for granted baby," Christopher explained. "I don't know how many men I have to dispose of before they'll realize you're mine."

"Typical, you should've stuck with girl squirrels instead," William chuckled.

Brittany desperately tried grabbing a hold of Christopher as he swiftly and uncontrollably tried getting at his rival. She eventually had him embraced in her arms, preventing a fight that could've turned as ugly as the fight in the arena. Not the least bit worried; William just sighed as he strolled over to get another glass of champagne.

"Oh grow up, will you?" William snickered. "You're acting like some kind of fatal attraction drama queen."

"If you ask me, men are the ones who are so overrated these days," Brittany protested.

CHAPTER SEVENTEEN

RYAN'S ARRIVAL

While Silver led the way to the stadium, he, Ryan, and Grace rode on top of Fangs as he flew his way around the city.

"It shouldn't be much longer now, we're almost there," Silver said merrily. "It's just approximately 3.2 miles away."

"Thank goodness, because we've got to stop this madness before it begins," Ryan cried.

"Even so how are we going to stop it?" questioned Grace. "There's going to be a lot of individuals to break up, even if we did they'd probably come after us too."

"Someone is going to have to break them away from their blindness," Ryan suggested. "To show them the truth."

"Who—you?" Fangs asked.

"Of course not me!" Ryan said.

"You act like you're in charge half the time," Grace commented. "Not to mention you're a fox and foxes are suppose to be clever and cunning. We thought you'd be the one who would tell everyone to put this thing to an end."

"I can't say a powerful speech that'll get people to listen," Ryan admitted. "I couldn't even get Russell to listen to me. He nearly killed me for crying out loud."

"Then who's going to stop them?" Fangs questioned.

"Umm—Silver," Ryan recommended.

"Me?" Silver said surprised.

"Sure, you're the one with the brains. You could tell everyone the truth about themselves," Ryan replied.

"Listen Vulpes, I may know a lot of scientific specifications but I don't think I can stop rivals from killing one another," Silver pointed out. "These characters must be brought to see their own sins and to hear a powerful message that will change their minds and make them regret the things they've done. Besides, my calculations say there's a 37% chance I can't do it."

"Terrific," Ryan grunted.

"Maybe it should be me," Fangs proposed.

"You? How would you do it?" Grace asked.

"Easy, I'll just breathe fire at everybody if they won't listen," Fangs said as he smiled with pride.

Ryan simply rolled his eyes in frustration and held on tightly to Fangs' back.

"Let's just hurry up and get there," he cried nervously. "We can't let this fight continue any longer or it will destroy everyone in the end."

Back at the stadium, from outside the building, Kyle and his friends ventured around the area. They were trying to find a secret entrance that could possibly lead them to another way in.

"Haven't found a weak spot yet and we've already been at this for hours," Ralph stated.

"We're just having the worst luck ever," Stan grumbled.

"We can't give up, we must keep searching," Kyle demanded.

"Kyle's right, let's keep up the search," Carlos remarked. "It should be pretty simple."

"That's so easy for you to say," Ralph moaned. "You perched yourself on top of our heads the entire time while we did all the work."

"It's just stress," Carlos replied. "Watch, I'll show you how it's done."

Carlos landed near the ground and slowly searched near the boundaries of the stadium. Bit by bit he hopped around the borders and pecked on the building. He kept his focus on pecking continuously until he accidentally pecked something else; which was Meeko's head.

"Ouch!" Meeko cried out.

Chapter 17: Ryan's Arrival

"Oops sorry, didn't see ya there," said Carlos.

Kyle and his friends were surprised to see Meeko, Miriam, and Rascal before them. They stared at each other in disbelief for a moment. Kyle's eyes instantly focused on Rascal, and Rascal equally did the same, remembering their last encounter at EATS which didn't turn out very well.

"YOU!" Rascal shrieked.

"You!" Kyle reacted.

"Of all the cartoons I had to encounter tonight, you turn up," Rascal growled. "I will take a lot of pleasure ripping you to pieces."

"Two hours ago I would've said the same thing to you but trust me, I don't want to fight you anymore," Kyle pleaded.

"Who the heck are you guys anyway?" Miriam questioned.

"You're not very smart are ya," Carlos said. "We're 2D animation. I'm a bird, that's a long neck, a triceratops, and a pterodactyl."

"Why do I even bother," Miriam griped slapping her paw across her face.

"You guys got trouble!" Meeko shouted. "That bird brain nearly pecked my brains out!"

"I said sorry, geez, you guys just can't drop it," Carlos criticized. "You hold on to too many grudges. It's no wonder you 3D characters got a lot of issues."

In a quick flash, Ralph grabbed a hold of Carlos and stomped his foot on top of him.

"Listen, we don't want any trouble," Ralph appealed. "We were just trying to find a way inside the stadium."

"On the other hand, we can all just go home and forget about the whole thing," Stan declared fearfully.

"Too late, we're going to have our own little battle right here, right now," Rascal ordered.

The anxious dog immediately jumped on Ralph's back, biting him on the neck while the poor dinosaur screamed in frustration trying to get Rascal off of him. Miriam attacked Stan by clawing at him but he defended himself by thrusting his horns at her. And Meeko charged at Carlos, biting and tearing his feathers off. Carlos cried, trying to flee for his life.

"Let's pluck them feathers off of ya," Meeko commented. "I think you'll look much better butt naked anyway."

"AWWW! This time I'm going to ram my beak so far down your head I'll puncture your brain!" Carlos shrieked.

"You've already perfected that," Meeko replied.

"Good, one less tragedy for me to worry about," said Carlos.

"STOP!!" Kyle yelled. "All of you! Stop it right now!"

But the fight continued, especially with Meeko and Carlos rolling all over the place looking like a bouncing basketball. Ultimately, Meeko and Carlos' bouncing caused them to crash into a basement passage that was hidden by leaves and plants. They both fell through the substructure of the stadium while the others immediately stopped their fighting when they saw what just happened. They peeked through the hole that Meeko and Carlos created which was so pitch black they couldn't see anything.

"Hey Carlos, are you alright?" Kyle called.

"Meeko, Meeko can you hear me?" Miriam cried out.

The gang could suddenly hear Meeko and Carlos moaning excessively from their pain.

"Ohhhh—I think I broke my wing," Carlos muttered.

"Owww—get your tail out of my face," Meeko groaned.

"That's not my tail," Carlos mentioned.

Kyle smiled with approval, ultimately proud that they had found a secret passageway. "Good work Carlos and—meerkat buddy, we've found a secret way inside the stadium," he exclaimed.

"A secret way? What the heck is going on? What are you guys talking about?" Rascal demanded.

"We're trying to find a way inside the stadium so we can get our friends out of there if anything goes wrong," Kyle said.

"Your friends—meaning 2D animation," Miriam declared.

"This may come as a shock to you but I mean everybody, including the 3D characters," Kyle corrected.

"Really? But why would you help our kind?" asked Rascal.

Chapter 17: Ryan's Arrival

"Because fighting is the last thing we need to worry about, besides we need to put all of this to an end," Kyle remarked. "I-I-I feel the need to bury the hatchet. Let's work together instead."

Rascal's ears perked up. The fact that he and Kyle had previously fought and nearly killed each other was enough, but hearing his enemy talking about a truce had him completely baffled.

"By the way—I forgive you Rascal—for the two black eyes you gave me," Kyle stated.

Rascal's ears instantly dropped down. "You do?" he whispered sadly.

After what Kyle said to him, he felt guilty and miserable. Sure he hated 2D animation but none of them ever made him feel this way before. For once his eyes were opened and he knew he had to make amends. After all, it made him feel like a better dog inside. Kyle slowly brought his claw out towards Rascal.

"Truce," Kyle said pleasantly.

Rascal had an ashamed look on his face but he eventually brought his paw out and shook Kyle's claw. "You'll forgive me if I'm a little uncomfortable with all of this," Rascal stuttered. "I still may not like you guys but... I-I-I'm sorry too Kyle, for everything."

Ralph and Stan instantly blew a sigh of relief, satisfied they were no longer caught in a brawl, though Miriam honestly didn't know what to make of the sudden arrangement.

"Well—I can't say it hasn't been pleasant but as much as I would like to challenge you guys, I'd rather get back at William instead," she stated.

"Great—I think," Ralph commented.

"Hold on Carlos, we're on our way down," Kyle shouted.

"Good, I can't wait," Carlos mocked back.

Back inside the stadium, the 3D characters slowly recovered from their first fight. Most of them wore bandages, drank water, and of course complained.

"I can't believe we let a bunch of low life ancient hand-drawn figures kick our butts!" a moose grumbled.

"They took us by surprise," said a chipmunk.

"We can't let them defeat us! People don't even care for them like they used to!" a giraffe shouted.

"I know, but how are we going to defeat them?" a rabbit asked. "They were pretty good in battle out there. I never knew they were so strong."

"It doesn't matter how strong they are," Russell moaned disturbingly, making his way through the rest of the crowd.

Everyone focused their immediate attention on him. There was something dark and black in his heart that frightened the rest of the gang. They knew he was to the point where he didn't care if anyone lived or died.

"Those 2D characters have been a walking sickness since the dawn of time. People don't care for the relic of animation anymore, they care for us—the new age of animation. They're selfish, jealous, and don't know what to do with themselves any longer because humans don't give a damn about them! They figured if they can't have the human's admiration, then no one can. They will do everything they can to wipe us off the face of the earth but they will be the ones who will be wiped off the face of the earth! After this day, 2D animation will be no more! We will rise up and fight! We are the ones that the people love and we will continue to uphold that reputation. 2D animation won't know the meaning of the word death until it confronts them in the face. Nothing will give me more pleasure than to get back out there and slaughter them all over the arena. This time we will be victorious and make our own history today! The day 3D animation destroyed 2D animation once and for all!"

After Russell's speech, all of the 3D characters went into pandemonium rooting his name over and over. Every individual who felt sore quickly recovered, forgetting about the pain, all they cared about was getting back into the stadium and conquering the 2D characters. They knew they would defeat them this time around and wouldn't go easy on anybody, the 3D characters weren't going to be merciful, and they were downright angry and full of rage thanks to Russell's lecture. "Remember our mantra? Who are we? 3D! Destiny to overthrow 2D! CGI is the force of the new time, listen to our rhyme. Technology at this rate will become our permanent state. Haha, 2D too late, you won't escape your fate, our public thinks we're great. You'll never forget this date! Just wait! Who are

Chapter 17: Ryan's Arrival

we? 3D! All hail to CGI, 2D we'll make you cry! We'll remove you from the public's eye." All the 3D animation roared and cheered and were pumped up by Russell's reminder.

"Now let's go back out there and take some lives," Russell finished.

The doors to the locker room opened up for the second round while Russell took the lead for the rest of the 3D characters. They slowly walked back onto the stadium with the audience cheering for them and 2D both. The furious rhino stopped dead in his tracks when he observed the whole 2D gang that were also ready for their next fight, but they had no idea Russell gave a pep talk to his teammates ensuring that the combat was going to be uglier than the first. Russell steadily stomped his foot on the ground and then angrily blew smoke out of his nostrils, his eyes were beaming bloodshot red, just like he looked at Ryan earlier as if he were ready to kill him. The 2D and 3D characters progressively stared each other down before charging off, they wanted to see which one was going to make the first move. Russell instantly made that decision for them. Like a speed of lightning, he charged his way through a whole crowd of 2D characters. They went flying through the air like a bunch of bowling pins being knocked over. The other 3D characters followed Russell and pursued their adversaries. Individuals emerged and began fighting from left to right. It was chaotic. A 3D elephant strangled a 2D ferret with its trunk, a 3D ostrich pecked the mess out of a 2D otter, a 3D Oryx smashed a group of 2D prairie dogs, and a 3D gorilla demolished many characters who were trying to get away. It looked pretty bleak for the 2D characters who were now losing. The 3D gang continued to annihilate and destroy as many of them as they possibly could. Russell constantly hurtled his way through the rest of the crowd making sure he left a hideous massacre and devastation throughout his stampede. There were wounded bodies everywhere. The 2D characters realized they were no match for the 3D gang anymore, but they still weren't going down without a fight.

A few feet from outside the arena, Ryan and his friends finally arrived. As Fangs effortlessly glided over the stadium they witnessed the entire crusade. Russell and his gang were literally trying to kill the 2D animation who didn't seem to have a chance of fighting anymore. Ryan gazed in horror as he watched his best friend continue his bloody rampage.

"I can't believe it!" Ryan cried. "Russell's gone off his rocket!"

"So has everyone else by the looks of it," Grace pointed out.

"How are we going to get in there?" asked Fangs. "The stadium is shielded with some kind of glass armor."

"Crash right through it!" Ryan yelled.

"What?" Fangs said surprised. "I doubt my strength can break that huge glass."

"Do it Fangs," Grace encouraged. "With those big and strong muscles of yours, I know you could do it."

Fangs blushed embarrassed, smitten with romantic feelings for Grace, he was pretty confident he could do anything after what she just told him.

"Alrighty then," Fangs stated. "Everybody hold on! I'm going to fly right through the glass!"

Ryan and the others held on tight as Fangs backed up a bit then swiftly plummeted down towards the stadium glass. What could've turned out to be a shattering of the glass shield, only turned out to be a collision, like when a bug hits the windshield of a car. Everyone stopped fighting for a brief moment and looked above them, so did the audience. They were shocked to see a large dragon located on the shield. Fangs, Ryan, Grace, and Silver eventually slid down off the shield like a slow slug then collapsed to the ground with a bad headache after the impact. Ryan steadily got on his feet, rubbing his head.

"I thought you were born for this type of action," he commented upset. "You star in all of those TV series where you wreck buildings and castles. How is this so hard for you?"

"The buildings and castles were all fake!" Fangs argued back. "That glass was like strong armor. There is no way I'm getting through that thing!"

"So much for big and strong muscles," Grace admitted.

Fangs' ears dropped as he put his head down in humiliation, full of shame.

Chapter 17: Ryan's Arrival

"Seems like we have a latecomer who's determined to get in," William observed from his office window.

William turned on the switch and opened the shield. Ryan watched, predicting they could be walking into a trap; even though he knew he had to stop the brutal fight one way or the other. He quickly hopped back on Fangs and directed him to go.

"Alright Fangs, let's do this again," Ryan said.

"So we're just going to go in there with no plan and no idea of how we're going to stop this," Fangs proclaimed.

Unable to give Fangs an honest answer, all Ryan could do was close his eyes and sigh in frustration. "I only pray well get through this somehow," he whimpered sadly. "Okay—Fangs, let's go."

"So much for the best-laid plans," Fangs complained.

Once more, Fangs flew over the stadium with Ryan, Grace, and Silver on his back as he steadily prepared to make a landing inside the arena. The audience roared with excitement when they saw Fangs make his appearance. Fangs felt a little embarrassed but then got confident and started bowing down. Ryan tried hitting him on the head to break him out of this state.

"Fangs you fool!" Ryan yelled. "We're not here for a show. Let's try to stay focused shall we."

Unexpectedly, a 2D bee dashed by and stung Fangs directly in the eye. He and the others crumpled to the ground straight into the ugly battle. Once Ryan and the others were inside, the shield slowly closed up again.

CHAPTER EIGHTEEN

JEWEL'S SACRIFICE

Ryan, Fangs, Grace, and Silver were caught up in the middle of the war. Characters were endlessly combating each other but the 2D animation couldn't hold on any longer.

"Oh no, what have we gotten ourselves into," Grace cried.

"Fangs are you okay?" Silver asked.

"Terrific Silver," Fangs grumbled as he held his painful eye.

"Did you know that about two million eye injuries occur in the United States annually," Silver explained. "The most common injuries are caused by blows to the eye, by particles that enter the eye, and by chemicals burns, explosions, and firearms. Many injuries can be prevented. For example, safety glasses or goggles protect the eyes from particles that may be thrown from electric saws, grinding wheels, and other power tools. In most cases, specks of dust or other particles that enter the eye can be removed by blinking gently or by flushing the eye with water. If the particle does not come out, it should be removed by a physician."

"Oh great, I don't happen to carry safety glasses or goggles with me! So, what are you, a physician?" Fangs asked sarcastically.

"Well I do have some experience as a medical doctor," Silver proclaimed as he grabbed Fangs' eyebrow.

"Hey, take it easy!" Fangs cried in agony. "That's the only right eye I have."

Chapter 18: Jewel's Sacrifice

"How are we going to get out of this mess Ryan?" Grace asked, frantically grabbing Ryan by the shoulder. "I'm not prepared to fight you know."

But before Ryan could answer Grace, the audience applauded. Ryan looked all around him and noticed most of the 2D characters lying injured and beaten to death. The second round had finally ended and everyone who bid on the 2D characters this time lost their money, while the others won, still the audience enjoyed the brawl. William decided to make his last announcement before the spectators as a conclusion to the final show of the day.

"Ladies and gentlemen. First round, the 2D won. Second round, the 3D won. It seems we will never know who the real champion truly is, but I hate to say, we've come to our final competition for the day. The cartoon characters have been through a rough combat and need to recuperate to regain their strength. Trust me… there will be more battles in the near future, I promise you that. You people may exit the way you came in. Thank you for your time."

The audience groaned in disappointment hoping to see another fight, nonetheless, understanding William's speech, they clapped for their last entertainment and eventually began to leave the building, which took quite a while due to it being a full house. Undoubtedly, William was pleased with all the money he made and wasn't going to foolishly gamble it away this time because he had a special project in mind. Once all of the people finally departed, the 2D characters remained lying on the ground unemotional and extremely impaired. Half of them moaned in pain and agony while the rest of them were completely unconscious. The 3D characters stood proud with victory, but Ryan's mind was not on victory. This display made him feel absolutely repulsive. It disgraced his heart even being part of the animation race. He gazed at all of the poor individuals who were injured and eventually came across Diana who was only a few feet away. Diana wasn't seriously hurt like the rest of her kind; on the other hand, she still was in terrible anguish. Ryan ran by her side trying to help her up.

"Here, let me help you," he offered.

"It's okay, I can do it myself," Diana scolded as she snatched away from Ryan.

"I'm not your enemy, I'm here to help you."

"Help me, why?"

"Because this fighting has solved nothing but has created calamity and disaster."

"I've got no argument with that. Maybe I should've stayed at EATS instead."

"You were all tricked as well as the 3D animation to come here. This isn't the way to solve our conflict between each other."

"How would you know how to solve it? You're only a 3D character. Why would you be talking to me in the first place?"

"Because I care for 2D and 3D both."

"You traitor!" a familiar voice screamed from the crowd.

After Ryan helped Diana get on her feet, he spotted Russell coming towards him. Still having his eyes fuming red with anger he didn't appreciate seeing Ryan assisting a 2D character. Ryan felt a little scared but he wasn't going to run away from his old friend this time.

"I should've known you'd be here helping them," Russell grunted.

"Russell, this fighting has got to stop. Please let it end," Ryan begged. "Can't you see it's causing nothing but more and more hatred? It'll eat you alive until there is nothing left but a shallow grave."

"The only grave I see is yours, Ryan. Since you care so much for 2D animation then maybe you should die with them."

"You won't hurt me, Russell."

"You don't know me as well as you thought you did. I've changed and so have you. I saved your life from 2D characters and this is how you turn out."

"Russell please!"

"No more pleading for mercy Ryan. Say good-bye, this is your last night on earth!"

Russell wasted no time rushing in tremendous speed towards Ryan. Once more, the frantic fox found himself running for his life, with Russell just a couple of inches away from him. Ryan was fast for his small size

Chapter 18: Jewel's Sacrifice

compared to Russell but it seemed he couldn't even outrun him. Russell's anger helped him charge at quick velocity and he charged his horn near Ryan's butt trying to pin him.

"Stop Russell! How could you do this to your friend?" Ryan cried out.

"You're no longer my friend Ryan! You're the enemy!" Russell yelled back.

Ryan suddenly bumped into the end of the stadium, trapped between a wall and an angry rhino. Ryan bravely stood up on his two feet and looked Russell right in the eyes.

"Russell stop!" he yelled.

Russell ceased his attack for a brief moment to listen to Ryan's last words.

"Russell, please listen to me. Why should this even be happening? There is no need for this fighting and destruction. Russell—I promised you since we were kids that nothing could ever come between our friendship and you're still my friend. Please try and see that. I still see the good inside of you. Please come back to it. Don't let this evilness destroy you. I beg you Russell, come back."

Russell stared at Ryan trying to think about what he just said. He could remember the good times they shared when they were children, even growing closer as brothers with Russell always protecting Ryan if he got into trouble. Ryan always repaid his kindness by being his friend but unfortunately, that was all ancient history now. Russell could only see the rival and anger of 2D animation getting in the way of everything. He roughly shook his head to clear his mind of all the memories of him and Ryan.

"The only Russell that is here right now is the one that is going to destroy you," he groaned.

"Hang on Ryan, we're coming!" Grace shouted.

Before Grace could help Ryan, she was tackled down by a 3D gorilla.

"You're not going anywhere," he laughed quietly.

"Great! I should've known Russell's backup squad would be waiting to help him," Grace wailed.

Back in William's office, Christopher and Brittany witnessed Russell about to attack Ryan.

"This is all wrong," Christopher said. "A 3D character is fighting his own kind. They have no remorse, not even for their own class. This could turn out a lot uglier than I realized."

"What's the difference," William remarked. "I made all the money I needed from them. Now they're of no use to me anymore, let them destroy each other for all I care."

"What are you talking about!?" Christopher yelled. "This wasn't the way things were supposed to turn out. What do you mean let them destroy each other?"

"Just what I said my fine chipmunk friend," William laughed. "I've got other plans anyway."

"What plans!?" Christopher shrieked angrily.

Unexpectedly, Jewel and Rex came through the front door of William's office with Jackson leading them inside. He normally stood outside guarding the office door and would only let anybody in if it was important. Catching everyone by surprise, Jewel gazed at William, Christopher, and Brittany while Rex growled furiously.

"Jackson, what's the meaning of this?" Christopher asked startled.

"They said it was urgent sir and they needed to talk to you," Jackson replied.

"Hey Christopher sorry we're late, did we miss a big battle?" Rex pronounced.

"Shouldn't you guys be downstairs in the arena with the rest of the gang?" Brittany asked.

"No, I was just looking for Ryan," Jewel stated.

"I don't know any Ryan," William said irritably, "but you better get out of here before I call security."

"Calm down William, I know Rex. It's alright if he stays," Christopher pointed out.

"Sorry but we can't stay, I'm just looking for a 3D fox whose name is Ryan," Jewel explained.

"A 3D fox? Why?" asked Brittany.

Chapter 18: Jewel's Sacrifice

"I can't say but it's urgent that I find him," Jewel cried frantically.

"Could you be talking about that 3D fox down there in the arena?" Christopher questioned as he pointed near the window.

"Where?" Jewel cried as she rushed over to the window.

She pressed her face against the glass trying to get a clear look and immediately caught sight of Ryan and saw Russell getting ready to charge at him. In the blink of an eye, Russell crashed into Ryan. The impact was so devastating it caused a big puncture in the wall of the stadium. All of the 2D and 3D characters couldn't believe it, they didn't mind trying to kill each other but they didn't know that Russell would literally destroy his own family. As smoke began to escape from the crash, Russell easily pulled himself out of the hole with Ryan hanging from his horn.

"RYAN!" Jewel cried in horror.

From the way Ryan was hanging it seemed like he was dead, but luckily he was still breathing. It was pretty fortunate for someone to survive an attack like that but his unresponsive body easily dropped off of Russell's horn and hit the ground. Everyone stared in terror fearing the worse, especially Grace, Fangs, and Silver, however, when they saw him breathing and trying to move, they breathed a sigh of relief. Unfortunately Russell wasn't relieved, he was furious.

"You're still alive!" he shouted violently. "Well—you won't be for long."

Russell quickly charged his horn up against Ryan's chest, trying to suffocate him. Ryan was already too weak and near death to fight back, all he could do was whimper like a puppy dog. Russell kept on pushing, trying to ensure he was dead. Fangs and Silver frantically tried to stop him but they were tackled down by more 3D characters just like Grace was. A lot of 3D characters had to hold Fangs down because he was the biggest individual there. With no one to stop Russell, it seemed that Ryan wasn't going to make it and Jewel just couldn't endure it. To watch Ryan die slowly was killing her inside. By this time she was willing to do anything to save his life.

"Please stop him!" she begged William.

"There's nothing I can do about it," William replied as he walked away from the window with no remorse whatsoever.

"You do have to stop this," Brittany protested. "Animation characters aren't supposed to kill their own family."

"Ask me if I care," William laughed.

"Why you no good, low life, rotten scum," Rex barked. "I'll destroy you-you-you—heartless, cold-blooded, monster! I'll chew you to pieces and leave your body out in the desert where the vultures won't be able to find anything left of you to eat!!!"

Jewel gradually put her paw on Rex to stop him from doing anything to William.

"Wait Rex! Listen William, please I'll give you anything if you just save Ryan's life," Jewel begged hysterically.

"You've got nothing to give me. I've already got everything I could possibly ever want. Besides why in the world would you want to give anything for a 3D character?" William asked.

"Because—because…" Jewel cried apprehensively.

Jewel could suddenly feel the pain come back inside of her. She swiftly held her stomach tightly and began to take a deep breath. Jewel tried concentrating real hard on Ryan and not the pain. He was her main concern right now. Little by little the pain disappeared and Jewel took a great big sigh then looked up at William deciding to finally let the truth out.

"Because…" William asked impatiently.

"Because… he's my husband," she revealed.

The room went into complete silence with everyone left in shock and flabbergasted at the same time. Rex was only surprised that she exposed the truth.

"Jewel—what have you done?" Rex said with concern.

But Jewel ignored Rex and kept her entire focus on William waiting to hear his response.

"You're kidding right?" William questioned. "Or is this some kind of sick joke?"

"No it's true," Jewel remarked. "We've been married for three months and got married in secret because of the conflict between our families. We

Chapter 18: Jewel's Sacrifice

knew they would never approve of us but Ryan is the best thing that has ever happened to me. I'm carrying his child and I couldn't bear it if he died. Please, I'll give you anything if you just save him! Save him please!"

"Awww, that's so sweet," Brittany stated. "It's just like Romeo and Juliet. I'd never thought I would be around to see anything like this. It's simply marvelous."

"And you've known all about this Rex?" Christopher asked.

"Yeah, so. I only kept this as a secret for Jewel's sake," Rex declared.

"Shut up all of you!" William interrupted. "Hold on a minute, didn't you say that you were carrying his child?"

"Yes I am," Jewel said sadly. "I wouldn't want my baby to grow up without a father. Please stop this torture before it's too late!"

William smiled devilishly. He knew if Jewel was 2D and Ryan was 3D that would make the baby a hybrid of both. It's not the first time a 2D and 3D combination was created on television by animators or a studio but it was the first time for an actual 2D character and 3D character to come together and conceive one. Something this astonishing could make William powerful. A new plan with an ugly scheme immediately crossed his mind.

"You'll do anything?" William asked Jewel again.

"Yes anything! Just save him please!" she cried.

William smirked at everyone and slowly walked over to his desk getting ready to press one of the switches. His evil smile could only indicate that he was up to no good. Jewel couldn't trust him but she didn't care as long as Ryan's life would be spared. Christopher and Brittany already didn't trust William anymore after his speech before Rex and Jewel interrupted. They prepared themselves for whatever he was about to do.

"Get ready for the grand finale," he acknowledged happily.

CHAPTER NINETEEN

WILLIAM'S SURPRISE

Russell continued driving his horn into Ryan and wasn't going to stop for anything until his old friend was completely gone. Ryan tried hanging on as much as possible but he was already fading out. Everything around him was getting blurry and black as he whimpered his last breath of desperation. He didn't want to be remembered for being killed by his friend, he'd rather think of Jewel before he died. Ryan tried focusing on her as much as he could before he could see the light. Seeing her in his mind brought the last joy of comfort to his heart. He felt he at least made a good life with her in this ugly world. She gave him a reason to go on and be happy. Before Ryan was just about to give out, a sudden rumble rocked the whole stadium. All of the 2D and 3D characters stumbled and fell all over each other from the impact of the great earthquake. They couldn't keep their balance because of the sudden shake. Russell even fell aside, leaving Ryan out of danger. No one even knew what was going on, no one except William, who controlled the whole stadium from the switch he activated from his monitor.

"It's showtime!" he announced contentedly.

From the left side of the stadium, a thunderous roar shook the ground from below. Suddenly something big erupted from underneath the arena and the cartoon characters quickly cleared a path to get away from whatever was coming. A giant claw abruptly crashed through the field. The claw resembled the forelegs of a praying mantis but had bat wings attached to it. The large beast gradually exposed the rest of its body as it climbed up

Chapter 19: William's Sacrifice

from the hole it made. The monster's head looked like a spider with six eyes, bat wings which were his ears, and spikes that resembled a mohawk on the top of his head. He also had two more arms just like a praying mantis on the side of his waist, legs, and feet similar to that of a Velicoraptor's, and displayed a long tail a lot like a Stegosaurus but much longer and sharper. He was a purple reddish color with black stripes and was a 2D character but a hideous form of a monster that was nearly as big as the stadium. He was so enormous that his head was cramped against the shield. Once he rose from the ground, he roared a frightening snarl which bellowed throughout the entire neighborhood. The monster gradually looked down at all of the 2D and 3D characters. No doubt everyone was in complete shock; this is something they were not expecting at all. Then if that wasn't enough, on the right side of the stadium another loud eruption shook below the ground. This time it was a 3D monster coming up from this section. Just like the 2D monster, he smashed his way through the field making his appearance. He had the arms and claws of a weird gremlin-like creature that were so long they dragged on the ground like an orangutan. His head gave the impression of a bearded dragon but he had a large underbite with jaws full of long sharp teeth and a dung beetles' claw on both sides of his jaws. He had big ears resembling a bat-eared fox, a medium-sized neck and his body appeared hunched over and emaciated with two large gargoyle wings on his back. His legs and feet seemed similar to that of a beetle combined with a dragon, shorter than his arms but strong and athletic. In addition, he had a long and slimy tail like an eel and large spikes on the top of his head to the bottom of his tail. He was black with green stripes while his stomach was a peach color. Once he fully came up from the ground he growled which shook the whole stadium as he glanced down at the cartoon individuals as well. Although the monsters were 2D and 3D animation, they seemed more advanced like something you would watch in a horror movie. The animation characters had never been so scared in their entire life; they were stuck between two large monsters which could easily wipe all of them out in the blink of an eye. Fangs who was the biggest character in the stadium now felt puny compared to the monsters. The beasts didn't do anything yet as everyone expected, they just remained patient waiting on William's command.

"We're dead," a gorilla cried desperately.

"Well, at least I went out as a coward than a hero," a rabbit blubbered.

"Hold on now," a cheetah protested. "Maybe each of them are on our side. After all, one is 2D and the other is 3D."

"Well, why don't you go up and talk to one of them?" Diana suggested.

"Me? No way, I'm a scaredy-cat," the cheetah replied.

"I'll do it," the gorilla volunteered. "I'm a silverback gorilla, I'm not afraid of anything."

Bravely the gorilla walked up to the 3D monster but nervously looked up at him. His frightening appearance and large size made the gorilla tremble. The monster just glared down at him with a terrifying stare and slowly snarled at him with drool sliding down his mouth.

"Hey there brother," the gorilla spoke steadily. "We 3D got to stick together, right? It's a good thing you've come along because we were just about to wipe out…"

The monster rapidly roared a hideous noise at the gorilla which made the fur fly off of his skin. The gorilla instantly ran away screaming like a woman and hid behind Diana like a frightened child.

"Men, so predictable," Diana smirked amused.

"Shut up," the gorilla retorted back.

William began to speak in his microphone throughout the stadium getting everyone's attention. "It's a shame you guys didn't know what you've actually done," he chuckled, "but I guess I have all of you to thank anyway. Without your help, none of this would even be possible."

"What do you mean without our help?" Grace yelled as she looked up at William from his office window. "What is this about!?"

All of the other characters began to agree with Grace by anxiously complaining. As though one voice the entire animated character group began to rapidly fire questions at William.

"Well…" William answered. "The monsters you actually see before you—were created by all of you."

Chapter 19: William's Sacrifice

"WHAT??!!" everyone yelled at the same time confused by what William just announced.

"It was very simple my cartoon friends. Your hatred for each other caused the mutation of these horrific beasts."

The whole stadium fell into confusion and uncertainty. It might have made sense of what he said but most of them were still unsure of what he was talking about.

"My friends don't you see. 2D animation, your hatred for 3D characters has caused you to create this 2D monster and you 3D animation, your hatred for 2D characters caused you to create this 3D monster. It was pretty simple and easy. Your loathing for each other has raged on for so long, it generated and produced the monsters you see before you. The same way animators create you guys, I simply did it with your help. What I didn't know is how you guys could ever construct such gruesome beasts. Without your knowledge that you were even creating these monsters, you helped generate them more and more with continuous revulsion for your rivals. These two monsters were designed by all of you and were small to begin with but kept increasing in size due to your endless wrath and racism. In a different realm they were born, and magically appeared on my computer. The only thing I did was bring them to life in the real world by rendering them out and I have all of you to thank because without your help, I never would've had these two monsters to begin with."

All of the animation characters in the stadium felt something that words couldn't begin to describe. They felt beyond stupidity and embarrassment. In a million years they never would've imagined they could create monsters capable of destroying mankind in the arms of an evil maniac.

"Now that you guys know the truth, I feel there's no more need for surprises except for one more. I had intentions of destroying you all right now but I've got other plans."

William slowly knelt down and picked up Jewel easily holding her in his hands as he presented her to the entire arena. Some of the 2D characters who knew her gasped in horror. Ryan was still badly hurt after his attack from Russell but was gently helped up by Silver. Ryan steadily stood on his four feet and looked to see what everyone was gawking at. When he witnessed William holding Jewel from his office window, his heart just sank into a black hole. Of all the places Jewel had to be, why here! His mind was in complete hysteria and horrible shock at the same time. For the whole day, all he cared about was getting back to her and being with her when the baby arrived. His emotions were eating him up inside. The thought of anything happening to Jewel would haunt him until the day he died. As injured as Ryan was, he forcefully limped his way through the crowd shoving individuals aside.

"JEWEL!!" he cried hysterically.

"Exactly my friend," William laughed. "To spare your life fox, Jewel exposed her secret, which is she's married—to you."

All of the cartoon characters were astonished again. Some of them laughed thinking it was a prank at first but when they saw that William was serious, they were left speechless. They stared at Ryan in disbelief; they had never heard something so absurd before and were literally at a loss for words. Ryan didn't care if the secret was out anymore; he just wanted to protect Jewel from William.

"Let her go!" Ryan shouted insistently.

"Sorry pal, can't do that," William smirked. "Jewel also told me that you two are about to have a kid. This will clearly make me famous. A 2D and a 3D hybrid conceived by actual parents and not created by an animator will remake the books as we know it. This is only the beginning my friend."

Jewel groaned heavily again feeling the pain coming back inside of her with the baby surely coming this time. As William easily put Jewel back on the floor, Ryan felt as if he was going insane. Not only was Jewel trapped in the arms of a corrupt man but his kid was on the way.

"Release her and take me instead!" Ryan begged with all of his willpower.

"She made the offer first," William remarked. "Besides, why would I want to give her up when I can take your kid once it's born? It'll make me legendary overnight and if anyone has a problem with it, then they'll have

Chapter 19: William's Sacrifice

to answer to my monsters. It's too bad you guys didn't suspect anything. I guess it's a good thing you cartoon characters are dumb after all, meaningless characters that have no purpose being here in the first place."

William grabbed a hold of Jewel as he placed her in a large suitcase which was shaped like a pet carrier. Dealing with the pain inside of her, Jewel couldn't even talk anymore. Sweating heavily, she rolled up into a ball as she forcefully grabbed her stomach. William picked up the suitcase and dressed himself up.

"Well, I guess it's time to go," he sneered with happiness.

Rex, Christopher, and Jackson rushed into his path to keep him from leaving. Rex growled at William while Christopher hopped on his head and Jackson snarled as he jammed his claws into the carpet. Of course they weren't going to let him get away with this.

"Drop the suitcase," Rex growled disturbingly.

"Or what," William retorted with no worries.

"Then we'll beat you to a pulp," Christopher replied. "I had a feeling I shouldn't have trusted you but this has gone far enough! You are not going anywhere with Jewel."

"Oh, aren't I?" William laughed wickedly.

Without warning, William pulled out a tranquilizer gun from his pocket and shot it at Christopher, Jackson, and Rex. In a split second, all three of them felt drugged and woozy and then instantly dropped to the ground falling asleep.

"What have you done?" Brittany shrieked upset.

"They'll be out for a while, nothing to worry about."

"You think I'm going to stand by and let you get away with this."

"I'd figure you'd say that."

Then unexpectedly William shot Brittany with the tranquilizer too.

"You idi… ooooo…." she unsteadily spoke as she immediately began to pass out.

William quickly grabbed a hold of her before she could hit the floor.

"You are going to be my wife," William chuckled to himself as he held her in his arms. "No more squirrels for you miss Garland. You'll forget all about nuts once you're with me."

Before William left his office he turned on a switch which opened the shield. Then he touched another one which activated an automatic helicopter that was placed outside the stadium. William made one more announcement in the microphone before he left.

"Alright my monsters, it's time to take off into the air. Toodoleoo my fine cartoon friends. It's been fun."

After hearing William, the monsters began to thrust their wings out. The 2D monster flapped his arms continuously until it ultimately lifted him off the ground while the 3D monster did the same by waving his gigantic wings from behind his back. A big gust of wind was created by the monsters flapping, causing most of the cartoon characters to fly all over the field and tumble on top of each other. Eventually, William, Brittany, and Jewel were inside of the helicopter which William maneuvered. Brittany remained unconscious while, Jewel, inside of the pet carrier was still in labor. The helicopter flew away from the stadium with the two monsters following closely behind it. With the shield still open, Fangs and other individuals who could fly saw this as a perfect opportunity to escape.

"Oh no you don't!" Fangs shouted.

He quickly brought his wings out and flew up into the air along with other characters but without warning, William rigged the stadium to close up again once he left. Fangs and the others hit the glass shield, descending back onto the field.

"Fools," William laughed ecstatically. "They didn't really think I was going to let any of them go. They're much dumber than I thought. I'll be back for them later and will ultimately eliminate them all."

William's helicopter flew high into the night air with his comrade monsters protecting him. As he disappeared high above the stars, everyone was dumbfounded by the chain of events that just occurred. First, William deceiving all of them, second, the surprising monsters they'd created, third, Ryan's secret marriage to Jewel, and now William trapping them helplessly. However, no one was more surprised than Ryan. No one could possibly begin to imagine what he was feeling right now.

CHAPTER TWENTY

THE REVELATION

Ryan rudely pushed and knocked over 2D and 3D characters just to try to get to Jewel. He desperately ran through the crowd screaming out her name. The emotional turmoil fox was experiencing a situation no one thought they would ever see. He made his way through a clear opening away from the crowd but it wasn't any good because he was still stuck inside the stadium just like the rest of them. All he could do was look up into the sky and see the helicopter getting smaller and smaller until it vanished.

"JEWEL!!!" he screamed insanely.

Ryan's body lunged to the ground as he folded his arms around his head. He cried in an agonizing state, full of hopelessness. He brought his head up and howled like a distressed wolf at night. Ryan's wounded expression touched everyone, his true and powerful love for a 2D character left them grieving and they felt his pain. They understood why Ryan kept his marriage a secret and watching his sadness; they would have never thought it would affect them so emotionally. It was as if an evil force had destroyed Ryan's heart and nothing could repair it. He was nothing without Jewel, and the fact that William was also going to take their newborn child made him even more melancholy. He would never see his first child or know if it's a boy or a girl. All of this left Ryan in such a tormented state; his heart was literally aching with pain as if someone was constantly stabbing it with a knife. Ryan's depression suddenly took a much darker side. His eyes opened to a sudden glowing intense red color, even more powerful than Russell's. His head then turned toward all of the 2D and 3D characters. He stared at all of them in a deadly rage. Ryan knew none of this would have ever happened if it wasn't for everyone's stupid hatred. All of his emotions made him speak from the heart and to finally let everything out in the open.

"YOU FOOLS!!!" he screamed from the top of his lungs. "ARE YOU HAPPY NOW!!!"

Everyone was taken aback by Ryan's temper.

"You all got exactly what you wanted! To fight and kill each other just because you can't learn to get along. William might have been the one behind all of this but you guys started it! You helped him become more powerful in the end. Tell me something… why do you guys hate each other so much! Huh? Why?! Because we're a little different. 2D is hand-drawn animation while 3D is CGI computer animation. Why do our appearances have to distinguish the way we have to be judged? You idiots, we are all ANIMATION! We're part of the same family from the same ink no matter what. Just because we're a little different you have to be prejudiced. You act just like the humans when they're prejudiced against each other because of skin color and race. You stooped to the lower levels of depravity. Your hatred has created two vicious monsters that will destroy this world by William's command and my beloved wife is gone because of you ungrateful, low life, ignorant, good for nothing hypocrites! I loved Jewel for who she was and that's all that ever mattered to me. I was always filled with overwhelming happiness with her and no 3D fox had ever captivated me as she did. I'd rather die than to live without her. I-I will never even see my firstborn child. You destroyed my family as well as my heart by only thinking about yourselves. But you also destroyed society with your hatred. Well, congratulations my friends, you've got exactly what you wanted and I hope you're happy with yourselves. You guys are a disgrace and you make me hate myself for just being a part of the animation race. I just want to die—I—I just want to die."

After Ryan finished his speech he turned his head away from everyone, then curled up into a ball and wept all over again. For once in their life, all of the 2D and 3D characters had finally awakened from their hatred and

Chapter 20: The Revelation

had a revelation. Ryan broke them down for who they really were and vengefully hated all of them for this disastrous state of affairs. It's true that none of them ever saw eye to eye but their hatred for one another had caused civilization to be in danger and risked the life of Ryan's family. Realizing all the sacrifices Ryan made just to be with Jewel made them feel extra guilty, also realizing that they'd stooped to the level of acting like wicked humans made them feel absolutely mortified. With all of the pieces now in place, all everyone could do was look at each other with tremendous humiliation and shame but Ryan's close friend's Fangs, Grace, and Silver weren't going to let this torment destroy their best friend. They helped him every step of the way and were going to continue no matter the circumstances. While the three of them made their way through the crowd to get to Ryan, Grace lifted him on his two feet and tried to get his attention.

"Ryan—listen to me. We didn't come this far to give up now. We'll help you get Jewel back no matter what it takes," she promised.

"That's right Vulpes," Silver remarked. "Your determination is what I admired and you've got to keep that faith."

"That's what friends are for Ryan and we will help you," Fangs added.

Ryan slowly stopped crying when he heard his friend's statements. After he felt there was no more hope, his friends were right there for him. Throughout the entire day, they stuck by him every step of the way and never gave up on him, and now when all seemed lost, they were still willing to help Ryan get through all of this.

"It's too late you guys," Ryan cried. "William's already won."

"Not on my watch," Grace exclaimed. "You're not going to give up Ryan because the one thing you are not is a quitter. I really appreciated having that in you as a friend and I will not let you give up now."

"Y-y-you guys are still going to help me?" he asked softly.

"Of course, why shouldn't we," said Silver happily.

"We're not going to stop until that William jerk gets what's coming to him," Fangs proclaimed.

Suddenly the rest of the crowd shouted, "Yeah!"

Ryan, Grace, Silver, and Fangs surprisingly turned their heads to everyone. All of the 2D and 3D characters seemed eager to get back at William for what he did but they also felt the need to help Ryan after hearing the news about his wife. For the first time in their life, they were finally putting their differences aside and thought of someone else other than themselves.

"All of ya?" Grace asked surprised. "But you all hate each other. A few minutes ago, you were almost ready to kill one another, now you want to work together?"

"It's not about us anymore, it's about helping get Jewel back," said a 2D hawk. "No one should be in the hands of a madman who is capable of taking away your own child."

"Besides, we caused all of this," said a 3D elephant. "The least we can do is fix it."

"We also helped create those horrible monsters," a 3D chipmunk cried. "Because of us, the entire world is in danger."

"We've never harmed a human in history," a 2D prairie dog howled, "and now the very things we've created could destroy every single human being out there. A lot of innocent lives could be lost."

"The only human being that's going to be destroyed is William," said a 2D otter.

"But the only way we can pull this off is if we work together properly, like a real team," Fangs pointed out. "We can't have any arguments or disagreements between each other."

"That's right," Silver agreed. "We need to work as a unit. We could successfully triumph if we work together. My calculations say there's a 75% chance we could win as a group of independent warriors."

"I like the sssssound of that," said a 2D snake.

"We should all agree to an alliance for now just until we take care of William," said the 3D gorilla.

"Agreed!" everyone in the entire stadium shouted.

Ryan was still furiously angry at everyone but for once he felt a little relieved. Everyone was finally coming to their senses and decided to unify. They probably still weren't comfortable working with each other;

Chapter 20: The Revelation

nonetheless, they all wanted the same thing, to punish William. They were not about to let William use those monsters to annihilate them or innocent people. Since Jewel's baby would be coming at any minute, they didn't want William stealing it for his own benefit. They dreaded the fact that William would use the baby the same way he used them or worse. A newborn baby shouldn't suffer from the price of torment because of the cartoon character's mistake. Jewel sacrificed her life to save Ryan, now he was willing to do the same thing for her. Ryan faced everyone in the stadium and stared at them for the longest time.

"None of you may survive," he warned them. "No one has to go if they don't want to."

"We were about to die just going into battle today," Diana responded. "We know what we're up against. At first, it was for our own pleasure but now if we don't make it, at least we went out as heroes saving the world—and your family."

CHAPTER TWENTY-ONE

THE ESCAPE

"I guess since that's settled, we just have to find a way out of here," Fangs declared.

"There's no use trying to get through that glass up there," said the 2D hawk. "That shield is as strong as a—shield."

"I'll dig us out!" a 2D prairie dog suggested.

Quickly, he began to dig his way through the stadium field. It didn't take too long because he was a fast digger, however, when it seemed like he was about to make it, there was a sudden clanking noise. The prairie dog became unconscious when he hit his head on a large piece of metal that was waiting for him on the way down. A 3D bat flew down the hole and pulled the prairie dog back out.

"William confined this place with elements that tend to lose electrons and form positive ions in chemical reactions, form bases in combination with hydroxyl groups and are lustrous, malleable, ductile, and good conductors of heat and electricity," Silver proclaimed.

Everyone was left completely confused and puzzled by Silver's statement. They had no idea what he was talking about.

"Say what?" asked Grace.

"What," Silver replied.

"NO, I mean talk English," she shrieked.

"In other words, he trapped this place with metal," amended Silver.

"That's just great," Diana complained.

Chapter 21: The Escape

"What about those holes the monsters came out of?" Grace asked. "There must be a way out from down there."

Most of the characters scurried into the holes and found nothing but a dungeon inside. It was big enough for the monsters but there was no way in or out.

"The monsters were right below us the entire time we were fighting and we didn't even know it," said a 3D giraffe.

"We really are the dumbest creatures on the planet, besides the humans," a 2D platypus remarked.

"You're not the only one who caught on slowly," Christopher commented.

Everyone noticed Christopher, Jackson, and Rex coming their way, exiting William's office, still feeling woozy and unsteady for a minute.

"Christopher, is that you?" Diana asked surprised.

"What's left of me I'm afraid. Where's that no good William gone to?" cried Christopher angrily.

"He's gone with Jewel," Fangs replied.

"And my Brittany!" Christopher exclaimed.

"Who?" Fangs asked.

"My girlfriend! He stole my girlfriend! When I see him again, he's going to wish he never messed with me. I'll punch his lights out!" Christopher screamed hysterically.

"Christopher, you made the deal with William to get us all here, did you know anything about this?" Diana questioned.

"If I did then I wouldn't be here!" Christopher yelled. "He set me up too which is why I'm stuck here just like the rest of you!"

"Well you're not the only one who is going to pummel William," Rex mentioned. "If he so much as harms Jewel and her baby, I'll kill that son of…"

"Rex?" Ryan said with admiration.

Rex was cut off by Ryan, who suddenly approached him.

"Yes—what do you want Ryan?" Rex said a little rudely.

"Jewel told you about us and you kept our secret for all this time," Ryan said. "I am forever grateful to you, always protecting Jewel for me even if it wasn't for my own benefit."

"Uh—yeah—whatever," Rex replied with not much enthusiasm.

Ryan brought his paw towards Rex wanting to shake in friendship. As much as Ryan loved Jewel he was very obliged to anyone who watched after her as Rex did. The aggressive Doberman still didn't like the CGI fox but he knew Jewel had been determined to find him even at the extent of risking her own life. He'd never known anyone to have such a compassionate relationship with their mate and he knew it was something he eventually had to get used to. Slowly, taking a deep breath, the dog calmly brought his paw out to Ryan's and shook on it. For some reason, shaking Ryan's paw gave Rex a warm feeling inside his heart, as if he was absorbing his positive and respectable nature. Rex couldn't help but return a positive smile to Ryan in satisfaction that they were okay and no longer rivals.

"Hey wait a minute, you guys came from William's office," Grace mentioned. "Isn't there a way out from where you came?"

"That's the first place we checked," Jackson spoke. "Unfortunately, William locked all of the doors after he escaped. Even if we tried to break through it, they're barricaded with metal."

"There's got to be a way out of here!" Christopher cried hysterically.

"How about our way?" Kyle called from the left side of the stadium.

Ryan and the others focused their attention on Kyle who was followed by Ralph, Stan, Rascal, Miriam, Carlos, and Meeko. The last time Ryan saw Kyle he was really angry but now, he was very excited to see him.

"Kyle!" he cried eagerly.

He wasted no time running up to him and when he made contact with Kyle they both tumbled on the ground like a bowling ball. As soon as they got back on their feet they both laughed because it reminded them of the films they made together.

"Where have you been?" Ryan asked.

"Long story, but what I should say right now is that I'm sorry for not telling you about any of this," Kyle admitted shamefully.

Chapter 21: The Escape

"I understand why you did it, to protect me. I just want to thank you for being a good and thoughtful friend," Ryan replied with gratefulness.

"I guess we missed a big fight," Rascal mentioned as he scanned the entire arena. "Too bad, I would've liked to get some of the action."

"I'm glad the fight is over," Ralph stated, "I didn't want to walk into an ugly battle to begin with."

"You should've put this kat into the fight, he wouldn't have lasted one minute," Carlos said as he landed on top of Meeko's head.

"Oh listen to the bird brain talk," Meeko said angrily. "No bigger than a man's…"

"Shut up you two!" Miriam interrupted. "Where's William?"

"He's gone!" cried Ryan. "But we're all working together so we can go after him."

"See, I warned all of ya this would happen!" Miriam shouted.

"Okay Miriam, we get the message," Rascal groaned.

"So far we can't find a way out of here," Christopher said anxiously. "If we don't, I'm going to lose my mind!"

Maybe everyone wanted to pay William back but Christopher felt the same way as Ryan. When he stole Brittany from him, he was full of so much rage and anger that he couldn't control.

"Well that's where we come in," Stan pointed out. "Lucky for us, we found a secret basement passageway that led us up here. If you follow us the same way we came in, we could easily lead you guys outside."

"I am forever in your debt," Christopher exclaimed as he repeatedly kissed Stan on the foot.

"Okay—this is awkward," Stan said embarrassed.

"You don't know how much I appreciate this Kyle," Ryan said profoundly.

"I wish I could do more to repay all the good you've done for me," Kyle replied gratefully.

Every single 2D and 3D character followed Kyle and the others outside. They came out from the basement doorway which Meeko and Carlos made earlier but Kyle and others made it bigger for everyone else to fit through. Fangs was the last one to come out because of his large size.

He tried squeezing his way through the hole which turned out to be too small for him.

"Fangs you're taking too long!" Ryan instructed. "You even give turtles a bad name by this pace. We're going to have to ride on you again; you can fly after William and head him off."

Fangs repeatedly tried to get out of the hole, but soon collapsed from exhaustion. "It's no use Ryan," he exclaimed. "I can't get out of this hole."

"Oh you pathetic lizard! You're supposed to be a strong dragon!" Ryan yelled.

"For the last time, I play a strong dragon in my television series," Fangs muttered. "I'm not that powerful in real life—I'm too weak."

Ryan was about to lose his temper and go off on Fangs, but Grace interrupted him.

"Let me handle it Ryan," she smiled confidently, "I know how to deal with him."

She slowly walked over to Fangs and looked down at him with an affectionate gaze.

"Now, I know you're not giving up," Grace said shrewdly.

"I don't want to buttercup but—I'm not as strong as I am on the parts that I play. I only wish I was stronger."

Grace grabbed Fangs by the face and looked at him deep in the eyes. Fangs started to shake nervously and didn't know what to say, all he could do was stare back at her. Before he and anyone knew it, Grace gave Fangs a great big wet kiss. All of the animation characters watching this were left in complete shock. Seeing a 2D character kissing a 3D character is something they'd never witnessed before. Some of their mouths dropped open from amazement while others covered their eyes from embarrassment. After Grace finished kissing Fangs, she stared deep into his eyes again and smiled. "I know you can do it—pumpkin."

Fangs' mind had completely left the universe. Her confidence in him had suddenly turned him into the same dragon he always played in his roles, strong and physically powerful in every way a dragon is supposed to be. Grace stepped back as she got ready for Fangs to make his way out. Steadily he paced his way back and forth, and then abruptly charged his

Chapter 21: The Escape

way out of the hole making a gigantic dragon roar. Some of the characters got scared by Fangs' sudden appearance while the rest clapped earnestly.

"Good work Grace," Ryan said. "Alright Fangs listen up, me, Grace, Silver, Christopher, and Kyle are going to ride on you. We're going to do whatever it takes to find William."

"Not without me!" Rex interjected. "I'm coming with you too."

"So am I," Carlos cried. "Wherever Kyle goes, I go."

"Very well," Ryan said not wanting to start an argument. "The rest of you are just going to have to track William on foot, I'm afraid."

"We can do better than that. How about that fancy limo you always had us ride around in Christopher? At least twenty characters can fit in there," Ralph considered.

"Good idea," Christopher thought. "I have at least five limousines in the parking lot already. Every single 2D and 3D character here could ride in all of them."

"Let's not waste any more time! Let's go and get William right now while we still can!" Ryan demanded impatiently.

All of the cartoon characters cheered enthusiastically and scattered off to their destinations; while Ryan and the others hopped on top of Fangs' back, Kyle said his farewells to Ralph and Stan.

"You guys be careful, you hear me," Kyle told them firmly.

"You're the one who should be careful, you're going after William in the air with those monsters for crying out loud," Ralph clarified.

"I'm well aware of that but not to worry guys, flying is one of my best skills," Kyle declared.

"Like at the mall," Stan brought up.

"Don't remind me about that again," Kyle said angrily.

"Take care Kyle, the others and I will try to catch up to you as soon as possible," Stan explained.

"Just don't be too late!" Kyle ordered. "Or else we'll all be playing the golden harp very soon. I don't want to grow angel wings just yet."

"See ya later little rat," Carlos taunted Meeko. "I'll see ya when you know what it feels like to be the underdog for a change. Oh I'm sorry—I mean kat. The underkat. Haa, haa, haa."

"Why you dirty little…" Meeko groaned with fury.

Fangs' large wings sprung out and began flapping. For the first time in his life, he felt proud to be a tough and resilient dragon, thanks to Grace returning his love for her. Without any further delay he launched into the air, however, Meeko quickly grabbed a hold of Fangs' tail at that exact moment. He had a beef with Carlos he wanted to finish and he wasn't going to let him leave his sight.

"Wow, you must be really desperate," Carlos said noticing Meeko hanging on Fangs' tail.

"The only thing I'm desperate about is getting back at you," Meeko shrieked. "You and I have a fight we didn't finish."

"I'd be sad if I were you. You're not in a very good position," Carlos claimed amusingly.

"Don't worry bird brain, I have my ways of getting around," Meeko maintained calmly.

Before Carlos knew it, Meeko swiftly scurried up from Fangs' tail and ran up front where he met Carlos face to face.

"Now—where were we," Meeko said wittingly.

Carlos simply giggled nervously.

CHAPTER TWENTY-TWO

THE RESCUE

William sat back in his seat all relaxed and comfortable while he left the helicopter on automatic pilot. The two monsters were still flying beside him; Brittany sat on the right seat still slumbering for the moment and Jewel who was still in labor desperately trying to deal with the pain but was able to talk to William.

"W-what are—y-you going t-to do to m-me?"

"First of all, I'm taking you and Brittany to my private island. I'm going to get you guys settled there while I'll make some arrangements."

"Arrangements—what arrangements?"

"I'm sorry you're the one who has to hear this but as I soon as we establish ourselves on my island; I'm going to order my monsters to destroy the rest of those good-for-nothing cartoon characters."

"Y-you c-can't!"

"Oh but I can, my dear. The only thing that can destroy a cartoon character is another cartoon character. With these two monsters I have, they can easily wipe out the entire cartoon population."

"I mean—you can't get away with this. W-what will t-the authorities s-say when cartoon characters are suddenly m-missing?"

"The authorities will have no choice but to go along with the things I do from now on. You see my dear, these powerful monsters can destroy a whole civilization. People will have no choice but to obey me or die."

"The only—monster around h-here is you."

"You are charming but it doesn't matter what you have to say because as soon as your baby comes I'll get rid of you. Once the baby gets comfortable with me, you'll never see it again."

"I'll die before—I'll let you take my baby and for it to be in the hands of someone as sinister as you."

"You really have no choice my dear. I've already won. So far my plans have worked out just as I predicted."

"Awwwww! I don't—know how much longer—I can take this! What a great time—to have a baby!"

"You're telling me. I'm glad I'm not in your shoes. Oh sorry, you don't have any. Haa, haa, haa."

"You're full of it!"

Only a couple of meters away, Fangs was getting closer to William than he realized. Until he got there, he kept his focus on flying as fast as he could. While Ryan and the rest of the gang were sitting comfortably, Carlos and Meeko were the only ones who were running and flying all over Fangs' body which was making it difficult for him to concentrate. Meeko ran around Fangs' waist then up to his face while Carlos flew a few inches above him trying to get away.

"Come back here and fight like a cartoon!" Meeko shouted angrily.

"You've got to catch me first," Carlos laughed.

"I will!" Meeko shrieked. "You can't fly forever. Pretty soon your wings will give out!"

"Will you two relax and stop fighting!" Ryan demanded. "That's all I can't take around here."

"Tell me about it," Fangs agreed. "Your running about on my body is starting to make me itch and you bird, you're making me dizzy with your constant flying. I'm the one who is flying here so will you remain seated."

"I'm the one who can't relax," Christopher grunted. "My baby is in the hands of someone like him. I swear if he so much as touches her…"

"I don't want to hear what you'll do to him," Kyle interrupted. "I know a ruthless gangster as bad as you will do gruesome, unimaginable things. I just don't want to hear the details."

Chapter 22: The Rescue

"Ruthless gangster, impressive," Silver said with amazement. "So what secret society do you represent?"

"Uhhh... that's classified," Christopher said.

"Of course it is. Ruthless gangsters are organized confidentially," Silver explained, "but I'm sure I can figure it out."

"William is going to get some action from my teeth," Rex groaned. "I hope he's delicate."

"Well we don't have to wait much longer. There he is," Grace said as she pointed in the distance.

Ryan and the others eventually spotted William's helicopter and the two monsters a few feet from them. After flying far from the city, down below them was a wide forest. Ryan was a little relieved because he didn't want people catching most of this action that was about to take place; it was going to be a suicidal battle against the monsters but all they cared about was getting Jewel and Brittany back. The 3D monster turned his head around and noticed Fangs getting closer then roared at William to get his attention. William looked at his monster confused for a moment then stuck his head outside of the helicopter. He was surprised and shocked at the same time never realizing that they could ever escape his stadium. Although he wasn't the least bit worried, he was kind of disappointed.

"How did they—oh it doesn't matter. This can work out to my advantage. If they want to die so soon then so be it."

Looking at both of his monsters, he just nodded to them by saying, "Finish them."

The 2D and 3D monster turned away from William's direction and headed straight for Fangs.

"Didn't we even have a plan to get us out of this!" Carlos cried with fear.

"Fangs do something!" Grace whimpered.

Fangs targeted the monsters closing in on him, got ready and took a very deep breath then fired a great big fireball. The monsters, not expecting an attack, were quite surprised. Fangs could see the attack was doing little physical damage, but seeing that it distracted them, he continued to fire at them.

"We need to get Jewel away from William!" Ryan ordered.

"I'm on it Ryan!" Kyle cried.

He immediately flapped his wings and flew off of Fangs but Rex suddenly hopped on top of Kyle's back. The poor pterodactyl could feel that same pressure weighing in on his back again which wasn't at all pleasurable.

"Hey, I didn't intend on you coming along!" shouted Kyle.

"If you're going to get Jewel back then I'm going with you!" Rex demanded. "Where her safety is involved, I always have to be there for her. Besides I want a piece of William."

"Rrrrrrrr—let's hope my back doesn't—give out!" Kyle cried as he sweated heavily.

"Yo Kyle wait for me!" Carlos yelled.

Carlos fluttered his wings as fast as a hummingbird then flew off of Fangs, but was immediately followed by Meeko who landed on top of his back. Meeko's large size was no match for Carlos, so they both fell. But Carlos quickly grabbed a hold of Meeko's two front paws trying to lift him as hard as he could.

"You—put us—in a really—bad position!" Carlos moaned anxiously.

"I'm not letting you leave my sight until I take care of you!" Meeko shrieked. "You owe me for that peck you gave me on the head."

"What—would you like—me to do—smash my—head against a rock—if it pleases you!" Carlos complained.

Suddenly without looking, Carlos crashed his head right into a tree while Meeko landed on the nearest branch safely. Carlos' head remained pinned against the tree like a pin stuck to a wall. Meeko finally smiled with satisfaction.

"Nope, a tree will do just fine," he replied happily.

"Destroy them until there is nothing left!" William shouted to his monsters. "I'll get us out of here in no time."

"Not before we crash your party," Rex growled.

William turned his head and noticed Kyle and Rex were flying right beside him. Rex jumped off of Kyle landing in the helicopter and knocked William over keeping him restrained.

Chapter 22: The Rescue

"Rrrrr, get off of me you stinkin' mutt!" William bellowed angrily.

"One false move and I'll bite your head off," Rex snarled viciously. "Kyle! Find Jewel and get her out of here!"

Kyle swiftly landed inside of the helicopter and searched for Jewel. "Jewel, are you here!" he called.

It didn't take him long to find her because he heard Jewel moaning and whimpering like crazy. He found the suitcase placed on the floor behind the back seat and opened it up finding her inside.

"Jewel, are you okay?" he asked.

"No I'm not okay!" she screamed. "This baby is about to burst out of me at any minute!"

Kyle felt nervous and worried, having no idea he was going to be dealing with a mother giving birth to a baby.

"Uhhh—alright—uh—just take a deep breath and hold on."

Kyle grabbed the suitcase by his feet and immediately rushed out of the helicopter. He flew at great speed but kept Jewel steady and secure for her safety. When William saw Kyle take off with Jewel, he was furious. "No! My money!" he screamed.

"I'm taking you and this helicopter down," Rex claimed.

He jumped off of William and brought his paws to the controllers turning off the automatic pilot and grabbed the front handle. Rex had never flown a helicopter before but he was pretty good at it for a first-timer. As he tried gliding the helicopter near the ground, William attempted to stop him. He wrapped his arm around his neck trying to strangle him.

"You think I'm going to let you stop me! I've come too far to let my plans be ruined by you fools. You're not bringing this helicopter down!"

Rex easily bit him and slipped through his arm with no problem because of his flexibility of being a 2D cartoon.

"Awwwww!" William yelled.

"Care to try that again?" Rex asked.

Holding her head and groaning with a bad headache, Brittany was finally waking up from her slumber.

"Ohhh—what's going on?" she asked woozily from the tranquilizer.

William pulled out his tranquilizer gun once more and aimed it at Rex.

"Say good night dog," William snickered. "When you fall asleep I'll throw your body out of this helicopter. No chance of you surviving a fall like that."

"I'll probably suffer a bad fall but it won't kill me," Rex informed. "Don't you watch cartoons at all? When's the last time you saw a cartoon character fall from the sky and only make a hole in the ground with an imprint on it. Besides you humans can't kill us."

"You're right. I can't kill you. But my monsters surely can. I'll feed you to them when I'm finished with you."

"Just try and catch me first."

William fired the first shot but Rex quickly avoided it, then he fired a second, and Rex avoided that one too.

"Is that the best you can do," said Rex amusingly. "I've seen babies that can shoot better than that."

William kept on firing as many shots as he could. Rex hopped in front of Brittany for a brief moment then rapidly dashed out of the way, however, in the process the poor girl got hit with another tranquilizer. She immediately passed out snoozing again. With no one attending the helicopter, it started flying recklessly. Ryan and the others became frantic and figured something might have happened to Rex but Christopher was more concerned about Brittany.

"Kyle got Jewel out of there, but who's going to get my Brittany!" he yelled angrily.

"I'll get her Christopher as soon as I get these monsters away from me," Fangs said. "I can't take on both of them when one is already hard enough."

"We'll distract them for you," Ryan explained. "Fly us close enough to the beasts then we'll jump on top of them."

"What do you intend for us to do?" Grace asked. "Put on a show for them."

"We're just going to sidetrack them long enough for Fangs to get Brittany and Rex out of the helicopter," Ryan ordered.

"Will you be alright buttercup?" Fangs asked Grace with much concern.

Chapter 22: The Rescue

"I've taken care of myself lots of times, you just go and rescue the others," Grace told him. "I'll be fine."

After listening to Ryan's idea, Fangs flew closer to the monsters. He flew over them to avoid their attacks so his friends could make a jump for it. Ryan saw a perfect opportunity to land.

"Alright guys—now!" he ordered.

Together, Ryan and Silver jumped on top of the 2D monster while Christopher and Grace jumped on top of the 3D monster. Fangs flew directly away from the monsters and tried to catch up with William. Ryan thought quickly and viciously pulled the monster's ears. Silver joyfully rode on top of the monster's mohawk like a cowboy.

"Yeeee haaaa! Howdy, howdy, howdy! Getty up there boy!"

"Silver this isn't the time for games. We're at war here!"

"If we're going to die tonight, why not enjoy our last few moments."

"Good point—I guess."

Feeling like there were ticks on his head the monster desperately tried getting Ryan and Silver off of him. The 3D monster was having the same problem with Christopher and Grace pulling on his skin annoyingly. He shook his head frantically causing Grace to lose her balance. She slipped and fell right between the monster's eyes and on his underbite. Staring at him directly in the eyes, she smiled at him fearfully.

"Hee, hee… hi… I'm Grace," she said uneasily.

The monster just blinked at her then opened his mouth, getting ready to chomp down on her.

"Hang on Grace, I'll take care of him!" Christopher shouted.

He quickly flew over the monster's head like a bullet and then headed straight into his ear. The monster roared in pain as he tried picking Christopher out with his claw.

"Sorry pal, I think you got something stuck in your ear," Christopher called from the inside. "You're going to have to dig deeper than that."

Grace swooped around the monster's teeth then was able to climb back on top of his head.

"Thanks Chris, I owe you!" she called.

Fangs dashed his way to the helicopter when he noticed it was still flying awkwardly. So awkward, it was about to hit one of the trees. William and Rex were still too busy fighting each other to notice. Full of frustration, William decided to try and catch Rex since the tranquilizer wasn't working anymore.

"Hold still you freakin' mutt so I can kill you!" he bellowed.

Right before the helicopter was about to collide with a tree and make a big explosion, Fangs grabbed the end of it just in the nick of time. With all of his strength, he lifted the helicopter and glided it to safety. After getting it airborne again, Fangs released the helicopter and checked inside finding William and Rex wrestling with one another while Brittany was slumbering.

"Rex, what the heck are you doing? You almost crashed the helicopter," Fangs stated crossly.

"I don't care as long as I take care of William," Rex growled.

To Fangs' surprise, Rex bit William on the butt and started pulling his pants and giving him a major wedgie. William of course shrieked in pain.

"That's enough action, it's time to leave," Fangs demanded.

He quickly grabbed a hold of Rex in his left claw while he grabbed Brittany in his right claw but Rex didn't let go of William. He still held onto his pants with a tight grip but eventually ripped half of it off with a piece hanging from his mouth as Fangs pulled him away. Without delay Fangs carefully flew Rex and Brittany away from the helicopter leaving William inside.

"NO!!" William shouted.

He was already angry enough that they took Jewel, but now he was furious when they took Brittany as well. With all the anger he was feeling right now he was willing to kill everybody, including the humans. The evil inside this man was revealing itself more and more deadly and was about to snap like a rabid dog. After rubbing his butt from the soreness that Rex gave him, he looked outside and realized the helicopter was going down. It made a brief spin near some trees, then took a nasty drop. Fortunately, the helicopter didn't collide with a tree but barely made contact with a large branch that broke its fall. Then it roughly landed on the ground next to a large tree. William was hurt, of course, but not to the extent where it

Chapter 22: The Rescue

could've been too severe. He was bleeding a tad on the head while his leg felt a little bit out of place. He grabbed his leg and limped out of the helicopter, then rested up against the tree.

"No one gets in my way and tries to defeat me!" he groaned. "From now on, things are going to be very different around here. When they feel my fury, this will be a day that no one will ever forget. My conquest will reign on this planet and no one is going to stop me!"

When he looked up, he noticed his monsters were still fighting in the air with Ryan and the others. He slowly smiled at the fact knowing the cartoon characters were no match for his giant monsters. This was a fight he knew he was going to enjoy.

CHAPTER TWENTY-THREE

THE FINAL FIGHT

Kyle was still carrying Jewel in the air hoping to find a good place to land. Although he was being careful with her, he was really nervous.

"How are you hanging in there?" he asked her timidly.

"Can I hold your foot!?" Jewel shrieked terribly.

"Uh—sure…"

Kyle continued holding the suitcase handle with his left foot while he let Jewel hold on to his right one. When she grabbed it, Kyle felt as if someone smashed an anvil on his foot. She was squeezing it so hard, he could hear the bones cracking and it immediately turned red.

"AWWWWWW!!" he screamed. "I'm never going to walk right again. I better hurry up and find a good place to land."

The monsters were fed up with Ryan and his friends, especially the 3D monster that still couldn't get Christopher out of his ear. He landed on the ground shaking his head viciously. Grace couldn't hold on any longer after the constant shaking and flew off like a slingshot but landed safely in the bushes nearby. The monster slanted his head to the right and started beating his ear where Christopher eventually fell out and hit the ground.

"Ewwww. I've seen places I never should've," Christopher commented feeling quite disgusted.

Looking down at Christopher with so much fury the monster lifted his foot ready to smash him like a bug. Ryan and Silver could see that

Chapter 23: The Final fight

Christopher had no chance of surviving this. They were still wrestling with the 2D monster in the air, however, Silver quickly thought of something.

"Ryan, pull his ears even tighter. I'll go for all the eyes," he ordered.

At Silver's command, Ryan pulled the monster's ears with all of his might while Silver slapped his bottom fin against the monster's eyes; all six of them. The monster roared frantically closing his eyes shut and couldn't concentrate on flying because of Ryan jerking him by the ears. He suddenly began to make an awkward landing near the 3D monster. Just as Silver predicted it, the 2D monster collided with the 3D monster. They both fell over each other and plunged together by crashing into a tree. Christopher was able to get out of harm's way safely while Silver and Ryan also made a quick getaway by grabbing hold of one of the tree branches and meeting Christopher face to face on the ground.

"Oh thanks you guys. I thought I was a goner for sure."

"Don't thank me, thank Silver," Ryan said. "He's the one with the brilliant brain."

"Really? Mmmm—with a brain like yours, I could use someone like you in my line of work," Christopher thought.

"Does that mean I have a job?" Silver asked happily.

"Hey!" Grace yelled.

When the gang looked up, they found Grace stuck in one of the tree branches above.

"Sure don't mind me, go ahead and celebrate right now, why don't ya!"

William observed his monsters were down for the moment but they were only trying to get themselves together after their brief fall. William carefully limped his way towards them.

"Get up you fools!" he yelled at them. "You're ten times their size and can easily wipe them out. I order you to destroy them all now! And no more slacking off!"

After William's order, both monsters were ready for the final battle. The 2D monster strengthened its advanced heavy muscles, its praying mantis claws enlarged, its tail sharpened like razor blades, its eyes started glowing bright yellow. The 3D monster's chest puffed up even more hideous than before, its broadening spikes stood up high and elevated, its arms and legs tightened with brute force, its tail extended like a large whip, and its eyes began glowing a vivid red color. This time they were out for blood. Before the next battle began, Ryan, Silver, and Christopher quickly helped Grace get out of the tree.

"Fangs would've killed one of us if you hadn't made it," Christopher stated. "You don't know what I had to go through by running into that beast's ear. I know I'm going to have nightmares for the rest of my life."

"Trust me Chris, I've seen worse things," she replied.

"I doubt it," he commented.

"All that matters is that we stopped the monsters long enough for, Kyle and Fangs, to get the others away from William," Ryan asserted.

"Uhhhh—how are we going to stop them now?" Christopher quivered.

He looked up in front of him as the gang witnessed the monsters lunging their way towards them. This time they had a much sinister appearance than before, something more deadly and fatal that they'd never seen in cartoon characters. But again these monsters were a manifestation of the hatred created by the 2D and 3D animation, so they weren't normal in any way. They were just an unfeeling creation that cared about nothing but torture and death.

"Ummm—Silver, got any ideas?" Ryan asked nervously.

"Just one—RUN!!" he screamed back.

Without blinking, Ryan and his friends left in a quick flash but the monsters were right behind them. Charging upon them at great velocity, they were smashing down all the trees that were in their path. No matter how fast Ryan and the others ran the monsters were closing in on them. The 3D monster stopped dead in his tracks and flapped his wings at an immense speed. A big gust of wind caused the characters to fly all over the area and the 2D monster rammed its claw into the ground right on top of Ryan trapping him helplessly. Ryan couldn't get up and felt like he was being suffocated by the moment. No matter how hard he moved nothing worked, it was like being locked in cement. The monster slowly brought his head down towards Ryan and smacked his lips tastefully knowing he was the perfect snack for him. He slowly opened up his mouth and brought it near Ryan's head. All Ryan could do was close his eyes and prepare for the

Chapter 23: The Final fight

worse but suddenly in the blink of an eye, the monster was immediately thrown back. He fell up against the 3D monster which was standing behind him. Ryan opened his eyes and gawked in amazement. His friend Russell just used all of his strength to ram the monster in his midsection knocking the wind out of him. Russell was inhaling and exhaling like crazy. He turned to Ryan with a mortified look. No one felt as guilty as Russell for what he previously did to him. Even now someone as tough as he could finally see the light.

"Russell?" Ryan said in shock.

"You have every right to dislike me," Russell stated. "But your hatred towards me can't compare to how much I loathe myself right now. The only way of redeeming myself to you is by helping you get through this."

"Russell—I'm just glad you're back," Ryan cried.

Russell steadily went up to Ryan and helped him get back on his feet. For the moment all they could do was stare at each other. Ryan gave his friend a confident smile to lift his spirits. Russell had a hard time smiling because of all of the hatred he had towards 2D animation. He had finally come to realize what Ryan tried to warn him about. He was in such a miserable state it was unbearable; nonetheless, he didn't want Ryan to worry about it so he gave him a little smile. Their heads immediately turned back to the monsters which were getting up. Russell stood in front of Ryan protecting him. Before the monsters could make their second attack they were unexpectedly knocked over again. This time they were hit by the arrival of the other 2D and 3D characters that rammed them aside with their limousines.

"I hope we're not too late," Stan cried as he stuck his head out the window.

"You just made it," Christopher said with much satisfaction.

All of the 2D and 3D characters exited the limos and surrounded the hideous monsters, standing as a group guarding Ryan and the rest of his friends. The beasts glanced all around them giving everyone a menacingly growl. They already knew they had to destroy every single one of them, so they weren't going to hold back on anything.

"It's time to face the very things we've created," Miriam declared.

"And this time it's not about us anymore," Ralph mentioned.

"We won't give up until we make sure nothing like this ever happens again!" Rascal shouted angrily.

"And it starts with destroying you manifestations," Jackson groaned.

All at once many of the cartoon characters took their immediate charge upon the monsters. They attacked the monsters the same way they fought each other earlier. Using all of their special skills and quick attacks they successfully had the monsters in sudden pandemonium. There were so many of them, they really didn't know where to start their attack. Christopher was going to join in the fight but suddenly turned his head when he noticed Fangs landing on the ground safely with Brittany and Rex still in his claws. Once he gently set them on the ground, he noticed Christopher coming his way.

"Brittany!" he cried anxiously as he scurried all over her body to see if she was okay. "Brittany Garland wake up! What has he done to you baby! Brittany! Fangs what's the matter with her!"

"I found her like that," Fangs admitted.

"Don't worry yourself to death, she's just snoozing," Rex assured him annoyed, and then immediately spit out William's pants which were still hanging from his mouth. "Yuck! The man needs to learn to change his underwear more often."

"I'm going to kill that William!" Christopher yelled aggressively. "Where is he?! Where is he?!"

William was still waiting out by his helicopter watching the cartoon characters trying everything to defeat his monsters, but he wasn't the least bit worried because he knew they didn't stand a chance.

"Spare no mercy!" he demanded. "Destroy them all until there is nothing left!"

The 2D monster shook at full force swinging while the 3D monster thrust his wings to blow all of the characters off of them. Every character took a bad beating, nevertheless, was still capable of enduring the battle.

"Whoa these guys are tough," Diana said rubbing her head.

"I've dealt with worse," Jackson muttered trying to butter it up.

"Trust me kitty cat, these guys take the cake," Diana responded.

Chapter 23: The Final fight

Crouching on his knees, the 2D monster swiftly lifted his enormous tail and swung it towards the 2D and 3D characters. Luckily all of them ducked but his tail was so sharp it sliced down many of the trees. Everyone was suddenly running for their lives as he continued swinging his tail at all of them. The 3D monster ripped one of the trees out from its roots and threw it, colliding with half of the cartoon characters. The result of this caused many unconscious bodies and characters scattering all over the place.

"It would be a good time to find a happy place right about now," Ralph cried.

"You and me both," Stan agreed.

Ryan ran for his life along with the rest of the gang who were still with him.

"How are we going to defeat these monsters?" Rascal cried. "They're way too strong!"

"Remember, we created these monstrosities," Miriam mentioned. "The only thing that can kill a cartoon character is another cartoon character."

"That's it!" Ryan shouted.

"What's it?" Miriam asked confused.

"We're too small and not strong enough to destroy these monsters" Ryan stated. "But they're big enough to kill each other instead."

"They work together as a team," Diana indicated. "There's no way they're going to fight against each other. Besides, they only take orders from William."

"Then we'll just have to trick them into killing each other," remarked Ryan.

A few inches away from the fight, Kyle finally set Jewel safely on the ground; however, he left her in the suitcase not wanting to mess anything up. Kyle painfully limped on his left foot still trying to assist Jewel through her labor.

"Just keep breathing—uh… that's right," he cried feeling worried. "Just take a deep breath and keep breathing. Uh… that's how they say it—right."

"You're not doing so badly for a first-timer," Jewel replied.

"Really—thanks—uh… what do I say next," Kyle requested.

"Oh Kyle—this is it!" Jewel cried. "It's coming! Please can I hold your hand?!"

Of course, Kyle didn't want to do such a thing but he knew he had no choice. He just took a big gulp and prepared for the next pain.

"AWWWWWW!" he yelled once he felt his bones cracking again.

Ryan could hear Kyle's voice in the distance fearing that something happened to him and Jewel. He was determined and frantic to make sure this plan would work.

"Come on you guys," he ordered. "It's now or never. Let's do it!"

Following Ryan's orders, all of the 2D and 3D characters got to work. First, all of them made an enormous counterattack against the 2D monster only. Second, everyone quickly dug a big hole in seconds. Using all of their strength everyone was able to knock the 2D monster into the hole. Before the 3D monster could do anything he was suddenly hit by a fireball directly in the eye. With his right eye swollen shut and burned, he presented a demonic stare at Fangs who gave him the black eye. After the 3D monster was shot in the eye and the 2D monster was thrown in the hole, they were unstoppable and furious. It was just as Ryan predicted it. He looked at Fangs and nodded his head to him. Fangs immediately took off into the air with the 3D monster following him at rapid speed. The 2D monster arose from the ground with the same demonic look. Ryan was the first character he witnessed. He didn't successfully eat him the first time so he was going to try it again.

"Spread out everyone!" Ryan shouted. "Here he comes!"

Everyone scattered for their lives and made a clearing for Ryan. The monster used his tail again by slicing through trees and ramming it at Ryan. Luckily Ryan was fast but not even he could dodge an attack like this. He just kept it up as fast as he possibly could while Fangs continued flying high in the air with the 3D monster right behind him.

"Come on wings don't let me down," he said to himself.

Once the monster got close enough he swung his long arm in midair, colliding with Fangs in the process. Fangs fell unconscious with his body plunging through the air while the monster tried to devour him. Before he could do so, Carlos arrived with Meeko hanging from his feet. Like a

Chapter 23: The Final fight

bullet, he threw Meeko on top of the monster's face as the eager meerkat scurried down his nose and bit him as hard as he could.

"You're messing with one of us, then you're messing with all of us," Meeko said excitedly.

The monster stopped heading after Fangs and tried shaking Meeko off of him. While Fangs' body was still falling in the air, Carlos tried to wake him up before his body would plummet to the ground.

"Yo Fangs! Wake up bro! Come on Fangs! You need to carry out the plan or else it won't work! You gotta get up bro!"

Carlos instantly opened Fangs' eye smacking it which woke Fangs up in a quick flash. When he found himself falling, he rapidly flew back into pace. Fangs looked upsettingly at Carlos then grunted. "Carlos, my eye was already sensitive being stung by a bee! You just made it worse."

"You'll heal brother," Carlos said cheerfully. "Besides I had no other way of waking you up compared to my small size."

Fangs flew toward the 3D monster who was still trying to get Meeko off. When Meeko saw Fangs heading his way, he scurried off of the monster's nose and ran up to his head, then he jumped off and landed on top of Fangs' back. After the monster rubbed his nose for a moment he noticed Fangs trying to get away and continued swiftly after him.

"It's about time you woke up from your beauty sleep," Meeko commented. "I didn't know how much longer I could hold on to that monster."

"I thought you guys hated each other," Fangs suggested.

"We still do but we knew you needed our help as much as you won't admit it," Carlos smiled gracefully. "You guys are just going to have to acknowledge you couldn't have made it without a handsome guy like me."

"Don't overdo it bird brain!" Meeko complained.

Back down below, Ryan was still scurrying for his life with the 2D monster hot on his trail. He constantly swung his tail at him with a massive force. As many times as Ryan dodged it, he eventually got hit. Ryan's body was in terrible pain by getting sliced on the back and falling over but he couldn't let it stop him now. If he didn't go through with his idea, then there would be nothing left for anybody. Ryan forcefully brought his body up one step at a time then persisted running. In his direction, he spotted William still standing by his helicopter.

"Foolish fox," William shrieked. "Why don't you just give up? Even someone like you is no match for my awesome beasts."

"The one thing I'm not is a quitter!" Ryan yelled.

"Then get ready to meet your doom, my little friend," William laughed. "Once you're gone, you'll never see your wife and kid ever again."

"The only doom someone is about to face is you!" Ryan shrieked.

Behind him, Ryan witnessed the 2D monster's assault at an alarming pursuit and when he looked up, he could see Fangs coming down their way with the 3D monster directly following him. He quickly ran towards William then passed him heading inside of the helicopter. William furiously chased after him as Ryan hid behind one of the seats.

"You impudent coward!" William called. "You know you're defeated so you're just going to run and hide like a sissy."

"If you're trying to drive me out, it won't work," Ryan claimed.

"Driving you out will be the least of my problems but I can smell your fear," William argued. "The fear that you and your whole family will soon face. The very end of 2D and 3D animation as we know it. Your emotions for them make you vulnerable and weak. That will be their downfall, especially your wife. Her death on your hands will have a full impact on you, knowing that your child will be my own grand prize. One that I'll raise and use for my own wager. Something you'll never be able to stop or prevent."

William's words were enough to make Ryan lunge out at him. Full of rage and anger, Ryan knew he had to calm down. When Russell lost his temper he almost did something he would've regretted, so Ryan easily took a deep breath and just sighed. He remained where he was without moving.

"Call it what you like but I know what I'm doing!" Ryan answered.

"So do I," William said amusingly.

In a quick flash, William unexpectedly whacked Ryan on top of the head with his tranquilizer gun. As soon as Ryan passed out, William easily grabbed him by the scruff of his neck holding at him like a rag doll.

Chapter 23: The Final fight

"It's a shame you guys don't know when you've lost," he moaned at him.

Ryan tried hard coming to but was extremely dizzy and weak. All he could do was shift a little and open his eyes halfway.

"Get ready to face your death," William said as he smiled at him with an evil look.

He gradually walked back outside and placed Ryan on the ground. The 2D monster was already awaiting his second chance to finish Ryan off. As he watched his master waiting for his command, William looked up at him and only said two words, "Kill him."

Ryan was aware of everything but was unable to do anything about it. The monster brought his slimy praying mantis claw in contact with Ryan's face then plugged it into his chest as he did before and raised his other claw in the air getting ready to smash him with it. In mid-air, Fangs was flying down directly towards the 2D monster. He immediately let out a fire breath upon the 2D monster hitting him on the back. The hideous monster turned and looked up at Fangs with uncontrollable fury. Disregarding William's order he took off and dashed into the air after Fangs.

"Come back here you fool!" William shouted. "I told you to kill this fox!"

As Fangs watched the 2D monster heading towards him he cautiously made sure the 3D monster was still following him. At that exact moment Fangs swiftly moved from the monster's position. In the process, this left the 3D monster flying directly at the 2D monster. The two monsters collided into each other making a thunderous sound like a lightning storm. Their impact was so tremendous both of them were bleeding actual blood from their foreheads. Just as Ryan predicated, the two monsters became enraged and began fighting one another in mid-air.

"NO, NO, NO!!!" William shrieked insanely. "I order you two to stop fighting each other and to kill the 2D and 3D characters!"

The monsters were so full of unmanageable rage they failed to even hear William's command. They continued fighting in a gruesome battle that made most of the cartoon characters turn away. From the way they acted these two monsters generally belong in a horror film from their destructive nature and ghastly personality. The two beasts grabbed a hold of each other as they began biting, clawing, and tearing each other to pieces. By this point, both of them weren't flying anymore and began to make a plummet towards the ground. William regretfully noticed the monsters were making their way down towards him and Ryan. But an abrupt move was taken when Russell came by like a speed of lightning. He incredibly shoved Ryan out of the way and took his place instead. At this point, the monsters were dropping at an incredible speed unable to stop. William was suddenly caught up in this death trap moment.

"NOOOOOOOOOOO!!" he screamed.

Once the monsters hit the ground making contact with William and the helicopter it caused an immense explosion. It was so powerful it erupted like an atomic blast up towards the sky. Everyone was thrown to the ground or blown into the trees from the horrendous force. After a while, the flames finally subsided and everyone was able to gather around to see what happened. The 2D monster and 3D monster were finally gone, along with William. Ryan's plan worked out just as he had hoped. He tricked both of the monsters into killing each other when they least expected it. The helicopter also caused the explosion to ignite the monsters completely. When cartoon characters are destroyed their bodies disappear like dust in thin air and to everyone's satisfaction, William was destroyed with them. He had no chance of surviving something like this. It also made the cartoon characters feel a little better because William didn't have to die by their hands, instead he died by his monsters. Before everyone could blow out into a big celebration they noticed Russell. He was caught up in the explosion too after he saved Ryan's life. Sadly it wasn't the explosion that wounded him, it was the two monsters for cartoons are only wounded by another cartoon. The terror of seeing him in the aftermath made everyone gasp in horror. His body laid in rubble under what was left of the helicopter. Ryan didn't want to believe it. He aggressively shook off his wooziness then quickly ran over to his friend who was still alive but barely.

CHAPTER TWENTY-FOUR

GOOD-BYE OLD FRIEND

Russell remained lying down on his side severely hurt from the explosion. All he could do was look at Ryan. Ryan placed his paw on Russell's head for comfort.

"Russell!" Ryan cried. "Don't do this to me! Please, Russell! Please!"

"I-I-I'm—just glad—it wasn't for nothing," Russell stuttered quietly.

"Russell—you—you saved my life," Ryan cried with grief.

"It—it—was the least—I—could do. After all—I can't forgive—myself—for what I—almost did to you."

"None of that matters, Russell. You'll always be my best friend."

"You were—right about me—the whole time. I was blinded—by—by so much hatred. I couldn't—see the truth anymore—until I—almost became something else."

"You just found your way out of the darkness. That's all."

"It's—too bad—I-I couldn't see the truth earlier."

"Save your strength old friend. We'll get you to a cartoon hospital right away."

"I don't think—it would make much of a difference."

"Russell! You're not going to give up on me now! You didn't have to save me you know."

"But that's what best friends are for."

"Russell…"

"Ryan. Even if I did survive—I wouldn't want to go on living. I can't stand—living with myself—after betraying you. It's better this way."

"Russell please. You're my good friend. Please don't leave me."

"I'll always be with you Ryan—always."

Before Ryan could say anything else to Russell, he watched in horror seeing him close his eyes as he desperately tried waking him up.

"Russell! Russell wake up! RUSSELL!!"

But Russell didn't respond anymore, he eventually stopped breathing and remained lifeless. Ryan felt the same pain come back to his heart as it did when he thought he lost Jewel. All he could do was stand still like a statue, in disbelief that his best friend was gone. Slowly he wrapped his arms around Russell's horn and quietly wept. Every single 2D and 3D character who had witnessed this event was sad enough to make them grieve as well. They already knew some of them probably wouldn't live through this war but they didn't think it would be this depressing. Russell might have tried to kill Ryan before, nevertheless, he redeemed himself by saving his life afterwards. As Ryan continued holding on to Russell, his body slowly began to fade away. Ryan desperately tried grabbing at what was left of him but he eventually disappeared completely. A white puff of smoke could be seen traveling along the tree branches above the whole crowd. Watching in amazement they didn't know what it was at first but they figured it was Russell's spirit. It slowly glided above the forest and then went up into the night sky. This was truly a wonder for them to watch because no one had ever seen an animation's spirit before. Ryan's eyes widened when he noticed the spirit was gradually taking a shape that turned out to be Russell's head. It was kind of hard to make him out at first but then they could see him clear as daylight.

Everyone's sudden sorrowfulness turned into pure happiness. Russell might have been dead, however, everyone was glad to see his spirit thriving. Nobody was more proud than Ryan, although he was still depressed. Russell's spirit looked down at Ryan and gave him a smile nodding his head letting him know that everything would be alright. Ryan managed to crack a smile. It was still hard for him to accept his death but as long as Russell's spirit was alive, he would feel a sense of comfort and hope in his heart. Ultimately his spirit disappeared altogether as it flew high into the air until it vanished above the stars. All of the 2D and 3D

Chapter 24: Good-bye Old Friend

characters cheered joyfully knowing that from this day forward, Russell will always be remembered. Ryan continuously watched the sky, hoping to see another glimpse of him but without luck. All he could do was stay confident and hope to see him again in the future. Ryan was suddenly interrupted when he saw Kyle coming towards him frantically.

"Ryan!" Kyle cried.

"Kyle?"

"Ryan, come quick! It's your wife!"

CHAPTER TWENTY-FIVE

A NEW BEGINNING

Ryan and all of the other animation characters followed closely behind Kyle who led them to Jewel.

"If anything happened to Jewel, there's going to be a death sentence around here," Rex complained.

"Gee whiz, you sometimes act like you're the one who's in love with her," Rascal commented.

"I'm just a bodyguard, nothing more," Rex replied.

"Don't you mean watchdog?" Ralph added.

"Whatever!" Rex yelled aggressively.

"Despite what happens we're going to help Ryan get through this as painfully as possible," Stan mentioned.

"Just how painful do you mean?" Grace asked confused.

Before the rest of the cartoon characters could pursue running, Kyle immediately stopped them dead in their tracks. He landed behind Ryan to the point where they should stop.

"That's as far as you guys can go!" Kyle ordered. "This is just for Ryan alone."

Everyone groaned in disappointment. They anxiously wanted to see if Jewel was okay, nonetheless, they knew Ryan deserved to see her before anyone else.

"Go on Ryan," Kyle said to his friend. "Jewel's waiting for you."

"Thanks Kyle," Ryan said respectfully patting him on the shoulder.

Chapter 25: A New Beginning

He walked ahead while everyone stayed behind. Jewel was still inside of the suitcase placed in the very same spot where Kyle left her. Ryan took a deep breath and walked slowly not wanting to excite Jewel or the baby by his panicky state. As he got closer, he could see Jewel's head sticking out of the suitcase giving him a satisfactory smile that brought warmth to his heart. He suffered all day being away from her, especially when William got a hold of her and the baby but now all of those worries were washed away and he was finally reunited with her at last. As soon as Ryan came nose to nose with Jewel, he gazed at her lovingly.

"Hey there handsome," Jewel said cheerfully.

"Oh—Jewel," Ryan cried passionately.

Jewel always gave Ryan an overwhelming sensation that drove him crazy. No other 3D character in the world could do it except for Jewel. Ryan immediately started kissing and licking her face nonstop. As much as Jewel was enjoying the moment, she didn't want this to be happening in front of an audience.

"Calm down honey," she warned him. "There will be plenty of time for this later."

"I can't help it," Ryan cried. "Just being with you again is enough to make me go crazy."

Before Ryan could continue he suddenly heard a baby cry. His ears perked up with amazement. Not knowing the baby had already arrived, Ryan started inhaling and exhaling at a fast pace while his legs began to tremble. This was the very first time he would see his child. He first looked at Jewel with worry but she smiled back at him with confidence. Ryan slanted his head to get a look inside of the suitcase but it was pitch black. Steadily he brought his paw to the handles of the suitcase opening it further so he could get a better glance. Once he did, it's as if a powerful force had possessed him. He couldn't believe what he was seeing. Ryan didn't just have a child; he had seven of them. Four of them were males and three of them were females. The genuine phenomenal gift about it was that they were 2D and 3D hybrids, with only two of them just being solely 2D and 3D animation. The first two males were a dark reddish color and a yellow stomach like their father. The third male was a light orange color like his mother. He kind of stuck out from the rest because of a cool mohawk fur on top of his head. The two females were a light red and orange color with yellow stomachs. The last female was only 2D animation but had a dark reddish color like her father and the last male was only 3D animation and had a light reddish-orange color. All of them gradually fed off of their mother's milk as all newborns do. Ryan was in a tremendous state of marvel and happiness. He never thought it would be anything like this; it was even ten times better than how he imagined. The true spectacle of this made it possible that 2D and 3D animation are capable of really being together as one. Ryan continued staring at his children with wonderment. At first, he didn't know what to say or do, all he could do was gaze at them for the longest time but he eventually brought his head up and looked at Jewel.

"Seven!" he said amazed. "I thought we were only going to have one."

"That's what I thought," Jewel said. "But they just kept popping out of me."

"I guess I was a little more intense with our romance than I realized," Ryan blushed embarrassed.

"I don't mind," Jewel chuckled. "After all, it was worth it."

"Jewel—they're—they're so beautiful," he cried happily.

"What should we name them?" she asked contentedly.

"Mmmm—let's see?" Ryan thought for a minute. "My first boy, how about—Ryan Jr."

"I like it," she agreed.

"Your turn, beautiful."

"Mmmmm—one of the females. I was thinking about—Jazelle?"

"I love it! Now the other female, how about—Rachael."

"Nice," said Jewel. "And how about we name our last female—Kelsey."

"Great—now for one of the males… let me see. Ummm—what about Ace?"

"Ace—perfect. I was also thinking about David for one of our boys."

"David, what a cute name for one of our sons. Last but not least is our runt of the litter."

Chapter 25: A New Beginning

"Why don't you choose a name for him, honey?"

"Let's see—how about—Rex. After the good and faithful dog who watched over you this entire time."

"Oh, that's so sweet of you Ryan."

"So there you have it. Ryan Jr., Jazelle, Rachael, Kelsey, Ace, David, and Rex. Our beautiful happy family," he sighed joyfully.

Ryan took another long look at his children which he adored as much as his wife. He at least wanted to hold one of them in his paws for the first time, so he gently picked Ace up first. He joyfully stared at him while Ace took a good look at his dad for the first time. He didn't do much except laugh with a cute baby squeal. It just made Ryan want to hug him even tighter. Before this bonding could continue, Ryan suddenly heard the whole crowd from behind him.

"AWE!!" everyone cried.

Everyone finally saw Ryan's baby for the first time when he took him out of the suitcase but they were in complete shock when they realized the baby was a 2D and 3D hybrid. Most didn't want to believe it, thinking it wasn't possible.

"That's a-a 2D and 3D hybrid?" Rascal said surprised.

"You ain't kidding," remarked Stan. "I thought those kind were only created by animators but Ryan and Jewel are the first to give actual birth to their kind."

"Awe, he's so cute," Grace squealed. "I just want to eat him up."

"How could you Grace!" Carlos shrieked. "He's just a baby."

"It's a figure of speech you idiot!" Grace wailed.

"Anything is possible beyond our own understanding," Silver explained. "Ryan and Jewel just proved to all of us that it can be possible for 2D and 3D to coexist as a true family."

After the ugly battle they just faced, along with losing Russell, the monsters they'd created and seeing Ryan's kids, it made them realize they must stop their racism. They carried this on for many years and it finally had to come to an end. They couldn't risk putting the whole civilization in danger again by continuing their hatred. Ryan had a point after all when he said they were all animation, part of the same family from the same ink and that's what's more important. Bit by bit the 2D and 3D characters began to make harmony with one another for the first time.

"Yo bro," said a 2D walrus to a 3D penguin. "Sorry for slamming my body on top of ya."

"It's cool man," the penguin replied. "But if you ask me, they'll love you in China."

"Forgive my rampage upon you guys earlier," said a 3D Oryx to a prairie dog family. "I just hope it wasn't too severe."

"Oh it was," said one prairie dog. "But luckily we 2D animations heal fast."

"It's okay deer," said another prairie dog. "We accept your apology."

"I'm an Oryx," he clarified.

"Whatever," said the prairie dog. "Hey, maybe you can return the favor by letting us ride your back half of the time."

"Great," the Oryx grumbled under his breath.

"That's one dangerous beak you've got there," a 2D otter commented to a 3D ostrich sitting on top of his back. "You nearly pecked my brains out."

"Trust me, it won't ever happen again," the ostrich replied. "Because in the process I bent my beak. You must really have a strong skull. I guess I deserved it anyway."

"Let's bury the hatchet and become friends," a 3D wolf happily said to a 2D sheep.

"Even if I do look tasty to you," the sheep trembled.

"Luckily for you," the wolf responded. "I don't eat 2D animation. You guys just don't agree with my digestive system."

"Well that's a relief," the sheep sighed. "Oh and one more thing. What would we want to bury a hatchet for?"

"Nice going with your quick flying skills Fangs," Grace stated.

"It wasn't really me," Fangs explained. "I was just following orders from Ryan."

"But we all couldn't have gotten through any this if it wasn't for you and you know it—pumpkin."

Chapter 25: A New Beginning

Without hesitation Fangs immediately scooped Grace up in his arms and gazed at her so lovingly. "Grace—will you—marry me?"

Grace couldn't believe anyone would've ever asked for her claw in marriage, especially a 3D character. She remained paralyzed for a brief moment, but she truly adored Fangs just the same. Throughout the whole day of going on adventures, they developed a relationship and it was one Grace wanted to keep on sharing with him.

"Oh Fangs—this is so unexpected—I—of course I will!" she cried gleefully.

Grace was so excited as she jumped up to kiss Fangs, she knocked them both to the ground.

Ryan gazed at the whole crowd and witnessed for the first time in history that everyone was finally putting their differences aside and becoming friends. This was more than he could ever ask for, however, he realized through hardship and struggle, things will eventually come out good in the end. Standing by patiently, Kyle eventually came up to Ryan wanting to take a closer look at the kids.

"Your kids are beautiful just like you and Jewel," he commented.

"Kyle, I owe everything to you for helping Jewel get through this," Ryan cried.

"I'm really sorry that I broke your hand and foot," Jewel said with sympathy.

"It's okay Jewel," Kyle remarked. "It's nothing that a couple of bandages and a first aid kit won't cure. Besides I get twice the pain on the episodes that Ryan and I make every day."

Rex instantly made his appearance known walking up to Ryan and the others.

"Rex, glad to see you made it," Jewel noted. "I can't thank you enough for guiding me throughout the entire day."

"It's my job," Rex replied.

"You'll be happy to know we decided to name one of our children after you," Ryan mentioned.

"Oh you didn't have to do that," said Rex embarrassed.

"Would you like to carry one of my children?" Ryan asked.

"Oh no! It's just that—I'm not the—affectionate type," Rex complained.

But without listening to him, Ryan placed his son Ace right in the middle of his arms. Rex was taken off guard and felt uncomfortable, having a hard time appreciating delightful moments such as this because of his hard personality. While he looked down at Ace with an embarrassing stare, Ace continued laughing with his baby squeal and warmly cuddled his head up against Rex's chest. Rex couldn't help but smile. This was a tender loving moment that was enough to even make him weak.

"Is that a smile I see?" Jewel said.

"Maybe outside you have a tough nature but I knew on the inside you were a compassionate loving animal," Ryan comprehended.

"Okay—so I guess everyone has a weakness," Rex groaned.

"And William's weakness was that he underestimated you guys," said Brittany who was wide awake and well. Slowly glancing at the entire area around her, she strolled her way over to Ryan and the others with Christopher on top of her shoulder.

"You know the media is going to be all over this," she commented.

"The only thing they have to know is that—our conflict has finally come to an end," said Ryan.

"But what if they start asking questions about William?" Kyle asked. "We could get into some serious trouble."

"Leave that to me," Brittany pointed out. "I have a way of persuading people to see things my way. I'll eventually get them to listen."

"My baby sure does know how to work on people," Christopher chuckled. "For future reference, no one is to evr talk about this event ever again. This will be an event that we'll bury and then move on."

"If this works out to our advantage, then things could be better than they were before," Ryan stated. "This could be a whole new beginning."

CHAPTER TWENTY-SIX

A WHOLE NEW BEGINNING

Four weeks following the big battle, the 2D and 3D characters completely made changes for the better. First, they had the stadium demolished, not wanting any reminder of that place that could've been their doom. Second, the 3D characters established a new proposal to the 2D characters. The 3D characters discussed with critics and audiences to give a little more respect to the 2D animation the same way they do them. And for once it made the 3D characters realize if they had done this from the very beginning, they could've learned to understand the 2D character's point of view. Third, they established Cartoon Studios with a better budget. Everyone put their brains together and worked as a team coming up with brilliant ideas, new episodes, and movies that audiences and critics both loved. Cartoon Studios started becoming so popular that it was the most famous animation studio around the globe. It even opened the doors for other cartoon characters like Stop-Motion animation, Flash animation, and many more. That way every animation of every kind could work a true race. As a result, Joseph didn't have to worry about his company getting bad criticism ever again. Ryan didn't star in movies anymore, not only because he was a father now but he became Joseph's new vice president and a director as well. Due to Ryan's kids, 2D and 3D hybrids born from actual 2D and 3D parents were the beginning of a new cartoon genre that had already captivated the world by surprise.

"I've got to hand it to you Ryan," Joseph said looking from his office window. "You really changed things for the better around here."

"I still couldn't have done it without any of my friends," Ryan said saddened when he thought of Russell for a brief moment.

"I'm sorry about your friend Russell," Joseph expressed sympathetically. "But he wouldn't want you to feel bad for him. He didn't die in vain, knowing what you did was right in the end. No matter what, he'll always be remembered and he'll always be your friend."

"I know," Ryan replied, "but I still miss him."

"Say, aren't your kids coming today?" Joseph inquired.

"That's right," Ryan announced happily. "I want them to see the new and improved Cartoon Studios. Not to mention, today is the day when other cartoon characters will apply at our studio for the first time. It will be a new beginning for all of us."

"Then you better get downstairs and make sure you make them feel as welcome as possible," Joseph ordered. "I won't allow any more prejudice in my company ever again."

"Yes sir," Ryan cried as he happily left Joseph's office and headed outside.

"I always knew I could count on ya," Joseph remarked. "Nice work little guy."

Outside the studio lot, Ryan glanced up at the new fabrication of the signs which was much bigger than before and polished nicely. He merrily strolled around the back lot which was full of humans and cartoon characters alike that were setting up their welcoming establishments for the new arrivals. Ryan could see all of the 2D and 3D characters finally getting along as a true family. Maybe some of them were bickering and quarreling with one another but cartoons will be cartoons. Ryan was even happy to know that his best friend Kyle was now a director and had his buddies Ralph, Stan, Carlos, Rascal, Meeko, and Miriam to star in his movies. A popular television series they made together was called, "Kyle of the Seven Seas" where they played wicked pirates with Kyle as their captain. Inside one of the sound stages, they were filming one of their episodes. Kyle posed on top of his gigantic pirate ship wearing a pirate's hat with Carlos hanging on his shoulder as his parrot-like pet, while Ralph, Stan, Rascal,

Chapter 26: A Whole New Beginning

Meeko, and Miriam stood below the deck as if they were getting ready to combat another ship.

"Arrr captain," Rascal barked, "unknown targets are approaching in the east! Let's steal their ship and take their booty!"

"I don't mind taking their ship," Meeko shrieked, "but they can keep their booty. Why would we want to take somebody's butt?"

"Booty, not booty!" Rascal argued.

"What?" Meeko said confused. "Here take mine to save you the trouble," he said as he shoved his butt into Rascal's face.

Rascal responded by biting him on the tail making Meeko cry out hysterically.

"Knock it off you two, we're not doing anything without captain's orders," Miriam directed.

"Needless to say, I get seasick," Stan cried miserably. "I'll never get used to this."

Kyle brought out his telescope and looked in the distance at the upcoming ship.

"Now is a good time to call out for the rum," Carlos cheered, "let's party!"

"We party after we take their ship," Kyle ordered. "I like taking them when they least expect it. Avast me lads, get the canons ready!"

Ralph, Rascal, Meeko, and Miriam immediately ran down below and set up the canons loading them with ammo. Once they were close enough to the ship, everyone waited for Kyle's signal.

"Surrender your ship mateys!" Kyle demanded bringing out his sword. "You've just come across Kyle of the Seven Seas and there is no escape!"

But in an abrupt move, the other ship fired an even bigger canon at Kyle's ship which ignited into flames. After taking a quick dive into the ocean they surfaced on top of deadwood from the damaged ship. Taken by surprise all they could do was float in the ocean while the other ship was departing.

"That's the third time this week captain," Miriam groaned.

"We need a new strategy captain," Rascal suggested. "It seems that everyone's aware of our status. Pirates are supposed to be feared but for some reason, no one takes us seriously."

"Why is everyone so eager to take people's butts?" Meeko asked. "I think we'd be more interested in taking their money instead."

"Stop it Meeko you're killing it," Rascal complained.

"The scurvy dogs!" Kyle complained at the other ship. "The devil take ya!"

"Thank God for the rum though," Carlos said happily holding a rum bottle in his wings.

"Yo ho ho and a bottle of rum," Ralph sang miserably as he sank below the ocean.

Back outside the studio Ryan continued walking around the lot and noticed the dolphins from the dolphin club who were briefly spending time at the studio, quickly spotting Silver in the bunch.

"Hey Vulpes, what's up?" Silver asked enthusiastically.

"Hey Silver, I'm glad you and your family could make it," said Ryan.

"We're just glad to be here but I'm afraid to say we'll be leaving."

"Why—where are you going?"

"Christopher wants me and my family to work for him. He's highly impressed with our advanced functions of intelligence believing it will help him with his private organization, besides we like going on adventures and solving cases. It's extremely exciting for us."

"Okay—I guess if it makes you happy," Ryan confessed. "What am I saying, you're always happy."

At that moment, Christopher, Brittany, and Jackson walked into the studio in front of Ryan and Silver.

"Hey guys," Ryan said. "Coming here to pick up Silver and his family?"

"I'm afraid so," Christopher admitted, "but I also didn't get a chance to thank you Ryan. Thank you and your friends for saving my girl—and me as well I guess."

"It was no problem Chris," Ryan replied. "And Brittany—thanks for shutting up the media."

"I told you I have my ways of persuasion," she chuckled softly.

Chapter 26: A Whole New Beginning

"Jackson, get the limo ready for our new employees," Christopher announced.

"I'll also get the saltwater ready," Jackson groaned annoyed as he walked away.

"Okay my dolphin comrades, let's get ready for your new mission," Christopher declared happily.

All of the dolphins cheered with excitement and began to head out of the studio towards Christopher's limo parked on the sidewalk.

"Take care of yourself Ryan," said Brittany as she walked away.

"You too," Ryan replied. "I'll see ya guys around."

Before Silver could retreat with the rest of his family, he took one last look at Ryan.

"Awe Silver, I'm—I'm going to really miss you," Ryan admitted. "You were really a big help."

"Don't worry Ryan, I'll be back," Silver assured him. "Until then, take good care of the company and your family."

Ryan gave his aquatic friend a big hug because he didn't know how long it would be until he saw him again, nevertheless, Silver was always optimistic so he wasn't the least bit worried.

"See ya later Vulpes," he said as he headed inside of the limo with the others.

Ryan watched Silver and the rest of his friends leave the studio as they drove far off into the distance. He smiled and waved good-bye to his intelligent companion then immediately spotted Jewel approaching the entrance of the studio. He wasted no time running up to her.

"I'm so glad you made it," he cried.

"Why wouldn't I?" Jewel noted happily. "Vice president of the company, I'm so proud of you Ryan."

"All my years, I've been dreaming of something like this to happen," Ryan replied. "I only hope it will remain this way for a long time."

After staying silent for a short moment, Ryan just smiled and wrapped his arm around Jewel's shoulder. Pretty soon, they caught sight of Rex coming their way. He had all of their children riding on his back. Not only was he Jewel's bodyguard but now he became the kid's babysitter. He grew a soft spot for them, so much that he couldn't refuse the offer. When the babies saw their parents they jumped off of Rex and ran towards them.

"Hey kids, did you miss me?" Ryan asked, giving all of them a hug.

"Thanks Rex, sorry if they were a handful," said Jewel.

"Nonsense," Rex replied. "They have respectable natures, just like their parents. Besides, they're too cute and cuddly for me to get angry with. I gotta get going; I have an hour before I get ready for my next filming."

Rex eventually walked into the studio lot leaving the kids behind with their parents.

"You see kids, this is where your daddy works," Ryan told them. "Pretty soon when you get older, this will be the place where you'll make movies too."

"And maybe your kids will star in the same movies with our kids," said Grace who abruptly came onto the scene. Fangs was right behind her, of course.

"Grace?" said Ryan surprised.

To Ryan and Jewel's astonishment, they were taken by complete amazement to see that Grace and Fangs miraculously had kids of their own. Just like Ryan's kids they were 2D and 3D hybrids as well except they were crossbreeds of an alligator and dragon. Grace and Fangs had six children that looked just as adorable as Ryan's kids. They had three boys and three girls. They all looked different from each other with beautiful color markings and dragon wings capable of flying.

"You guys had kids!" Ryan said bewildered.

"Last week I had them," said Grace. "After the events of our horrific battle Fangs proposed to me. We spent the whole month in Las Vegas for our honeymoon."

"It was the best time of my life," Fangs cried out happily wagging his tail. "You should've been there."

"If you call scaring people in Las Vegas a fun time, then I don't know what you consider to be a disaster," Grace implicated.

Once Grace and Fangs' kids saw Ryan's kids the children immediately became friends and began playing with one another.

"Your kids are so adorable," Jewel smiled.

Chapter 26: A Whole New Beginning

"Thanks Jewel," said Grace. "I knew our kids would get along with yours just fine."

"You know the thing about kids, they're never prejudiced about anything," Jewel acknowledged. "It's the lifestyle they're around of whoever raises them to hate."

"So Ryan, did we miss the new arrivals?" Grace asked.

"Nope you're just in time," he remarked. "As a matter of fact, they should be coming at any moment now."

Suddenly, near the entrance of the company, everyone witnessed the new cartoon characters arrive. Everyone had their own qualities from their different genes of animation which were stop-motion, flash animation, Anime, and even old silent cartoon drawings. Some were even so mysterious no one knew what age of animation they could have possibly come from. They seemed shy and unsure of taking this chance to work at this studio. After all, they already heard of the previous 2D and 3D reputation, but Ryan smiled with confidence and just sighed.

"Let's give them the warmest welcome possible. Let's make this a brighter future for all of us."

After Ryan's comment, every character in the studio ran up to the newcomers and introduced them to Cartoon Studios. It was a new experience for the cartoon characters to finally see eye to eye with each other and to rapidly make new friends with no exceptions. Someone can always make a difference by changing things for the better but never without sacrifice. The yearnings to be accepted in society are often filled by a world that is buried deep in the hearts of creatures whose lives often drift towards antagonism. Individuals who are willing to make a difference can simply stay immune to these emotions. Accepting others for their true race is a challenge; however, it will enable you to see the happiness of other lives, creating a new experience of life that could not have possibly been known.

The End

Printed by Libri Plureos GmbH in Hamburg, Germany